DEVILS
&
THIEVES

DEVILS & THIEVES

BY JENNIFER RUSH

LITTLE, BROWN AND COMPANY
NEW YORK BOSTON

Cover design by Karina Granda. Cover illustration © 2017 by Luke Choice/ Velvet Spectrum. Cover copyright © 2017 by Hachette Book Group, Inc.

Little, Brown and Company

Hachette Book Group
1290 Avenue of the Americas, New York, NY 10104
Visit us at lb-teens.com

First Edition: October 2017

Little, Brown and Company is a division of Hachette Book Group, Inc. The Little, Brown name and logo are trademarks of Hachette Book Group, Inc.

The publisher is not responsible for websites (or their content) that are not owned by the publisher.

Library of Congress Cataloging-in-Publication Data

Names: Rush, Jennifer (Jennifer Marie), 1983– author.
Title: Devils & thieves / by Jennifer Rush.
Other titles: Devils and thieves
Description: First edition. | New York : Little, Brown Books, 2017. | Series: Devils & thieves ; 1 | Summary: "In a world of magical motorcycle gangs, eighteen-year-old Jemmie Carmichael taps into her magical abilities to stop an evil spell before it can be fulfilled" —Provided by publisher.
Identifiers: LCCN 2016049238| ISBN 9780316390897 (hardcover) | ISBN 9780316390866 (ebook) | ISBN 9780316390903 (library edition ebook)
Subjects: | CYAC: Magic—Fiction. | Self-confidence—Fiction. | Love—Fiction. | Motorcycles—Fiction. | Gangs—Fiction. | Missing persons—Fiction.
Classification: LCC PZ7.R89535 Dev 2017 | DDC [Fic]—dc23
LC record available at https://lccn.loc.gov/2016049238

ISBNs: 978-0-316-39089-7 (hardcover), 978-0-316-39086-6 (ebook)

Printed in the United States of America

LSC-C

10 9 8 7 6 5 4 3 2 1

To Sarah Fine, who saved me and this book
when we both needed saving

ONE

I hated the mall. I hated the smell of fast, cheap food. I hated the windowless walls, the cavernous space that somehow made me feel trapped. Most of all, I hated the echoing cacophony of a thousand voices.

There was already enough noise in my own head.

"Jemmie?" Alex called. "What do you think?" She spun around in the tenth dress she'd tried on in the past hour.

"I like it," I answered, pressing my fingers to my brow in an attempt to ward off a headache. Then I let my hands fall into my lap and smiled at her.

"You said the same thing about the last dress, and the one before that," she said matter-of-factly, not at all put out by my fogginess. She was used to it. "But I think you'll *love* this next one."

She disappeared into the fitting room again, not bothering to ask if I was going to try anything on. She already knew the answer—and how to pick her battles.

I was more comfortable trailing along in her shadow anyway. As long as I was with Alex (which was just about always), eyes would never be on me. She was the only daughter of the Medici family, arguably the most powerful kindled family in the US. Her place was here in Hawthorne, New York, with the rest of the Medici clan. She knew where she stood, and what lay ahead for her.

I wasn't envious of Alex's beauty. I was, however, envious of her certainty.

Magic was the currency of our world, and Alex was rich. I...was not.

The dressing room door creaked open and she stepped out, this time in a low-cut black dress that barely covered her butt.

"Your brother would kill you if he saw you in that," I said. "So would your mom. And if you weren't dead when they were done, then the rest of the Devils' League would finish you off."

Alex rolled her eyes. "As if I'd wear it in front of Crowe."

There was a reason Alex mentioned only her brother

out of that long list of potential dress code enforcers: He was the only one who had even a scrap of influence on her.

Crowe Medici was just twenty years old, but he was already notorious in the kindled world. The Medici name carried a lot of weight as it was, but after Alex and Crowe's father, Michael, was killed in a motorcycle accident down in New Orleans last year, Crowe had ascended to president of the Devils' League, the one and only motorcycle gang in Hawthorne comprised entirely of kindled. Since then, he'd had a run-in or three with rival gangs in the tristate area, enough to cause whispers about how dangerous he was, how volatile. Not many people had the power to break bones and raise plagues with a simple arch of an eyebrow. Rumors had spread about how he was unstable, but those of us who had known him all our lives knew better. He wasn't crazy.

He was grieving.

The first anniversary of Michael Medici's death had just passed. It probably wasn't such a good time to test him.

"Are we not shopping for an outfit for the Kindled Festival?" I asked Alex. "And will your brother not be in attendance there?"

Alex ran her hands down her hips. "I can wear a coat or something over it until I ditch my brother. He's not going to be paying attention to me anyway, not with all the other available distractions. The Sixes rolled in last night, and the Curse Kings got here before noon. The Deathstalkers should be here by now, too, I think." She frowned for a moment before shaking it off.

I had the opposite reaction to the mention of the Deathstalkers. A tiny, forbidden thrill raced up my spine.

"Anyway," she continued breezily, "I saw Crowe stumble into an alley with one of the Six hangarounds last night. They were all over each other."

Thrill forgotten, I scowled. "Figures."

The Kindled Festival was an annual gathering. It was a chance for the families to swap curses and enchantments, celebrate who we are...and make new connections. This year, the Devils' League was hosting the party in Hawthorne. The Deathstalkers had hosted it in New Orleans last year, and I remembered that time with a special kind of agony. Crowe never should have attended, not so soon after his father had died. He went on a three-day bender and pretty much turned into an asshole. But I recalled the festival with another, more private emotion: euphoria. It had marked the beginning of something promising, but also the end of something that had never had a chance to begin, the death of a wish I'd had for years.

It was complicated.

Alex patted my arm. "My brother's a hound, Jem," she said with a wink. "None of them mean anything to him."

"Is that supposed to make me feel better? Which Six girl was it?" I remembered a bunch of them from the previous year.

"I'm getting this dress," Alex said, sliding her fingers along the hem at her thighs.

"You're dodging."

"Am not. I like this dress."

"Which. One." I shouldn't care. I totally shouldn't care. "Was it Katrina?"

Alex swiveled back toward the dressing room. "I'll change real quick, and then we can leave!"

I grumbled, reading between the lines, and wandered to the front of the store. I was being an absolute hypocrite, and I had no claim on Crowe whatsoever. What the hell was wrong with me? After browsing the racks of sunglasses and taking a few deep breaths, I slipped on a pair of aviators and peered at myself in the mirror. The faint scent of leather and flowers drew my attention away from my appearance.

"Good grief. Speak of the devil," I muttered as the mirror's reflection revealed a tall, willowy figure walking by just outside the store. "Katrina freaking Niklos."

Katrina and a few other Rolling Six girls meandered toward the candy shop across the corridor. One of the girls said something and Katrina hung her head back and laughed. Her *animalia* magic spiraled around her in faint purple wisps that I knew from experience only I could see. That had been the scent I'd detected, too. Sometimes— scratch that, always—the sensitivity I had to magic was a real pain in the ass.

"Whoa. It's like you have the power of conjuring," Alex said in my ear.

I jumped. "Christ. What, did you fly out on your broom?"

"I've been standing here for a whole minute. You were just too busy staring razor blades at the girl to notice."

My shoulders sagged. "I don't care who Crowe sneaks into alleys with."

"Keep telling yourself that." She gave me a mischievous look that made my stomach drop. "Should we mess with her?"

"No."

She slung one of her shopping bags over her shoulder and started digging in her purse. "I only have a handful of cuts on me, but I'm sure we can find something. Or I could just make her puke all over herself."

Alex's power was the same as Crowe's—*venemon*. Magic of the body. Both brother and sister had it running thick through their veins.

"As much as I would enjoy that," I said, "I say we don't. Please."

Alex dug deeper in her purse. "Why not?"

Because I could already feel the heavy scent of at least three different kinds of magic wafting up out of her bag as she pawed through it, mixing with the lingering hint of Katrina's magic and the honey and smoke scent of Alex's. Because my vision was already going hazy with swirling colors.

"Katrina isn't dumb," I said, taking a few steps away from Alex in an effort to reach fresh air and sanity. "She'll figure it out, and then she'll tattle or something."

"Who cares what she says?"

"What if she tells Crowe?"

Alex looked up and bit her lower lip, considering. Technically the two gangs were allies, but after Crowe's last encounter with the Rolling Sixes, the peace was fragile at best. We shouldn't be stirring up crap with them. But Alex automatically hated all of Crowe's girlfriends, and I did, too, because . . . well, there were reasons.

Again with the hypocrisy. I tried another tack. "What if she tells the *Syndicate*?" I asked. "We can't use magic in front of drecks!" That was our word for non-kindled people—who were all around us right now.

Alex rolled her eyes. "Really? If Syndicate agents are coming, their focus is going to be on the real action at the festival, not a prank at a mall."

Now I was starting to feel ill, and not just because of the sight and sound of mixing magic. "Maybe you're right, but if anyone finds out—"

Alex shrugged as she peered between two mannequins standing in the storefront partially concealing our position. "We'll use something innocuous. Come on. Look at how smug she is. I bet she's telling everyone she got into his pants."

I followed Kat's progress down the corridor, her dark hair shining like oil in the light. I couldn't help but picture Crowe's fingers sliding through it and the thrill it would have given her like it had once given me. "Fine," I said.

Alex smiled, baring her teeth in a way that was more maniacal than pleased. She dropped to the floor so she could get a better look into the bottom of her purse. "Aha. This will work." She held up a small plank of red wood, about the size of a stick of gum. Scrawled across the length of it in silver sharpie was SMELL: BAD.

The wood plank was called a cut, or charm, and I could immediately tell that it'd been created by Thom Flynn because of the handwriting, and because it was so unadorned. Most kindled created cuts like they were art, etching them with rune symbols or hand-drawing their labels in heady oil paints. Flynn's cuts were like Flynn: simple and straightforward.

"Why do you have a bad-smelling charm?" I asked, and got a weird look from a passing guy. I pressed my lips together. We weren't supposed to *talk* about magic in front of drecks, either.

"You never know when a stench will be called for," Alex answered. "I like to be prepared for anything."

Once activated, cuts were easy to use directly, like for protection or as tools—or weapons. It was a little trickier to use them remotely, on a target that wasn't close by, but Alex was a pro at by-proxy magic.

"Do you know what the smell is?" I asked, nerves creeping in once again.

"No." Alex was crouching just inside the entrance to the store. "But knowing Flynn, I'm sure it's uproariously foul." She set the charm in the palm of her hand and whispered the short incantation, giving it a target. As she stood up, I shifted behind her and grabbed the bar of a nearby clothing rack, just in case. Even though I wasn't the magic's target, I never knew how the scent and sight of it would affect me, and I didn't want anyone to know it could affect me at all.

The wooden cut glowed green with Flynn's *inlusio* magic, and despite the fact that it had been created to give off a bad smell, my nose filled with the scent of autumn leaves and cigar smoke—the smell of the *inlusio* magic itself. Emerald filaments laced my vision, and I clamped my eyes shut in the hope of clearing them away.

"Hey, you okay?" Alex asked.

I forced my eyes open. "What? Oh. Yeah. Headache."

"Again?" She lifted the charm from her hand, and the light burned out. Once again, it looked like nothing more than a normal sliver of wood. "Want me to—"

"No," I said quickly as she started to reach for me, ready to use her own *venemon* magic to heal. "I'm fine." There was enough magic in the air already.

"Oh, here we go," she whispered, peering at Kat.

I followed the line of her gaze with a mixture of dread and giddiness. This was the way of our relationship. Alex always did the dirty work, and I always let her. She had enough power and caused enough trouble that there was almost never pressure on me to use my own magic, for which I was very thankful.

The first to catch a whiff of the curse was the shorter girl at Katrina's left. Her nose wrinkled and she brought a hand up to cover it. "Ewww," she said. "What is that smell?"

Kat caught on next, and her mouth turned down at the corners as she tried to wave the smell away. "I don't know. God, that's awful."

10

The dark-haired girl trailing behind Kat said, "I don't mean to be a bitch, but I think it's you."

"Of course it's not me, you idiot." Katrina scowled. "I showered this morning."

"Oh God, it smells like rotten tuna," another girl said.

Alex barked out a laugh.

Katrina's head turned, and her eyes immediately found us hunched in the entrance of the clothing store.

"Shit," Alex said.

"I told you!" I said.

"Go!" Alex pushed me out the door.

"You haven't paid for the dress!"

She threw it over the shoulder of the nearest mannequin and gave me another shove. "I'll come back for it later."

"Alexandra!" Katrina yelled. "Jemmie! I will kill you!" She stormed toward us, her sleek ponytail whipping behind her.

Shoppers slowed to watch our drama. A cluster of dreck girls from Hawthorne High held up their phones, ready to film if a fight broke out.

"Faster!" Alex gave me another shove.

"Don't push me!" I said over a shoulder.

Kat was gaining ground on us. "Goddamn it, you two! Undo it!"

"Not a chance!" Alex said.

"Hey! Ladies! Stop right there!" A mall cop stepped into our path, his hands held up like he was trying to soothe a bucking horse. Or, more likely, stop a suspected shoplifter.

People pressed up against the storefronts, throwing protective arms around their children like we were first-rate criminals. Laughter bubbled up my throat.

Alex snapped her fingers, and her magic, sweet and smoky and shimmering with golden flecks, hit my senses in an instant even though, once again, I wasn't its target. She dodged to the left, yanking me with her as I stumbled. The cop—who *was* the target—doubled over, his face waxen.

Just as Katrina was running past the cop, he straightened and puked all over her. The gathered onlookers took a collective breath. Katrina froze, vomit dripping down her leg and sloughing from her billowy tank top.

"Time to go," Alex whispered just as Katrina snapped back to life and let out a demon-like snarl.

Alex and I laughed. And laughed and laughed and laughed until we were far away from the mall and Katrina Niklos.

"I definitely need to trade for another of Flynn's cuts," Alex said.

She turned her car off Reddman Road and onto a graveled one-lane. The woods hugged the drive that wound back to Sable River, and the little cottage that sat on its shore. We were officially on Medici property now, which made us safer than almost anywhere else.

"Because that has got to be the second-best revenge strike we've ever put in motion."

"I think you mean *you*," I corrected. "I get dizzy if I even try to cast like that."

Alex blew out a breath. "It takes practice, Jemmie," she said quietly. "Don't tell me you can't do it. Remember that time Crowe was chasing after us in the woods and you put up that barrier—?"

"We were eleven. I was scared. It was a reflex." And I'd gotten so dizzy from the rush of my own magic, plus the intensity of the sight and smell of it so close by, that I tripped and fell on my face a second later. Crowe was after us because he'd discovered us in his room and threatened to pull our lungs out through our nostrils—a threat I actually took seriously. But he bounced off my barrier right after I fell. He landed on his butt, already laughing about the instant karma while I wiped mud from my face on the other side.

"That was one seriously badass reflex, my friend," Alex replied.

I turned toward the window, thinking of what had

happened the very next day, how it had changed my life forever, how it had cemented my decision to avoid using magic whenever and however I could. "It was a fluke."

"You have greatness under all those layers of denial, Jemmie. Someday we're going to dig it out."

Alex's constant faith in me felt good, like a warm fire on a cold winter's day. If only it were actually warranted. The magic that ran in my family, the Carmichaels, was protective *locant* magic. My dad had it in spades. The barrier I'd thrown up that day was so wide and so stubborn that Lori, Crowe and Alex's mom, had to call Dad in to remove it, and it had convinced him that I would be as powerful as he was... but he was wrong. And so was Alex.

Sure, I might have magic. I just can't use it.

And in the kindled world, that made me about as useful as a dreck.

The road curved inward and the Medici cottage came into view. It was a slouching, one-story house surrounded by flowers that looked as if they'd been planted deliberately in a neat rainbow of color. They hadn't. Lori Medici was originally a Stoneking and had the *terra* magic many in her family were known for. She could walk into a forest and speak to the trees like they were old friends. She'd used her magic to coax the heart of the woods to beat stronger around the cottage.

On either side of the front door, giant hydrangea bushes bloomed all summer long, even in the heart of the hottest months. Wildflowers had sprung up between the hydrangea blooms in purple and yellow and cornflower blue. A twisting rose bush had been creeping for years up a peeling white lattice on the corner of the house, and although it was an antique rose, meant to only bloom once a year, it kept producing buds from spring to fall. On the far side of the house, facing the river, a magnolia tree hung heavy with flowers. Only a dusting of loosed petals lay in the grass.

Alex parked at the head of the driveway. We got out and walked around the house to the river's edge. The Sable River here was narrower and shallower than it was in town, but it was no less beautiful to look at. Here the sandy bottom glittered in the sunlight. Water trickled over a cluster of rocks, producing that spa-like tranquil sound of gurgling water.

I lay on the ground beneath the magnolia tree, sunlight peeking through in crosshatches. I kicked my shoes off and dug my toes into the grass. Alex lay down beside me, closed her eyes, and breathed out. This was our happy place, the cottage and the woods. In this place, with my best friend at my side, I felt like I belonged.

"Have you thought about what you're going to do this fall?" Alex asked after a moment.

"No." I closed my eyes, too, and let the sun warm me, my hands splayed across my stomach.

"Why not?"

"Because I don't know what I want to do." I didn't have to see her to know she was now looking at me, frowning.

"Are you considering moving to the city, maybe following in your dad's footsteps?"

"Are you kidding me?" I fought to keep a sneer of disdain on my face, but I couldn't hide the tremble of my lower lip that said this conversation was getting to me.

"Aw, Jemmie," Alex said. Her fingers brushed my arm. "I shouldn't have mentioned him."

Dad had left Mom and me the day after Crowe chased us through the woods, and he'd barely been involved in our lives ever since. A founding member of the Devils' League along with Crowe's father, Owen Carmichael now worked for the Syndicate, of all things. That agency served as a check on kindled powers, and they'd been down on the Devils ever since a brutal gang war with the Deathstalkers that had ended seven years ago with the violent death of the Stalkers' president, Henry Delacroix. Just after it happened, my dad left the Devils—and our family—to work for the other side.

And I was pretty sure it was at least partly my fault.

I pulled my arm out of Alex's reach. "It's all right," I said, laughing to hide the catch in my voice. "I just don't think a job with the Syndicate is in my future."

People with *locant* magic often worked for the Syndicate, using their power to protect others and even bind criminals' magic so it couldn't be used against innocents. If the Devils' League wasn't my chosen family, a job with the Syndicate might have been a natural choice for me... assuming I could actually cast.

So what was I supposed to do now that I'd graduated from high school? Go to a dreck college and pretend I was like them? Marry a dreck who had no clue about the world I'd been raised in? No thanks. But I wasn't so sure I could stay in Hawthorne, either. It wasn't exactly easy for me to be here, and living in a less magical place would be a relief in some ways. Except—I would have to leave my mom and Alex, the only two people in this world who really cared about me, with or without magic.

"You know," Alex said, and the way her voice crept up an octave immediately caught my attention. She sounded uncertain, and Alex was rarely uncertain.

"What?"

"Now that you're eighteen, you could apply to be a prospect."

I laughed. "You know I don't have a bike."

"And you know there's one in that shed behind your house."

The one that had been my dad's. "If you think going for a patch is so awesome, why don't you do it?"

"Ha! As if I'd join a club where my brother was the president. No freaking way. Bad enough being part of his family."

I knew she was mostly joking, but also that she'd never be able to take orders, especially from Crowe. She just wasn't built for it. I wasn't sure I was, either. "So you think I should join even though you never would? Hypocrite much? Gunnar told me all about the hazing, by the way. I can't believe you'd wish that on me."

"Oh, you wouldn't be a prospect long. Crowe would make sure you moved up to full patch fast—it's not like anyone would vote against having you. Your *locant* power is something the Devils haven't had access to since your dad left."

In dreck motorcycle clubs, women weren't always allowed to be members. But with the kindled, parts didn't matter—power did. "I'm sure they can find someone else if they really want to. Someone useful."

"Stop that," she snapped. "You always put yourself down."

I sighed. "Just being realistic."

"You know you have more magic than you're willing to use. I wish you'd tell me why."

I wished I could. "It's just...I'm not good at it. Practicing doesn't help."

"I'd buy that if you ever actually practiced!"

"It doesn't matter, okay? Crowe doesn't need me. He doesn't want me, either. He barely even notices when I'm in the same room with him."

"That might be the biggest lie you've told all day."

I squinted against the light as the wind shifted, pushing the branches of the magnolia tree out of line with the sun. My rebellious heart pounded eagerly in my chest. "Did he say something?"

Alex sat up and folded her arms around her legs. "No. Nothing out loud."

"Isn't that the way one says things?" I pushed myself up on my elbows. Part of me wanted to coax more from her. Part of me wanted her to say that what Crowe and I had had before was not completely broken.

One moment had changed everything between us, the thread that connected us burned away—and he'd been the one to set it on fire. He'd chosen that moment just to hurt me, too. Or maybe he'd never cared at all. Which made me lucky, I supposed. I'd surely dodged a bullet.

At least that's what I told myself whenever I crossed paths with him, because admitting the truth would be worse.

I missed Crowe Medici. But telling myself I hated him was much, much easier.

Alex pulled a tube of lip gloss from her bag and drew the wand across her lips. "Forget Crowe. I'm the one who needs you."

I hung my head back. "Now you're being ridiculous."

"It's true. I would wither and die without you." She smiled, her lips bright red and glittering. "Or, more accurately, I'd be in jail with no one to bail me out."

I laughed. The wind subsided and the sunlight faded as the tree branches settled again.

A single magnolia petal fell from above, drifting back and forth like a feather.

Alex had it all wrong. She didn't need anyone. It was me who couldn't survive without her.

"You'll figure it out, Jemmie," Alex said softly. "But if you want my opinion, you belong right here in Hawthorne."

Glints of her golden magic sparked in my vision, forming an aura around her face—she had so much that sometimes it just wafted from her unbidden. I closed my eyes to shut it out. If Alex knew what I felt every time I was around kindled power, she'd probably tell me I should leave town and live somewhere else, far away from the magic that made my vision blur and my head ache. Though I knew she'd say it out of concern for me, it would still kill me to hear. And no matter what I decided, it couldn't erase the truth that ruled my life:

It was freaking painful to love something that didn't want you in return.

TWO

ALEX AND I SPENT THE BETTER PART OF THE AFTERNOON at the Medici Cottage. It wasn't until the sun started to set that we left the house and followed the river three miles south to the Schoolhouse.

It, too, sat on the edge of Sable River, and although it hadn't been an actual school for a century, going there was always an education.

One I both looked forward to and dreaded.

The two-story structure, which served as the Devils' League clubhouse and party headquarters, had been constructed of red brick, with white trim around the doors and windows. The old leaded glass windows were still intact, as was the bell tower and the giant bell inside. Just the thought of it made me cringe a little. Last summer after so many things had fallen apart, I'd managed to get drunk enough to climb up there and try to ring it. Crowe had had to rescue me after I got stuck, and I wished I could forget the sad, disgusted look on his face as he did. I'd stayed away from the Schoolhouse for nearly six months after that out of pure shame. Since then I'd been back a few times, but never for more than a drop-in.

Alex pulled into the lot and drove past a row of parked Harley-Davidsons. They were lined up equidistant from one another, the front tires all cocked to the right. Parked Harleys always reminded me of stacked dominos—kick one and they all go down. Not that I'd ever try something like that in a place like this.

Alex parked in front, in the spots reserved for her and her family. An old oak tree loomed over us, and in the murky evening light, it looked like a giant with a thousand gnarly hands. The old gas lamps were lit up, too, casting golden halos on the cobblestone path up to the front door. Music spilled out open windows—and so did magic. I blinked as my vision hazed with it, as my stomach rolled with its heavy, multifaceted scent. Alex skipped along next to me, oblivious and happy. Why was I the only one who seemed to be allergic to the stuff? It was so unfair.

I breathed through my mouth and focused on the song that was playing. Something old, something rock-and-roll. Familiar and grounding, even if it wasn't my favorite.

" 'Lord knows I can't change!' " Alex sang along with the music, her arms raised above her head. "I love this song," she added when the lyrics gave way to a guitar solo.

"Me too," I lied, and stepped aside as Boone, a giant of a man, ambled past, his body clad almost entirely in black leather.

"It's the little banshee!" he called over his shoulder.

Everyone at the Schoolhouse called Alex "the little banshee," because when she was a baby all she did was wail.

"Your brother was in a mood today. Fair warning, sugar," Boone said as he made his way toward his motorcycle.

Alex and I shared a look.

I pulled the heavy wooden door open and Alex slipped in ahead of me. Better she go first. Crowe wouldn't kill his flesh and blood. Besides, I welcomed the chance to adjust to the onslaught that greeted me. Like many of the kindled motorcycle clubs, the Devils' League was a small, single-chapter club with only twenty full-patch members and a handful of prospects and hangarounds who might prospect in the future, but there were a few hundred friends of the club, members of the kindled community who gathered to support them, which was what seemingly all of them had done tonight. The Schoolhouse was packed, swirls and splashes of amber, green, pink, purple, and orange haloing the kindled, hanging in the air. Just the sight made me clutch at the wall. I willed my feet to be steady.

The music was even louder inside, thrumming through the floorboards. In the first classroom we passed, everyone had abandoned the billiards tables and danced to the guitar solo that was somehow still carrying on, punctuated by quick, frenetic drum riffs. They were a motley crew of men and women, gyrating and jumping, hair whipping, arms raised and flailing. When the lyrics picked back up, the entire room broke out in song.

This was the double-edged sword of the place. There was something intoxicating about seeing this crowd here, something so *us*. And yet it also made me ache because I couldn't be fully part of it. Unlike everyone else, I couldn't just let go and revel. A ringing had picked up in my ears, and the colorful aura signaled a major headache coming on. Perhaps sensing me falter even though she couldn't possibly know why, Alex threaded her arm through mine and tugged me toward the bar—and that was right where I needed to be if I wanted to survive the evening.

To get there, we had to walk past the library, which was situated in the far left corner of the building. The room was fronted by thick double doors that were always closed and locked. That was the casting chamber and meeting place, accessible only by members of Alex's family and trusted members of the Devils' League, as well as a few select kindled who were allies of the club.

I could smell the magic inside even now, so potent that it collected like a film on the back of my throat. There were notes of something metallic and steely, but it was overwhelmed by something sticky and sweet. *Venemon* magic—specifically Crowe's, which had a musky, masculine undertone that distinguished it from Alex's. It made me want to breathe deep. It made me want to run.

No magic in the kindled world was inherently good or bad. But Crowe could turn a hex as easily as a child could cast a handful of rocks. Of course, the *venemon* magic that ran in the Medici family lent itself well to being twisted. They could heal, but could just as easily inflict pain, or crush bone, or make someone ill.

Crowe was devastatingly good at both healing and hurting—and didn't hesitate to do either.

A lot of conservative kindled said that made him a criminal. Crowe once joked that it made him talented. After all, his ancestors had been renowned for their poisons and antidotes, which were really just well-cast spells. The better-known Italian Medicis were assassins and court enforcers and aristocratic warriors, but many were also skilled physicians and healers. Crowe parlayed his inherited abilities into a gold mine like so many of his ancestors before him.

The Devils' League sold his magical healing cuts through trade lines all across the continental United States. They also sold mild hexes that might cause someone to vomit for a week or lie in bed in anguish for a day. But the top sellers, by far, were Crowe's amplifying cuts. The charm gave the user a temporary boost, much like a shot of adrenaline, and that included making whatever magic the individual cast about ten times stronger.

I didn't have to be a conservative to know that what Crowe created and sold toed a dangerous line. It gave more people the opportunity to use their own magic for crooked purposes. And one time, I admit, I sort of did exactly that— I had tried to use one of Crowe's amplifying cuts myself. I had stolen it from his room the day he found and chased us, actually. My dad had just announced he would be moving away, and I thought, maybe, if I could convince him I had magic as powerful as his, he would stay. He would stop looking at me with that furrowed brow that signaled a mixture of concern and disappointment.

Thanks to that reflexive barrier spell, I had gotten away with the amplifying cut. The next day, as my dad packed his things, I tried it out, thinking I could throw a containment spell around the entire house and keep Dad with us, where he belonged.

This is the way eleven-year-olds think, unfortunately. It was also the way I ruined everything. I activated the cut the same way I'd seen some of the grown-ups do at summer gatherings—cradling the wood close to my face, whispering the incantation just so—but what I thought would boost my magic only boosted my sensitivity to it. Suddenly, I was retching, writhing, the containment spell I'd tried to cast wrapping around me like sky-blue ropes, the minty, stinging scent of it closing my throat. Choking me.

I remember the horror and confusion in Dad's eyes when he found me. I remember my mother calling 911. I remember my father having to destroy the spell I'd cast in order to allow the dreck paramedics to make it through the door.

The doctors told them it was an allergic reaction, probably to something I'd eaten. My parents thought I had misused a cut I'd stolen from my dad's bag, and he moved out that very night. Mom told me it really had nothing to do with me, but how could I believe that? He couldn't even look at me as he said good-bye.

That was the last time I'd intentionally used magic. But when I was in a place like the Schoolhouse, it didn't matter.

By the time Alex and I slid into our booth in the back corner of the barroom, my body was practically buzzing with it. Magic of all types crept up my spine, across my skin, into my ears and nose.

Alex gave me a look. "You okay?"

"I need a drink *stat*."

She frowned, but before she could dig further, one of her cousins called her name and sidled over to our table, coaxing Alex into a conversation about the upcoming festival. I headed to the bar and furtively ordered a shot of rye from Dara, the bartender. She arched an eyebrow. "Sure you wanna go down that road again, darlin'?"

I winced, thinking about my last drunken night here. "Nope. Not at all. But this is just to take the edge off, okay?" I offered her my best puppy-dog eyes. "It's been a rough day."

Dara was a sucker for the puppy-dog eyes. "You know I'm not supposed to serve you...."

"It'll be our secret," I whispered. "And make it two. Alex wanted one as well."

That sealed the deal, because no one refused Alex Medici. "Sip on it, all right? Take it slow."

"Will do," I said as she slid two shots of the amber liquid toward me. Relief was already singing in my veins— alcohol dulled my sense of smell and dampened the killer rainbow aura of kindled power in the room. It was the best way for me to survive the night. I whirled around, smoothly downing the first shot as I did. Quickly walking back to Alex, glad as ever that she was monopolizing the gazes and focus of half the people in the room, I tossed the second shot back and set the two glasses on a table that needed to be bussed.

Alex hated rye anyway.

Smiling as the liquor burned my throat, heated my belly, and sent a wave of heavy relaxation along my limbs, I sank onto the seat next to her. She didn't seem to notice I'd been gone and was engaged in animated conversation, so I pulled my phone from my pocket. Turns out I'd missed a text earlier—one I'd been waiting all day to receive.

I'll meet you at your house later, it said.

Fingers trembling, I texted back: **Can't wait.**

Putting my phone on vibrate, I dropped it back in my pocket and turned my attention to the library again. Just because I could sense Crowe's magic didn't mean he was here—the Schoolhouse always smelled like him. When I didn't see him, I relaxed a little.

With our table now full, and Alex talking about her mother's plans for the Medici tent at the festival, I turned to the room to people-watch. At a table in the far corner, Jackson Niklos, a Devil member in his early twenties, was showing off his *animalia* magic using a butterfly. The monarch flitted in between three women, the wings brushing against their cheeks like a chaste kiss, making the women blush and giggle, sending up purple puffs of magic only I could see. Behind the bar, Brooke, one of the Devils' League prospects, a Warwick with the *invictus* power her family was renowned for, carted in two kegs, one balanced on each shoulder. The weight was nothing for someone with that kind of magic, which hung around her in a faint orange haze. I knew from experience it smelled of cloves, pungent and biting. Fortunately, all I could smell right now was the lingering hint of rye. It let me enjoy this place for what it was—an oasis of wonder in a not-so-wonderful world.

Within the walls of the bar, our magic wasn't a secret, guarded and tamped down like it was in the outside world, among drecks. Even before my dad split, all my holidays and birthdays were spent here with the Devils' League. They were my family. And even as I got older and my sensitivity to the magic grew, I never wanted to stay away *too* long— and so I'd figured out how to cope.

"Little banshee!" Thom Flynn called as he shuffled over and leaned in to kiss Alex's forehead. Although he wasn't related to Alex by blood, she considered him her uncle, and he treated her like she was his favorite niece.

"Hey, Uncle Flynn," Alex replied quickly before snapping

her fingers as Dara walked by. "Jack and Coke for me, please. Jemmie, what are you having?"

Dara gave me a hard look, and I grinned in what I hoped was a charming way. "Uh...a Tom Collins, maybe?"

"Good idea," said Alex. "Keep it light."

"Absolutely," I said, turning away so she couldn't smell the liquor on my breath. "Wouldn't want to get crazy."

Dara paused for a moment, and I tensed, wondering if she was going to call me on my antics. But then Alex cleared her throat and the waitress scurried off.

Flynn scooted in next to me and put his arm over the back of the booth. "So what's new, Carmichael?"

I shrugged. "The usual."

He grabbed a handful of peanuts from the bowl on the table and started cracking them open. "The usual good or the usual bad?"

"Just the usual-usual."

Flynn laughed. His overgrown salt-and-pepper hair was tied back in a bun, revealing what might have once been an extremely handsome face. Freckles dusted his nose. His eyes were big and blue. Gray stubble covered his jaw and the skin wrinkled around his eyes, but a lot of the older women who orbited the club went after Flynn. I guess to them he still had something worth pursuing.

I'd known Flynn as long as Alex had, which was to

say, since we were babies. My dad, Michael Medici, and Flynn used to be best friends and had founded the club together back when it was more about the riding and the freedom. I got the sense that their feud with the Deathstalkers had ruined all of that. The club Crowe inherited last year was a completely different animal, more about doing business and fending off threats. More about basic survival.

Someone called out to Flynn from across the room, poking fun at his recent loss at the poker table. Flynn cursed at the guy, whispered an *inlusio* incantation, and tossed a peanut his way. I held my breath to protect myself from the cigar smoke scent, but saw the telltale trail of cast magic as the peanut arced through the air and burst into a thick green haze when it hit the table—revealing a coiled viper as it cleared. The guy lurched to his feet, eyes round with terror as his body reacted instinctively to the illusion. If the snake struck, the bite would hurt him almost as much as the real thing.

Flynn laughed again. "That one deserved it," he said to me, and grinned.

I returned his smile and swiped my drink from Dara's tray when she returned to our table. Alex shoved aside her straw and took a healthy gulp. She chuckled as I sucked down half of mine in the same amount of time. "Looks like we'll need another round soon," Alex called, even though Dara had already turned away. "And add two shots of tequila!"

"Slow down, little banshee," Flynn said to Alex.

Alex rolled her eyes and exchanged a conspiratorial glance with me behind his back. My cheeks burned with guilt—if she'd known I was two ahead of her, she wouldn't think it was so funny.

I sipped my drink, determined to do exactly as Flynn advised, especially because my head was already starting to swim. I needed to slow down if I wanted to stay in this zone of pleasant, numbing buzz without toppling over the edge into crazy, drunken Jemmieland. "So," I said to Flynn, leaning close so he could hear me over the pulse and pound of the music, "I heard you finally got that old 1938 Crocker road-worthy. Are you going to show it off at the festival?"

Hearing my interest in his dearest love, Flynn's eyes lit up, but before he could answer, the library doors began to open and the entire Schoolhouse turned their attention in that direction.

The doors creaked and scraped as they swung wide, heavy and loud. The library had always held my fascination—and fear. Ever since I was a child, it had seemed like a forbidden world separate from my own, where magic was a beast tamed by grown-ups, easily unleashed if someone misbehaved. For me, even setting foot in that room was likely to end badly, so I'd never tried. Though I was older now, far from being a kid anymore, my dread of the library had only increased—because now Crowe commanded it.

"Tell you about it later," Flynn said over his shoulder as he hurried from the table.

Crowe was the first out the double doors. From where I sat, he stood in profile when he paused in the hallway to scan the bar. A lock of his black hair hung rogue over his forehead. He was clad entirely in black, save for the trio of cuts hanging from a leather cord around his neck.

All eyes were on him. At six foot three, he towered over most, but it was more than his height that made him stand out, even to kindled who couldn't sense Crowe's magic the way I could.

Crowe was the kind of person who didn't need to demand respect—it was automatically given to him.

"Oh, great," Alex muttered next to me. "He *does* look pissed."

And he did. He looked really, really pissed. I didn't even have to see the whole of his face to know it. The tendons in his arms stood out sharply, clenched just like his fists. His jaw flexed, teeth grinding. I wanted to shrink the way he swelled, and disappear into a puff of dust beneath the table. If I had *that* ability, I'd probably try to use it.

Flynn settled in behind Crowe, on his right, and curiously enough, on his left was Old Lady Jane Vetrov, clad in a patchwork dress and motorcycle boots, and wearing a black bandanna over her long white hair. Jane was stuffed to the gills with *omnias* magic that ran in the Vetrov family and made her Hawthorne's resident psychic, the best of the best. And weirdest of the weird, if you asked me. But that was probably just a side effect of having access to the Undercurrent, what drecks called the spirit world. Old Lady Jane wasn't a Devil. She kept herself on neutral ground, believing that her gift belonged to everyone, and therefore owed allegiance to no one club or family.

Seeing her in the Schoolhouse, with Crowe of all people, was rather uncharacteristic.

She rose to the tips of her pointy boots and whispered something into his ear, and he acknowledged her with a shift of his chin. She nodded, squeezed his arm—protected from her powerful clairvoyant touch by the thick sleeve of his motorcycle jacket—and headed for the bar.

Crowe's best friend, Hardy Warwick, took up the spot vacated by Jane and, like a pack of wolves, the three men faced the room together. "Gunnar still hasn't turned up,"

Crowe announced. "I don't know where he's tucked himself this time, but if any of you come across him, tell him to sober up and get his ass to the festival tomorrow. I need him."

Ah, Gunnar. He and I had shared a few wild nights at the Schoolhouse in the past, seeing as he could drink me under the table as easily as breathing. His *arma* magic enabled him to forge weapons out of anything—mud, a pile of rocks, a handful of drinking straws—and I guess Crowe thought that was pretty important for the festival, which made me wonder what exactly he thought was going to go down.

I didn't have much time to ponder that, though, because that was the moment the president of the Devils' League noticed me. If Alex was a pearl, then her brother was obsidian. Black volcanic glass. Pretty and shiny, quick to cut. As our eyes met, it all came back, his hands and his mouth, and then the moment I realized he had used me as a momentary distraction. I hunched in my seat, once again wishing I could disappear.

The jukebox switched albums, and something loud and bass-heavy started up, allowing me to pretend that the thumping in my chest was the music and not my traitorous heart.

Crowe started toward us, and I took a long draw from

my drink, hoping the burn of the alcohol would override the other burn sinking lower and lower in my gut.

"Alex," Crowe said when he reached the table. He shed his jacket and hung it on a hook nailed to the side of the booth. He leaned over and kissed Alex's cheek, then slid into the booth beside me. Hardy slid in on the other side of Alex, effectively trapping us between them. Flynn grabbed his drink and leaned against a nearby post.

"Hey, Jemmie," Crowe said. "What are you drinking?"

I concentrated on enunciating my consonants as I said, "None of your damn business."

He reached over, grabbed my glass, and drained what was left of my drink in one gulp. "Tom Collins."

"Hey!" I said.

Hardy chuckled. I scowled at him, but it only made him laugh harder, sharpening the lines of his cheekbones.

I waved at Dara as she passed. "Can I get another Tom Collins, please?"

"No, Dara," Crowe said. "She can't." He didn't take his eyes off me. "You reek of whiskey, Jem."

I turned to him, glad that the heady burn in my gut had formed into something useful: anger. "Bullshit." But my cheeks were also burning—and probably bright pink.

"Dara, how many drinks have you served Jemmie already tonight?"

The waitress shifted her weight from one foot to the other, biting her bottom lip.

"It's okay," said Crowe. "You won't get in trouble. Just tell me."

"Three," she said quietly.

"That's totally not true," I snapped, but Crowe ignored me.

"And how long has she been here?" he asked.

"'Bout twenty minutes," Dara replied, throwing me an apologetic look.

"She's done for tonight," he said over me.

"No, I'm not, Dara," I said, my throat tight. With Crowe next to me, all the magic inside him was pressing on my senses, making my entire body ping with alarm and dizziness. It was going to take another drink at least to tamp that down. "You were supposed to bring ush shots of tequila anyway."

Dammit. I'd slurred my words. Crowe's brow pinched with disapproval.

"Dara," Crowe said. "Jemmie is done if I say she's done."

Dara gave him a quick nod before scurrying away. Next to me, Alex heaved a disappointed sigh. I clenched my jaw, so the next words that came out of my mouth were ground between my teeth like grain beneath a pestle. "Why are you such an asshole, Crowe?"

At least I hadn't slurred it.

Everyone within earshot fell silent. It was the kind of quiet that comes before a storm hits, an eerie stillness charged with anticipation. The table was almost buzzing with it, everyone wondering how Crowe would react.

Crowe smiled and pretended I didn't just call him an asshole in front of everyone. "Last time you drank here," he said, "you ended up puking all over our bathroom. Or did you forget already?"

Worse than Crowe yelling was Crowe chastising.

Now *I* looked like the asshole.

I sagged against the back of the booth, defeated, and as I did, I felt the heat of his arm through the thin material of my vintage T-shirt. It brought on a flashback of that night I'd gotten so sick, of Crowe, his voice soft and reassuring as he held my hair back while I vomited. His hands on me, on my stomach, and the instant relief that spread through me as he worked a spell to settle my queasiness. The cold that lingered when his hands finally pulled away.

Why did he do these things to me? Being around him made me feel like a rabid animal. I wanted to tear him apart and devour him all at the same time. His magic overwhelmed me more than most, even when he wasn't using it on me, but it also felt like heaven to have his hands on my skin. His gentle attention was like the sun on my face...but the way he'd looked at me afterward, the worry and puzzlement over why I'd had too much to drink yet *again*, the frustration and irritation when I wouldn't tell him why... that felt like being lost in the darkness of space.

I understood why girls fawned all over him. And it wasn't just the pull of him, or the power. He was also ridiculously gorgeous, and the scars that marred his face only managed to make him more attractive. A small one cut his left eyebrow in half. There was another slash just beneath his right eye, and a third and fourth ran along his jawline. Both were the result of brawls with interlopers from other gangs who tried to encroach on Hawthorne in the past year, thinking that because Michael Medici was dead and my dad had gone, the Devils' League would be ripe for a patch over. They hadn't bargained on Crowe's power in their takeover attempts, though, nor were they wise to his determination to keep the Devils independent, his willingness to get down in the mud and fight, and his utter brutality when he did. He could have healed himself after literally crushing the guys who tried to take him out, or he could have had Alex do it. But he'd chosen to let his wounds heal naturally. Alex had joked that it was because Crowe hadn't been able to stand looking so perfect all the time, but I had a feeling there was a different reason—the scars were a visual reminder of who he was now, of his responsibility, of what he'd lost.

Looking at him was reminding me of what I'd lost, too. Or, really, of what I'd never had.

"Crowe," Alex said, finally cutting through the obvious tension despite Crowe's seemingly relaxed smile, "give Jemmie a break."

As he turned to his sister, that smile disappeared and he just looked at her in that way of his that could destroy cells at the nuclear level. Alex rolled her eyes.

Crowe took in a breath. It wasn't a normal breath. It was the kind of breath that said he was preparing to light us on fire. Despite the alcohol rolling through my veins, I could already smell it. Smoky. Sweet. Deadly.

"I heard a rumor about you today." He turned in the booth to face us both, stretching his other arm, the one covered in a sleeve of tattoos, out on the table. His fingers rapped against the wood.

"A rumor?" Alex parroted, feigning disinterest.

Crowe scooted in closer, until his chest was practically pressed against my shoulder. Our legs bumped together beneath the table. I rubbed my eyes in an attempt to clear the shimmering threads of amber magic drifting off his skin.

"Did either of you cast at the mall?" he asked.

Alex pinched her straw between two fingers and twirled

42

it around and around in her drink. "Like I would be so stupid?"

Crowe gritted his teeth and turned his gaze on me. "Jemmie?"

"Uhhh…"

More than just the table was silent now. The whole barroom was quiet.

The hair on the nape of my neck stood on end.

"Twice!" Crowe barked, and I jumped. He clearly already knew the answers to his inquiries.

"This is bullshit," Alex started, but Crowe cut her off.

"You used it on two people. At the mall, of all fucking places."

"I did not!" was all the challenge Alex could muster.

"There were witnesses!"

Alex snorted. "Who? Your new girlfriend? Are you going to believe her over your own sister?"

As Crowe leaned in more, I pressed my back into the booth, wishing I could melt into it. No one wanted to be caught between two warring Medicis, but right now it was to my advantage. Once again, maybe I could hide in Alex's shadow.

"I shouldn't have to remind you of the rules," Crowe said. "And I also shouldn't have to remind you not to cast against an ally. Katrina is a Six and you know it."

"Well, I'm not officially a Devil and neither is Jemmie," Alex snarled, "so she's not *our* ally, is she?"

I grimaced. Why had she brought me back into it?

Crowe slid out of the booth and stood. "Get up. Both of you."

Alex folded her arms over her chest. "What? Why?"

"Get up. *Now.*"

I obeyed. After a mutinous pause, Alex did, too. I wasn't sure where Crowe was going with this, but it didn't feel like it would be anywhere good.

The people in the middle of the barroom shrunk away from Crowe as Alex and I stood in front of him.

"Do I have to remind anyone else here of the rules?" he said as he turned a circle. "What is the consequence for casting recklessly in front of the drecks?"

"Binding," someone called out.

Oh no.

Crowe began to pace. Alex set her hands on her hips, like she was bored. I put my hand on my stomach, suddenly feeling sick.

"Exactly," Crowe said. "Binding. And there's only one person in this town who can do a binding spell." Crowe stopped. His heavy gaze settled on me.

"No."

He kept staring.

44

"No. Absolutely not. You probably have cuts my dad left behind that you can use. You don't need me."

"Nah. Fresh out," he said, giving me a tight smile. "You're up, Jemmie."

My whole face felt like it had been set on fire. Every gaze was on me, like needles digging under my skin. "I can't," I whispered.

"Now that's bullshit," he said. "You seem to forget that I've experienced your magic. I know what you can do."

"Crowe," Alex said, her tone softening. "That was a long time ago. I don't think—"

"Shut it," Crowe ground out. "She's going to do this, or you're both going to be banned from the festival."

"What?" Alex wailed. "You can't do that!"

I coughed as Crowe and Alex's smoky-sweet magic billowed around me, as the golden skeins of it roiled around their bodies, loosed by their rage. "Stop," I pleaded.

"If she doesn't bind your power with her *locant* magic, I'll happily leave you both so sick that it'll take you a month to start eating solid food again," Crowe said. "And if you even try to heal yourself, Alex, wait and see what starts to grow on your face."

"You wouldn't!"

Crowe laughed. "Try me."

"Remember that grayish fungus thing Gunnar was

sporting after New Year's?" Hardy asked. "That was Crowe being gentle."

Alex huffed and took me by the arms. "Just do it, Jemmie." I started to shake my head, then gasped as she squeezed painfully. "Do. It."

I gave her a pleading look, but she was now too full of fury to realize what she and Crowe were demanding. My heart was beating so fast I could barely get the words out. "Please. I can't."

"If you won't do it," Crowe said as he turned away, "then I suppose I'll have to report her, and the Syndicate will send its *locant* specialist to do it."

Goddamn it.

Goddamn him.

The Syndicate's *locant* specialist was my father.

"Fine," I muttered.

Maybe with three drinks on board, I could make this work. Maybe it would be okay.

I glanced at Alex. She was avoiding my eyes now, but the rosiness in her cheeks told me enough. Her own brother was embarrassing her in front of all her friends and family, and she wanted this over with.

My cloudy head tried to look for an alternative solution, but I came up with nothing. If the Syndicate was brought into this, my dad would bind her for a month. I could probably only muster a binding spell that would dissipate after a few days—if I could cast it at all.

Would she hate me for being the one to do this, or was it a favor to her? What if I was about to make even bigger fools of both of us?

"Time's up, Jemmie," Crowe said, and pulled out his cell phone.

"I said I'll do it!" I shouted.

Alex whipped her head my way, a scowl deepening the dark line of her brow. I turned to her, giving the room my back. "I'm sorry," I mouthed, but Alex's frown didn't lessen. If anything, it became more pronounced. I had no idea what she was thinking.

I wrapped my hands around her wrists. Although alcohol dulled my senses, my magic still came rushing forward, answering the call, wreathing my body with sapphire ribbons that slithered like cobras and were just as dangerous, to me, at least.

I'd been born with this magic. Using it should come as naturally as eating or sleeping. But without practice, it was a blunt instrument instead of a scalpel. And now the scent of it was on me, sharp and overpowering. I held my breath. My palms were slippery with sweat as I tightened my grip. Strands of blue magic waved and coiled in the air, growing from my skin like weeds. My stomach rolled. Sweat started to bead at my temples and the small of my back. The attention of the room made my skin crawl and burn—and so did my own magic.

I wanted to curse Crowe to an eternity of hell for doing this to us.

My head had begun to buzz with lack of oxygen. If I didn't cast quickly, I was going to pass out. With the blue twists of my *locant* power wrapping around my best friend, I mentally clamped the lock closed on Alex's magic and felt the flicker of it die out. It wasn't gone for good—there was only one way to take another's magic forever, and it was completely forbidden—but it was blocked from her use until the spell ran its course.

It wasn't until Alex yanked her arms from my grasp that I realized my hands had gone numb. She turned and walked away while I leaned on the table with my elbows, the only way to keep myself from hitting the floor. People were still staring. I wanted to cry and scream and kick and rage, but instead I said, "Alex, wait."

She didn't.

"It's not like she didn't deserve it," someone said behind me.

I whirled around, recognizing the voice. "You bitch," I said as I caught sight of Katrina. She smirked at me while she sipped a beer. My breath sawed from my throat. As soon as I got the feeling back in my hands, I was going to strangle her. "You should leave."

Katrina snorted. "And if I don't?"

"Jemmie," Crowe said when I started for her, my footsteps heavy and clumsy.

Amber ropes, invisible to everyone but me, wound around me. Every part of my body froze, my hand raised in midair. I growled at Crowe as he stepped between me and my target.

"Let me go," I said, fighting against his magic, silently berating myself for letting my guard down, for leaving a door open so he could step right through it. The sweet-smoky smell was making my stomach turn. Or maybe that was the rye.

He got in closer so when he spoke, it was loud enough that only I could hear. "Not until you stop acting like a brat."

"This is all *her* fault," I said. I gave Katrina a death glare as she inched closer to Crowe.

He frowned. "Is it?"

It suddenly felt like we were talking about something else entirely, and we both knew what that was.

"Yes," I said. "And yours, too."

His magic pulled back, freeing me. I sucked in a deep breath and shoved him away. He barely staggered an inch. It was like trying to displace a mountain.

With a curl of my lip, I swiped a shot of something clear off a nearby table and downed it in one burning gulp. Then I stormed out of the barroom.

THREE

As I hurried down the Schoolhouse's front steps, the double doors burst open behind me. I didn't have to turn around to know who it was.

"Jemmie, wait."

"Screw you."

Crowe quickly caught up to me. "There are rules. Without rules, we'd descend into chaos."

I stopped abruptly and Crowe had to backpedal. "That's rich, coming from you."

He cocked his head to the side. "The difference between Alex and me is that I know how and when to break the rules. She disregards them entirely."

He had no idea what he'd just done to me. No idea why I was so upset.

I started walking again. The Schoolhouse music faded behind us. There wasn't a lot of civilization in this part of town save for a few workshops that had long since closed. It was one of the reasons the bar got away with its rowdy crowd and thumping music long into the night.

"You shouldn't have made me do that," I said, my voice wavering.

"If anyone else could have, I wouldn't have asked you to."

We reached the street. I'd headed this way simply to escape, but now that I was out here, I realized I didn't have a ride home. If I wanted to go anywhere, I'd have to walk.

"Did Alex drive?" Crowe asked, reading my frustration easily.

"Yeah." I crossed my arms over myself and rubbed my hands over my bare skin. The night had cooled off since I'd been inside the bar, and goose bumps rippled down my forearms. Still, the fresh air was nice. And necessary. Finally, my head was starting to clear from the muddle of magic and alcohol.

"Let me take you home."

"I'm not riding on the back of your bike." Too soon for that, in so many ways.

"I have my car."

Spend time in an enclosed space with him? Ha. "Not riding in your car, either."

He ran his tongue along the inside of his bottom lip. Crowe didn't have a lot of tells, except for this one. It was what he did right before he put someone in their place.

I braced for it. It'd been a long day, and I wasn't sure I had enough left in me to fight him.

Hoping to cut the tension, I added, "I like walking."

"It's three miles."

"I'm in great shape." I peered down at my sandals. I was going to have blisters for days.

He sighed. "Just wait here. Please?"

"Fine."

He jogged back toward the Schoolhouse, disappearing in the shadows on the north side, swallowed whole like a specter.

Less than a minute later, he pulled his black 1967 Nova into the street. He crossed the centerline, driving up alongside me at the curb, then leaned over and opened the passenger-side door.

Inside, the chill in my bones seeped away immediately, despite the fact that the car's heater hadn't had enough time to warm up. A heavy scent of cinnamon hung in the air, along with tiny pink shimmers. He'd used a cut to kindle a warming charm. Probably from his mom.

I glanced at Crowe as he shifted the car into gear and pulled back onto the road. "What?" he said, without looking at me.

"Thanks."

"You're welcome."

We rode in silence for a while, and I tried to calm down. Crowe had no idea why I didn't use magic, or what it did to me—and that was because I kept my problem to myself. He'd wanted to make an example of Alex and me tonight, and he had succeeded. He couldn't have known how scared I had been, how awful it felt to cast. Those thoughts cooled my rage and humiliation, making room for other realizations. I had managed to do a binding charm, and I hadn't ended up on the floor or in the hospital. That...was actually a good thing. And if Alex would let me know that she wasn't pissed or hurt, then I'd feel even better. Needing to turn my anxious thoughts away from my temporarily powerless best friend, I asked, "What was Old Lady Jane doing at the Schoolhouse?"

Crowe's thumb tapped against the leather steering wheel while we waited out a red light. "Club business."

"About the festival?" With a half-dozen other clubs in town, there was a lot of business to do.

The intersection was empty of traffic. Crowe tapped out a quicker rhythm, as if sitting still in the car, the brake engaged, was making him restless. "Jane's been consulting for me on a few things."

"Such as?"

"The future."

I sighed. "Obviously. That's what Old Lady Jane does. So what's happening in the future?"

The light finally flicked to green and Crowe stepped on the gas. The car's engine roared to life as we lurched through the intersection.

"Bad things," he said quietly.

"You planning to break more bones?"

He leaned back on the headrest. "If I have to. But this is bigger than a few fistfights."

"A lot of fistfights, then?"

"We haven't run up against the Deathstalkers since last year."

I sat up in my seat. "But hasn't it been seven years since the Devils took their president down? I thought you guys had made peace."

"Hardly. The Devils didn't just take down the Stalkers' pres—they took out all five of the officers, too."

"Whoa," I said quietly. "I didn't know—"

"You were young. I'm sure your dad didn't want you to know."

"You were young, too."

"I was old enough." Weariness had seeped into his voice. "Anyway. I don't think the fight is over."

"But the Deathstalkers hosted us last year in New Orleans." My hands got clammy as the memories poured in. "They didn't seem to hold any of that against us," I said lamely.

"Yeah, they were perfect gentlemen," Crowe said.

"Your sarcasm is loud and clear," I said.

"They murdered my dad, Jem." His voice had gone low and husky.

"What? I—" I swallowed hard. Talking to Crowe about his dad's death felt like playing catch with a loaded gun. "I thought it was an accident."

"Wouldn't it be easy if we all believed that?"

"Flynn told me that's what it was."

"Flynn wishes that were true. But I saw my father's body. I know different."

I stared out the window into the night. "How could you tell it wasn't, um...natural?"

He sighed and shook his head. "I shouldn't have mentioned it to you."

"Why did you?"

A one-shoulder shrug was all I got for an answer. I let my vision go unfocused as I considered that Michael Medici might have been murdered—by Deathstalkers, no less. And if Old Lady Jane was right and something big and bad was going to happen, I could see why he was tense. With the Kindled Festival coming up, it was the perfect time for someone, anyone, to try to get revenge on Crowe for the pain he'd inflicted in the past year. The perfect time for someone to strike out at any of the Devils. Any of the Medicis.

"You just had me bind Alex's magic—what if she needs to protect herself?"

"I'll have people watching her back. Don't worry about this, okay?" Crowe turned onto my street. "Whatever is going on, I'll handle it."

My phone buzzed in my pocket. I scooped it out, hoping it was Alex.

Crowe glanced at the phone before pulling up in front of my house. "Who's 'D'?"

"None of your business."

"Girl or guy?"

"Guy." It was true, but also, I wanted to see his reaction.

He shut the car off and leaned back in the bucket seat, his body angled toward mine. A streetlight cast half his face in shadow and half in bright, silver light. Crowe had that perfect Italian skin and bone structure. The way he lived—drinking regularly, sleeping little, high stress and anxiety—you'd think he'd look haggard and older than he was. He didn't. He looked like he drank kale smoothies for breakfast and ran ten miles a day. I didn't know how he did it. Maybe his appearance was doctored by Flynn. Maybe Crowe Medici's handsomeness was just an illusion.

"This D guy a dreck?"

"Not all of us get off on dating for power." I pushed the car door open. "Why?"

He looked away from me, out the windshield to the empty street beyond. "I just want to be sure you're safe is all. Seeing a dreck is an unnecessary risk."

"So you think I should date only kindled?"

A half smile turned him devilish in the light. "I think you should embrace girl power and all that and stay single for a while."

"You're a shitbag." I stepped out and slammed the door shut.

"Jemmie. Wait."

I stalked around the front of my house to the back door. On the porch, I dug in my bag for my house key but didn't find it fast enough. Crowe caught up by the time I turned the deadbolt.

"Why are you still here?" I said as I dropped my bag on the kitchen table, giving the house a quick scan. It was dark save for the light above the stove. It cast a soft golden glow around the room. A package of thawing ribs and another of sausage were sitting out on the counter—clearly Mom was planning on making her special slow-cooked *feijoada*—but from what I could tell, she wasn't home. Thank God.

"I think we've had enough of each other for one night," I said.

I rummaged around inside the fridge and pulled out a takeout sandwich left over from last night. When I turned around, Crowe was standing in the middle of the kitchen, his car keys hanging from his index finger. He just stared at me.

The house seemed to shrink in size around him, and I took a step back, pressing myself into the counter so I didn't have to crane my neck to look at him.

"You always going to treat me like this?" he asked evenly.

I set the sandwich down and propped my hands on the edge of the counter. "Treat you like what?"

"Like you hate me."

"Maybe I do."

"Jemmie," he started.

I cut him off. "I should have walked home."

I moved past him for the living room. His hand snapped out and grabbed me by the wrist. Heat spread out from his touch, engulfing me, and I wondered if he felt it, too, this volcano that erupted between us whenever we touched. Only some of it had to do with magic, but I was already

59

breathing it in as it snaked out in amber streaks around us, dark and dangerous and pulsing.

He hadn't touched me purposefully in a long time.

A strange smell hit my senses, not magic. It was acrid and sharp, slicing through the sweet amber haze. It was accompanied by a very distinct sound.

The ribs and sausage were sizzling, the plastic around the packages melting onto the meat, smoke curling up toward the ceiling. Crowe cursed, his eyes sliding shut.

Crowe Medici rarely ever lost control of his magic.

"I'm sorry," he said when he finally looked at me again.

"For the meat, for following me into the house, or for something else?"

The question was baited, and he knew it. He took a step closer to me, and I stepped back until I was pressed against the doorway between the kitchen and living room and Crowe was pressed against me.

I could have sworn the earth shook.

"You don't know the whole story," he said, his voice low and throaty.

"I know enough of it."

"No, you don't. Otherwise we wouldn't be having this conversation."

"Then tell me."

"I can't," he answered.

"Of course not. Because it's complicated, I'm sure. Or maybe it's club business."

He exhaled with frustration. "Everything is always complicated in our world. You know that."

"Except what happened had nothing to do with magic, and everything to do with us." My voice rose as I went on. "You kissed me that night and I kissed you back, and what did you give me for it? Silence. Absolute fucking silence."

"Jemmie," he growled. I could barely see him through the shimmering fog of his magic. My tongue was coated with it. The meat on the counter popped and hissed some more—and then the sausage caught fire.

With another curse, Crowe stepped away, crossing back over to the kitchen counter. He swept both packages into the sink and turned on the faucet. "I'll have someone bring over more."

"Don't bother." I leaned over beside him and shut off the tap. "It's just one more reminder that you ruin whatever you touch."

His expression turned into a hard scowl. "Fine," he said, and the meat caught fire again despite having just been doused. I coughed from the mixture of smoke and sweet magic, holding on to the counter to stay upright.

"I hope it's reminder enough for you." He turned away

from me, tore open the back door, and slammed it shut a second later.

I couldn't help but watch him through the windows as he strode away, a dark shadow in a dark night.

I was better off without him.

Kissing him that night at his house, over a year ago now, had been the biggest mistake of my life. We had both been drunk, too caught up in each other. I wouldn't make that mistake ever again.

FOUR

I FINALLY BREATHED A SIGH OF RELIEF ONCE I HEARD
Crowe's car start up and tear off down the street. I made
my way down the hallway to my bedroom, wanting desperately to peel off my jeans and get into a pair of comfy
pajama pants. But as soon as I stepped inside my bedroom,
I knew I wasn't alone.

I flicked on the lamp on my dresser. Darek lay in my
bed, half propped up on an elbow, his phone in his hand.
"When did you get here?" I asked.

"About fifteen minutes before you did. Parked my bike
up the road." He nodded toward my open window, which

I'd left unlocked just for him. "And for a second there, I thought I was going to have to come to your rescue."

"You heard all that?" I dropped on the bed beside him and lay flat on my back.

He slid his arm over my middle slowly, like he was waiting for me to push him away. I didn't. Instead, I sighed and sank into the mattress as my muscles unknotted from the tension of the last hour or so.

"How could I not hear it, Jem?" A backward baseball cap covered most of his sun-bleached blond hair, but a few loose strands had managed to escape.

"Well, I'm glad you didn't intervene." I scrubbed at my face, suddenly sleepy. "You and Crowe in the same room would be a very, very bad idea."

After all, Darek was a Deathstalker prospect, due to be voted up to a full-patch member of the club in a month or two. To Crowe, he was the enemy, straight up. Even if the two gangs supposedly had a truce.

Darek offered me his easy, sweet smile, one I'd seen through video chat at least every week since last summer. We'd met at the festival—right after I'd seen Crowe with Katrina for the first time. I'd needed a distraction, but he had become more than that. "I think I could take Crowe Medici, don't you?"

I laughed. "When did the Deathstalkers get into town?"

"Few hours ago."

"Seen any of the Devils yet?"

"Oh, yeah. I ran into one at that ice cream place by the library."

I sat upright. "Are you serious?"

He hung his head back. "You think I'd be sitting here if I crossed paths with a Devil all by myself? I can't hurl a hex to save my own skin—you know that."

"God. Don't do that to me." I collapsed again on the bed. "Tensions are high right now. I don't want you to get hurt." I debated telling him about Old Lady Jane meeting with Crowe but decided maybe it could wait. Even though I was pissed at Crowe, blabbing about it felt a little disloyal. Besides, I didn't want to think about it now. I was just happy Darek was here.

The night we'd met, I'd tried to escape the festival after drinking too much. I'd been trying to cope with both my heartbreak over Crowe and Katrina, and the extreme amount of magic in the air. I'd accidentally wandered off the path and into a swamp, where Darek found me buried up to my knees in muck, still clutching an empty bottle of Jack.

To say I had been messed up was an understatement. By all accounts, I was a pathetic disaster. But Darek, all blond, blue-eyed, sunbaked, and lean, merely asked me which

I'd like first—a piggyback ride out of alligator territory or another drink.

I chose the piggyback ride. When we got back to the festival, he got me a huge cup of lemonade (nonalcoholic) and we talked for hours, just wandering the edges of the grounds. We had more in common than I ever expected. Our fathers gone, our powers a disappointment, our lives spent in others' shadows. He handled it more gracefully than I ever could.

And now he was lying next to me, the line of his body pressed against mine, and I knew the time had come to make a decision. Anything less was unfair to Darek. We'd never progressed beyond the friend zone, but our e-mails and phone conversations had circled ever more tightly around the possibility that we would. Both of us knew this year's festival would bring us together again. Neither of us knew exactly what to expect, though.

Sometimes I liked to daydream about how Crowe would react if he found out I was seeing a Deathstalker, and one who looked like Darek at that.

He'd die.

I'd die with delight.

But starting a romantic relationship with Darek needed to be about a lot more than making Crowe jealous. It shouldn't be about Crowe at all, really. So why was I still thinking about him?

"Are you hungry?" Darek asked.

I blinked up at him, shaking off the image of Crowe stuck in my mind. "I have a sandwich," I answered.

Darek jumped out of the bed. "How pedestrian. I'll make omelets."

"Are you serious?"

"That seems like a stupid thing to be unserious about. Do you want one or not?"

"Umm...yes?"

"Is that a question?"

"Yes, I would like an omelet. Please."

I followed him into the kitchen. He tore off his black-and-white flannel shirt and tossed it over a kitchen chair, revealing his fitted black T-shirt underneath. "Whoa," he said, peering at the burned hunk of meat and plastic in the sink. He poked at it gingerly. "What happened?"

"Crowe happened." I sighed as I stared at the new scorch mark on the counter.

Darek dug the carton of eggs out of the fridge, along with the butter, cheese, a green pepper, and an unopened package of ham. "What did you mean when you said tensions were high?"

"Oh, no big deal," I said airily. "Crowe just thinks your club killed his dad."

He cursed. "Why would he think we would do something like that? It would be suicide. The Devils already wiped us out once. Killian wants us on the straight and narrow, especially as we rebuild." His hands shook a little as he buttered a pan and set it on the stove a bit harder than necessary. "When is this going to stop, Jem? It's the twenty-first century, for God's sake. We're not fucking barbarians anymore. Why do all our problems need to be solved with violence?"

"I don't know. You do sort of look like a Viking."

"I'm French. Not Scandinavian."

"Could have fooled me." I smiled and slid his cap off his blond locks. Darek was a Delacroix. He was a distant relative of Killian Delacroix, who became the president of the Deathstalkers at the age of twenty—right after his older brother Henry and, I now knew, the entire leadership of the Deathstalkers had been killed by our very own local club. I knew it was because Henry had been trying to do something majorly evil, but killing all their officers seemed over the top.

The Delacroixs were known for the *animus* magic that ran strong in their veins—the ability to sense and manipulate emotions, and sometimes thoughts. I might have been nervous about hanging around with Darek as a result, except that I already knew he didn't have that kind of magic at all. Not all people with kindled parents manifested the same power that was dominant in their family tree. Sometimes there were surprises, like a kid might take after his mother's side of the family instead of his father's if both had magic, or he might even inherit a type of magic from even further back, like Gunnar did when he got his great-grandmother Kitsamura's *arma* power. And sometimes, unfortunately, a kid didn't inherit any magical ability at all, or just a trace of it, not enough to actually call upon and cast at will.

My mom was like that. So was Darek.

As we maneuvered around my mom's tiny kitchen, I couldn't pick up anything in the room but the slight sting of my own magic and the ashy, acrid stench of burned meat. I didn't know how Darek coped, not being able to cast like nearly everyone else around him, but he seemed to take it in stride and had still chosen to be a part of the kindled world.

I was a little envious at how easy he made it look.

The eggs sizzled when he poured them into the hot pan. "Don't repeat this," he said, "but I think Killian plans to reach out to Crowe directly during the festival. See if they can't improve ties between the clubs."

"He's got some work to do, then."

Again, I considered mentioning Jane. The fact that

she'd seen bad things in our future likely meant the Devils' League and the Deathstalkers would not be besties anytime soon. But why? If Killian extended the offer, why would Crowe turn it down?

"And you?" I asked Darek. "What do you think about a truce?"

He diced up the ham and green pepper with quick efficiency, and threw it, along with the cheese, over the bubbling eggs. "You know how I feel. I want fences mended. I want peace. Families have died out before, you know. Magic lines have been crushed out like cigarettes, or have just dwindled to nothing...." He trailed off. The eggs started to brown.

"Hey. You okay?"

"What? Yeah." He scraped the eggs, folding them into an omelet. "I was just making the point that we should all get along. The kindled have this amazing heritage, you know? I don't understand why they can't work together to preserve it."

"Darek, it's our heritage, too."

He looked over at me and smiled, but it didn't reach his eyes. "Good point. But how about this—I also don't like the fact that I have to hide our relationship just because we're from two different clubs with a bad history of killing each other."

I grinned and threw a scrap of diced pepper at him. He heroically caught it in his mouth. "Relationship, huh?" I asked.

He bowed his head, wearing a genuine smile as he chewed. "I guess we haven't really hashed that out yet. Let's do it on a full stomach."

The burner clicked off, and he slid the giant omelet onto a plate. We sat down at the kitchen table with our feast between us, forks in hand. The omelet was delicious. He'd once told me he dreamed of being a chef in New Orleans but had felt the call of the club after the Deathstalkers were nearly wiped out. His father had once been a member but had died a long time ago in an accident. He never talked about his mother, but I'd gathered she'd died, too, long before his father, leaving him an orphan. Unable to stomach the idea of his father's club dying out, he joined up, and here he was. I smiled across the table at him. "I'm glad you're here."

Our eyes caught and held. "I wouldn't have missed this chance for the world," he said softly.

I was still caught in his stare when the back door opened and my mom shuffled inside wearing her Denny's uniform, her thick black hair frizzy and disheveled. She took one look at the mess in the sink and cursed. "So much for my plan to bring about world peace with amazing *feijoada*. You must be Darek."

He held out his hand, and she gave it a quick shake. "I guess Jemmie told you about me."

"Just a few things. You be careful out there in our little town, Mr. Deathstalker Prospect."

"Will do." Darek winked at me. "I think Jemmie's going to take good care of me."

"Okay, then," she said, drawing out the words. "Remember to use a condom. I'm going to bed."

"Mom!"

She snorted. "I'm just kidding." She walked toward her bedroom and paused in the doorway. "Seriously, though. Condom. Good night."

She closed the door softly behind her, and I buried my head in my hands. "Ugh."

"I actually found that delightfully supportive. I'm glad she's so accepting."

"More like she's utterly exhausted after a ten-hour workday and barely even knows what she's saying." I took our empty plate to the sink. When I turned around next, Darek was inches away. He cornered me, his hands planted on either side of me, on the counter.

"Are *you* supportive of our relationship?" he said.

My breath caught in my throat. The scent of him, cigarette smoke smothered with mint, clouded my better judgment. I pressed my nose to his chest and breathed him in as his hands rose to rest on the sides of my neck. That warm sense of relaxation drew a sigh from my mouth. "I don't know," I said honestly.

He pulled my hand down and placed it on the hard muscles of his waist. "Happy to let you take a test-drive."

I looked up to see him wearing a mischievous grin, and I was embarrassed to smell my own frosty, minty magic. Usually I could keep it contained, but I guess he was affecting me more than I was willing to admit. I closed my eyes to avoid the sight of *locant* sparkling like stars as it floated between us. "Don't tempt me."

He licked his lips and leaned in closer. My eyes dropped to his mouth.

Crowe's stupid face flashed in my mind, and I tore my gaze away, biting my lip.

Darek sighed. "Message received."

"What?" It came out as a yelp.

"Jemmie, you can't fool me. I mean, I know we've had this long-distance thing going, but I still know you. And I know you haven't made up your mind. You're still thinking about Crowe, aren't you?" Now his handsome face was hard, jaw clenched.

"That's not fair. I hadn't talked to him for weeks, and then tonight—"

He put up his hands. "I'm not in the mood for details right now. I heard you guys in here earlier, after all."

I pressed my fingertips to my temple, where a headache was taking shape once again. "Fine. I'm sorry. Like I said, it's been a shitty night. Not the best time for me to be making serious decisions about anything." I turned to walk back to my room, and Darek followed.

"I'm sorry," he said as I plopped down on my bed. "That wasn't fair, and the last thing I want to do is pressure you." He laughed. "Especially because you're probably the only Devil in Hawthorne who wouldn't kill me as soon as you looked at me."

I hung my head. "They're not that bad. We'll figure it out." I yawned. "Tomorrow." I pulled my phone out and sent a quick text to Alex. **I'm sorry about what happened. It should only last a day or two. Please tell me you don't hate me.**

"What did you do?" Darek asked, reading upside down.

Exhausted, I silenced my phone and laid it facedown on the bedside table. "Magic," I said, stifling another yawn.

"And it worked for you?" he asked. I'd told him all about my avoidance of magic, just not why.

"Believe it or not, it did." A small smile crept onto my face.

"Jealous," he said in a singsong voice as he sank onto the bed beside me. As if we'd been doing it for a year, we both lay down, me in his arms. It felt peaceful and safe. The opposite of being around Crowe. That had to mean something, right?

"Will you start practicing now?" he asked. "I think you're more powerful than you're willing to admit."

"You sound like Alex," I said sleepily.

"Alex is a smart girl," he replied, stroking my hair. "You going to introduce me?"

"Let's take it slow, seeing as her brother blew up my mom's plans for edible world peace or whatever she said."

Darek snorted. "Fair enough. And Jemmie? Thank you."

"For what?" I was drifting now, right on the cusp of deep slumber.

He tightened his arm around me, his fingers finding a bare sliver of flesh above my jeans; my stomach thrilled at the touch. If I couldn't have my best friend right now, at least I could have my second-best friend, who was very hot, and very warm, beside me. "For being who you are."

I squeezed my eyes shut and pressed a smile into his shoulder. Maybe this could work. Maybe all of it would work. The Devils and the Deathstalkers would shake hands and become allies. I could love Darek. I could practice my magic. Alex and I would smooth things over, and we'd go right back to having fun. The next few days were full of promise and possibility.

Of course, this was how I'd felt last year, just before the festival, when my hope for a relationship with Crowe fell apart—and just before Crowe's father crashed on that lonely road in rural Louisiana. But in Darek's arms, sliding into a river of dreams, I couldn't help but hope that Old Lady Jane's dire predictions were dead wrong.

FIVE

I woke to the sound of my mother cursing at the coffee machine in the kitchen. I rolled over and found the other side of the bed empty. With bleary eyes, I checked my phone. One text from Darek and none from Alex.

Had to go join the guys for a breakfast gathering, his text said. **I'll catch up with you later.**

At eight in the morning? I threw the blankets back, unreasonably sad and irritated that he'd disappeared without waking me. I hadn't slept so well in weeks.

"What's wrong?" I croaked when I shuffled into the kitchen.

Mom sighed. "I'm exhausted, and I can't get this stupid

coffee pot to work." She stood there in a raggedy old band T-shirt and men's boxer shorts, glaring at the coffee maker as if considering all the terrible things she wanted to do to it.

"Move," I said, and she stepped aside, pulling herself up on the counter, well out of my way.

Our coffee maker was possibly older than I was and just as stubborn. There was a trick to getting it to work. I unplugged it, flipped the On/Off switch a few times, then plugged it back in. It gurgled to life and a huff of steam escaped the crooked reservoir lid as hot coffee finally dripped into the pot.

I grabbed us each a mug.

As I spooned sugar into the cups, Mom gestured at the scorch mark on the counter. "That has Crowe Medici written all over it. You introduce him to Darek?"

"Not a chance in hell."

I avoided looking at the evidence of Crowe's being here, the reality of it in stark daylight somehow more troubling than it had been in the semi-darkness of night. "Crowe gave me a ride home."

"And he was so overcome with joy at seeing you home safely, he left a permanent scorch mark on my glorious counter?"

"It's orange laminate, Mom."

"You are avoiding the question."

"That was a question?"

She frowned. The morning light filtering in through the window at her back rimmed her in a pearlescent haze. She'd scrubbed the makeup from her smooth, light brown skin and tied her ebony hair into a messy topknot. There were faint shadows beneath her brown eyes, but they only served to make her look delicate instead of haggard.

Sometimes it hit me out of the blue how gorgeous she was when she wasn't trying to be.

Both of my parents were beautiful beyond reason, but the older my mother got, the more slowly she seemed to age. My mom might not have had a lot of her family's Cabrera *merata* magic, which made the people who possessed it invincible, but she must have inherited a few scraps. She'd never been sick in my entire life, and she looked better at thirty-five than I usually did at eighteen.

"What's going on with you two?" Mom asked, and it took me a second to realize we were still talking about Crowe.

"Nothing."

Mom hopped off the counter and poured her coffee, stirring in a truckload of powdered creamer. "What's Darek think about it?"

I side-eyed her. "Why?"

She shrugged innocently. "Just wondering. I mean, from

the look of it, the two of you have a thing, and I have to wonder how he felt when Crowe drove you home and then things got heated enough to barbecue without a grill."

"It wasn't like that."

I'd never told her what had happened between Crowe and me, that we'd kissed, that it'd seemed like there was more to our relationship, only to have him ignore me afterward and act like a total jerk at last year's festival and ever since, but she could sense that something had gone wrong, and she had obviously taken my side.

She looked thoughtful as she sipped her coffee. "Well, Darek seems nice. And safe." For a moment, she stared out the window, toward the shed where Dad used to work on his bike. "Not a bad thing, especially for you."

I poured myself some coffee while my throat tightened. "You mean because I can't cast. Because you think I can't keep up with Crowe or anyone like him."

"I didn't mean it that way."

"What did you mean?"

"You think it was easy for me to be with your dad? I loved the guy." Her chuckle was laced with sadness. "So damn much. But he had power oozing from his pores, and I've always been..." She raised her arms, as if to say *just look at me*. "He never tried to make me feel bad about it."

"But you did anyway," I said quietly.

She gave me a sorrowful smile, and her thoughts were so obvious that I had to turn away from her. She didn't want me to end up the same way she had—with a powerful guy, whom she had to watch from the sidelines. The idea stirred something rebellious and ragey inside me. I didn't want that, either.

Was a guy like Darek, who was from a kindled family but had no power of his own to speak of, the answer? It didn't feel right to make a choice because of that.

Or maybe I just had to admit to myself that I wasn't ready to let go of Crowe quite yet. That I never had let go of the hope that he'd realize what an idiot he'd been, that he'd come back to me. "God, I'm so stupid," I whispered, then buried my nose in my cup, breathing in the bitter fumes.

"No such thing. You've got a good head on your shoulders. Just make sure you use it." She gave me that motherly look of hers that I rarely saw but always took seriously when I did.

"I will," I said, and she smiled and nodded. The one thing I could count on my mother for was her ability to let secrets lie. Most people poked at them, prodding them from the shadows so they could see them standing naked in the light.

"Oh, by the way," she said as she disappeared into the hallway, "your father will be here within the hour."

"What?" I shouted, but she was already gone, her bedroom door clicking shut behind her.

I couldn't believe my mom hadn't given me more advance warning. Then again, the last time he'd visited, I'd hidden out at Alex's, and when he'd done a locator spell to find me, I'd refused to speak to or look at him. Yeah, I'd been a typical pissed-off fifteen-year-old girl, but I guess Mom didn't trust me. "He's trying," she'd told me.

He hadn't tried much after that, but now he was coming to Hawthorne. It must be for the festival—the big party tonight was the kickoff and day one of the three-day event that would bring thousands of kindled to our town, and I guessed it made sense that the Syndicate would send someone to check it out. Just my luck, my dad was the law now. As if being basically powerless wasn't enough, this would cement my status as the most popular girl at the festival.

Ugh.

He arrived an hour later in his ridiculous and totally not inconspicuous black Audi. I peered at him through a crack in the curtains, torn between locking myself inside my bedroom or climbing out the window and trying to sneak into the woods behind the house. He paused halfway to the door and looked at my curtained window like he could see me spying. His mouth twitched into a little smile, and I lurched back, my eyes stinging, my fists clenching.

"Mo?" he called as he let himself inside.

"Don't call me that," I blurted out, loud enough for him to hear me through my closed door.

Mo was the nickname Dad had given me when I was a kid. It was short for *mo ghrá*, which was Irish Gaelic for "my love." I used to like the name. Now I hated it. If he loved me so much, he would've stuck around.

"Come out here and say that to my face," he said, humor infusing his voice. "Or else I'll never call you anything else!"

"Big threat, considering I hardly ever see you."

I listened to the sound of his footsteps coming up the hall. He knocked softly on my door. "Come on, Jemmie. I'm here now."

I could barely speak past the lump in my throat. "Yeah, for the festival, right? Did you draw the short straw to get this assignment?"

He was quiet for a moment. "Not exactly. Will you come out, please? I don't care if it's just to punch me in the face. I want to see my little girl."

"A funny thing happens when you barely stay in touch. Little girls grow up."

"If you come out, I'll take you for ice cream. If you don't, I'm just going to wait until you open the door. You're going to have to come out at some point."

Especially because I'd had all that coffee. "Ugh. Fine." I whipped open the door.

Dad looked startled. "Whoa. You're a lot taller than you used to be."

"Screw you," I said, stalking past him and heading into the bathroom, where I slammed the door.

"Trying to sleep," Mom shouted from her bedroom. That was probably a lie, considering she'd gone in there with a cup of coffee, but she hadn't come out to see Dad, and he wasn't trying to make her.

"Sorry, Gina," Dad called.

When I came out of the bathroom, he was rummaging in the fridge. "Does your mother not feed you?"

"I'm eighteen, Dad. I can feed myself."

"Mostly prepackaged garbage, from the looks of it."

"Is that why you came over here? To lecture us on proper nutrition?"

The fridge door squeaked shut. "How about we go grocery shopping?"

"Right now?" I asked.

"Is there a magic hour for grocery shopping?"

"No. There is no such thing as a good time to go grocery shopping with your father. Especially when that father is you."

He nodded. "Good. Expressing your feelings is healthy. Now get dressed."

I huffed. We *were* getting low on coffee and ice cream, the basic necessities. "Are you buying?"

"If I say yes, will you come?"

"Yes."

"Yes."

Less than twenty minutes later, we were heading inside Delmore Grocery, Dad a few paces ahead of me. Like my mother, my dad had naturally dark hair, but he spent hours in the sun, so it was blonder on top and dark brown closer to the roots. He was wearing it longer than when I'd seen him last, and he seemed to be styling it now so that it stood up from the top of his head in a disheveled pompadour.

As we entered the store, at least four sets of eyes tracked him, like they couldn't decide if he was someone famous, or just someone unfairly handsome.

Or maybe just a jerk who'd abandoned his family seven years ago, simply because his daughter couldn't follow in his footsteps. I knew that wasn't the whole reason, but as I trailed him through the store, the resentment bubbled up inside.

A dreck lady gave him an appreciative look, her gaze sliding down the length of his full-sleeve tattoos, watching his muscles flex as he bagged a few apples and set them in his cart.

I rolled my eyes and grabbed a bunch of bananas. "How long are you here for?"

"A few more days. I actually got here yesterday. You know how these festivals are. People start to gather before the formal stuff starts to happen. I'm just here to observe."

"Oh, yeah. Because the Syndicate is so neutral." Flynn had told me they'd been gunning for the Devils for years, just looking for an excuse to take them down a peg. He'd always stopped short of insulting Dad to my face, but I could tell what he really thought.

"We *are* neutral, Mo." He took in my sour look. "We've got the Sixes, the Kings, the Devils, and the Stalkers, all of which have feuded with each other in the past decade, as well as a handful of smaller clubs. Not to mention all the other kindled folks who just come for a good time. The Syndicate's just here to keep the peace."

I arched an eyebrow. "Yeah? And you're the best person for the job?"

His nostrils flared. "I am, actually."

I made a grumbly, skeptical sound in my throat as I poked at the tomatoes.

"So, have you been hanging out with the Medicis much?" He picked through the onions, like the question was insignificant.

"Around Alex, yeah. I don't see much of Crowe anymore."

Dad tossed an onion in the air and caught it again. "Crowe is a great kid, but he's a great kid who does bad things, and I worry about him without the guidance of his father. I think it's smart to keep your distance."

Sometimes I forgot that the death of Michael Medici affected more than just Alex and Crowe and their mom. My dad and Michael had been best friends since they were kids—until my dad took off, that is. I hadn't talked about Michael's accident or death—or murder, if Crowe was right—with my dad, but that was mainly because he hadn't even come back to town for the funeral. And though I was pissed at him for leaving, I couldn't believe Dad didn't care. I could see the loss etched on his face now, the pain that flashed through his eyes before he turned away. It sort of took the wind out of my anger.

We made our way through the store, and Dad grabbed the necessary items to make chicken fajitas, my favorite, which told me he was either a) sorry for being such an absent dad and hoping cheesy Tex-Mex would heal all wounds or b) planning to use spicy deliciousness to lull me into opening up.

Dad grabbed a six-pack of beer off the shelf. "You been practicing at all?"

Well, there it was. His fake-casual tone dragged me back eight years, to when he would try to coax me into showing him what I could do and then pretend not to be disappointed when anything I tried fizzled out halfway through because I was too overwhelmed to hold it together.

Instead of answering, I turned the corner to enter the aisle for frozen food. I needed ice cream. Like, the most salted-caramel-chocolate-dipped-pretzel-terrible-for-me kind.

"The perimeter on the house is practically nonexistent," he said. "That should be easy for you by now."

A mom, prodding along two young kids, stalled for a second as my dad passed. She smiled at him. He ignored it.

I tossed a carton of my chosen vice into the cart. "Is that really any of your business, since you don't live there anymore?"

"Maybe it should be, if Crowe Medici is showing up and trying to burn down the house that I still own. His dad used to get worked up like that from time to time. Like father, like son."

"It was a few pounds of meat, for God's sake."

"Not really the point."

The point was that he'd caught me in a lie. Or at least, a half lie. I'd said I hadn't seen Crowe much, and I hadn't. But I had seen him the night before in the kitchen of my own damn house, and *both* Mom and Dad had noticed.

"He drove me home," I explained.

"Uh-huh."

"Dad," I said, part warning, part whine.

He glanced at me, leveled his stare. "Just don't lie to me, Jem. It's as simple as that. I'm your father, you know."

"Oh, really? I hadn't noticed, what with you moving hours away!"

He turned into the next aisle. "I keep a roof over your head, don't I?"

I grabbed an extra carton of frozen comfort, grinding my teeth. "That's it? That's what you have to say?"

He was waiting when I entered the aisle where he was loading up on pasta. "Jemmie, someday, when you can talk to me like an adult instead of like a toddler throwing a tantrum, I'll tell you why I left."

"Fuck you," I snapped, tears starting in my eyes. "I have a right to be mad."

He bowed his head and pinched the bridge of his nose. "Okay. You're right. I'm sorry. Look—let's go home. We'll cool down and talk later."

"Whatever," I mumbled, but followed him to the checkout line. I didn't want my ice cream to melt before I could get it to a freezer. I also didn't want to break down in the middle of Delmore's.

The girl behind the register greeted us in a too-high-pitched voice. I tossed a few things on the conveyor belt. She rang up a total of three items before saying, "Wow. Your tattoos are incredible."

"Thanks," Dad said. He fished his wallet out.

"How long did it take you to get all that done?"

She was stalling now. The conveyor belt had stopped moving and our milk sat, waiting to be scanned, the plastic sweating in the heat.

"A few years," Dad answered vaguely, probably used to having these conversations.

It was so weird to stand there next to him. He was only in his mid-thirties; he and my mom had had me so young. Didn't mean I was cool with a girl my age stumbling over herself to flirt with him.

"They're incredible," she said again. Her cheeks flushed when she noticed me staring at her, my lip curled in disdain. She scanned the milk. The sun beat through the windows, momentarily blinding me. If only it'd deafen me, too.

The girl finished scanning the groceries. "I'll be in the car," I said, and grabbed a few bags.

"Wait, Mo," Dad said, but I was already gone, the automatic doors rushing open in front of me.

Outside, in the parking lot, I slid my sunglasses on and sighed against the sudden warmth of the sun. As I made my way to the car, I smelled something heavy in the air. The hair on the back of my neck stood up. *Magic*.

Dad ran up behind me. "I said to wait. You never listen to me."

Three motorcycles sat parked in the back of the lot, with three members of the Devils' League perched atop. Hardy, Flynn, and Boone.

Dad had his sunglasses on—great big aviators with mirrored lenses. But I could tell he was staring at them, and they were staring at him, and something tense and hostile thrummed between them.

"Dad?" I said, my voice sounding young and unsteady as the scent of his magic hit me, mint so strong it burned the inside of my nose.

"Get in the car," he said, so I hurried to it and climbed inside, locking the door behind me. I didn't think the Devils' League would hurt Dad, not now, and especially not out in the open, not in broad daylight. At least, not if they were sober. But the power was so thick and pungent that my head throbbed with it. I pressed my face into my hands and breathed through my mouth.

Dad slid in behind the wheel a second later and started his car up with the push of a button. "You all right?"

"What did they want?" I asked. I could still feel the Devils behind us, like a storm cloud growing on the horizon.

"Tensions are high right now," Dad answered, echoing what Crowe said last night. "They just wanted me to understand that they know I'm here. A welcome party, if you will."

"Um. They didn't look that welcoming."

"Yeah, well. It's just a game. I know how to play it, and all I want is for folks to keep to the rules." Fake casual again. He couldn't fool me.

"You're not here just to watch the Devils, though, are you?"

"No, not unless they're breaking those rules."

"Dad, of course they are. Everyone knows that."

He let out an exasperated sigh. "Some rules are more important than others."

"What are you talking about?"

"Jem, it's Syndicate business, and I can't discuss everything with you. Especially not when you're still obviously in Crowe Medici's orbit."

"Believe whatever you want, *Dad*," I said, more harshly than was probably necessary. "It's not like you actually know me or anything about my life, after all."

His jaw clenched. He put the car in gear and pulled out of the parking lot.

I crossed my arms over my chest and said nothing on the drive home. I didn't want to get between Dad and the Devils anyway. Maybe Mom was right. Maybe I should just stick with a guy like Darek who could understand our world but wouldn't be fully immersed in it.

Maybe I should just walk away from all of it and teach myself not to care.

Or maybe I should grow wings and fly to the moon. Sadly, that would have been easier.

SIX

ALEX FINALLY TEXTED ME AFTER MY TENSE CHICKEN FAJITA
lunch with Dad, which had ended with him kissing me on
the forehead and promising he'd catch up with me later
before taking off in his shiny car. When I saw her name
flash across my screen, I was equal parts relieved and terrified to read the message.

I don't hate u, u loon. Pissed @ Crowe tho. Like to stuff that
bird and hang him above the fireplace. R we still heading over to
the property together? Have smthing to tell u. Can't txt it.

The relief that ran through me was nearly palpable.

I'm glad, I replied. I was worried. Stupid rules. Stupid Crowe.
Yes lets go together around 4?

Yup I'll pick you up.

I showered and dressed, and by the time I came out of my bedroom, Alex was having a cup of coffee in the kitchen with my mom. She'd kindly brought me a frozen latte, since I only drank hot coffee in the mornings.

"Is that what you're wearing to the festival?" Alex asked.

I glanced down at the outfit I'd picked: black leggings, black motorcycle boots, and a loose-fitting gray V-neck tee. "What's wrong with this?"

"Show some leg!" Alex said. "Maybe some butt cheek. I mean, it's the Kindled Festival. It will be crawling with hot, powerful guys."

Mom sent me a meaningful look. She thought I should tell Alex about Darek, but I wasn't sure it was a good idea. Admitting that I was friends with the enemy seemed like a risk I didn't need to take—especially now. I wouldn't be able to forgive myself if I put Darek in danger.

"I think I'm fine on my own, thank you very much," I said.

"Yes, but Crowe would be jealous if he found you hooking up with another kindled. He would pretend otherwise, of course. Imagine if you hooked up with Katsuya Kitsamura? Crowe would die."

Katsuya was a Curse King—the vice president of the

95

club, actually. They were based in Minnesota, and he was not only incredibly hot—he was also packed with the *arma* magic that ran legendary through his family line. I'd met him last year, and nearly choked on my tongue because of both. He had the same power as Gunnar except a lot more of it, and his pale yellow magic was so thick and reeking of sulfur that I'd almost puked on his boots after shaking his hand. He probably thought I was a freak, but that was okay, since the stench kind of put a damper on the attraction.

I laughed. "I don't think Katsuya and I are meant to be."

"Certainly not in that outfit," Alex said.

"I'm not changing."

Alex frowned. "Fine. I guess that'll save Katsuya a few more broken bones."

Crowe had crushed both of his legs with a curse when the Kings rolled into town a few months ago hoping to take over. He'd sent Katsuya to the hospital and the rest of them packing. There were more than a few people who had an ax to grind with the Devils.

"Are we ready, then?" Alex asked.

I grabbed my bag and my coffee. "Oh, one minute. I forgot something." I took my stuff and scurried down the hallway, guilt beating inside me. But I needed this—I was about to be in a place seething with magic, and I wasn't going to make it if I didn't prep ahead. I closed the door to my room and knelt next to my bed, reaching behind the headboard to pull out a bottle of Jack. I poured a generous measure into my frozen latte and snapped the lid back on the cup. After one or two deep pulls that led to a burn in my throat and major brain freeze, I rushed back down the hall. "Ready!"

Alex's eyes narrowed briefly, but then she smiled and turned to my mom. "Gina, are you coming later?"

Mom folded herself into a kitchen chair, her paper coffee cup clutched between her hands. "I'll try, but I might have to pull a double. We're understaffed."

Alex planted a kiss on Mom's cheek. "My mom would love to see you."

Mom smiled. "I'll see what I can do. Be good, girls."

"We always are," Alex sang, and followed me out the door.

"I doubt she'll come," I said once we were outside the house.

Alex pulled a pair of large, round sunglasses on over her eyes. "Why?"

I shrugged. "Mom doesn't really feel like she fits anymore."

"Well," Alex said, "I hope she does come, because she belongs there no matter what anyone thinks."

Hearing that from her warmed me inside—Alex might have disliked certain people, but she never dissed members of our community just because they didn't have as much power.

We climbed inside Alex's Range Rover, and when she pressed the starter button, the air-conditioning burst from the vents like a winter wind.

I turned the AC down as Alex backed out of the driveway. I had planned to press her on the *something* she had said she wanted to share, but she beat me to the punch and asked, "So what's with the giant scorch mark on the counter?"

UGGGHHH.

I took a long, slow drink from my spiked latte. "I was playing with matches."

"Well, that's one way to set a guy's loins on fire."

"Oh my God. You said 'loins.'"

"Seriously, though. After what Crowe did to us, you let him in your house?"

"He drove me home after you ditched me."

She winced. "I totally did. I'm sorry. I kind of short-circuited. I was so pissed at him."

"It's okay. I get it."

"So he drove you home and set your kitchen on fire. My

brother is such a gentleman. You know what I'm going to do? When I get my magic back, that is."

"I suggest you do nothing."

"I'm going to give him boils. All over his ass."

"That might be a bit harsh."

"Better than that fungus thing he threatened to do to me! Did you see Gunnar's face afterward?" She shuddered.

"Has Gunnar turned up?"

"Nope. And fungus is nothing compared to what Crowe's gonna do when he does. At this point I wonder if Gunnar's just gone into hiding to save that pretty mug of his. Can't say I blame him."

We spent the better part of the ride complaining about Crowe and bitching about Katrina and the other girls Crowe had gone out with, and it felt ridiculously good. I liked that Alex was on my side. She wasn't just mad that he'd made me bind her magic—she was also pissed that he'd forced me to cast in front of everyone. "I mean, I know you can, Jem, but it was such a dick move the way he did it."

I closed my eyes. "I was afraid I wouldn't be able to."

"But you did," she murmured. "I can't feel my magic at all. I've got nothing, Jem."

My eyes popped open and I turned to her. She was frowning as she stared through the windshield. "I'm sure it'll wear off soon," I said. The guilt was back. "Do you want me to...?"

I wasn't sure I could undo the binding I'd placed on her, and dread squirmed in my gut at the thought of trying, but for her, I would.

"It's okay," she said. "Maybe tomorrow when the formal stuff begins? Tonight I just want to get drunk and party. Don't need magic for that!"

I grinned, relief sweet on my tongue. "Sounds like a plan."

The Kindled Festival was taking place this year on two hundred acres that the Medicis owned. It was the same property that the cottage and the Schoolhouse sat on, but the festival would be set up far enough away from both places that no one would wander to them. The grounds were bound on three sides by thick woods with a single one-lane road running through to the old abandoned logging mill at the edge of the Medici land, on the bank of the Sable.

The property would give everyone the privacy they craved and needed to be using so much magic away from the drecks, especially in a town as small as Hawthorne. Drecks might notice an influx of "tourists"—there would be at least four thousand people attending this year, according to Crowe's mom—but that was *all* they would notice. For the most part, the kindled coming into town would be sleeping in tents or campers on the property, and those who didn't care for camping would stay in hotels outside of town.

Lori had done most of the planning for the festival, which meant she'd coordinated all the logistics, and hired a bunch of stronger people—mostly Devils—to do the hard labor for her. Last-minute preparations were still under way when Alex and I arrived. A huge tent had been erected in what would likely be the center of the gathering. The roof rose to a pointed steeple with a Medici banner flapping from a short flagpole. The flag depicted a crow with its wings spread, clutching a human skull with its talons. A gold dagger pierced the skull through the left eye socket.

The Medicis had never been known for their subtlety.

Smaller tents in shades of gray, red, and white dotted the rest of the field as far as the eye could see. Each had its own banner: Some bore family symbols, and others were club logos. I could see the Deathstalker scorpion flying above a tent at the very end of the path right at the edge of the woods, and wondered if Lori had deliberately put them as far from the Devils as she could.

On the south side of the property, also near the tree line, a large fire pit had been built, with benches and chairs circling it. The chairs were empty, but by tonight, people would be fighting for a place to sit. And in case of rain, I was pretty sure either Lori or her brother Boone were ready to use their *terra* magic to make sure the grounds weren't hit by a single stray drop.

Somewhere in the maze of tents, metal rang out against metal, followed by a string of curse words. We tracked the sound to a white tent in the far back corner of the field and ducked inside to find Crowe hammering away at a tent support with a massive sledgehammer.

Lori stood over his shoulder supervising. "You have to hit it harder," she said.

"Ma." He straightened and wiped the sweat from his forehead with the sleeve of his T-shirt. "If I drive it in any farther, I'll fucking bury it."

"Don't talk back to me."

Though Crowe's eyes were hidden behind a dark pair of vintage sunglasses, I could tell he was glaring at her by the deep V of his brow. "I have people for this," he said, slightly breathless, his shoulders heaving. "And I have shit to do."

"I do, too," Lori countered. "Now get back to work. The tent is sagging in the middle."

I glanced up. The tent looked fine to me.

"If they aren't secure, they'll collapse with a puff of wind," Lori added.

"Can't you make sure that doesn't happen?" asked Alex.

Lori put her hands on her hips. "I can't be everywhere at once!"

"Lori!" someone shouted outside.

"I gotta go. Don't cause trouble," she said, pointing a finger at each of her kids before hurrying off to solve whatever problem had arisen.

"So are you two pests gonna behave tonight?" Crowe said casually, the sledgehammer resting on the ground by his boot. Without missing a beat, Alex said, "Why? You planning to threaten us with fungus again?" She dropped her mouth open and clapped a hand over it. "Oh, wait. Or maybe you'll go *full* asshole and threaten to have Jemmie bind my magic?" Her hand fell away, revealing a sneer. "Been there, done that."

"Careful, little sis." Now his teeth were gritted. "I've had a shitty day and if you add more shit to it—"

"You'll leave scorch marks all over our houses?" she countered.

Crowe glanced at me, and I was glad he was wearing the sunglasses. I was glad *I* was wearing sunglasses, so I could pretend I wasn't looking right at him. Secrets were paramount with Crowe, and apparently this had been one he thought we'd silently agreed to keep. I hadn't told anyone, but somehow everyone seemed to know. Why? Because the scorch mark was evidence I couldn't hide. That was Crowe's fault, not mine.

Still, somehow, in some way, I felt like I'd betrayed him.

"Come on," I said, and grabbed Alex by the arm, dragging her from the tent and into the daylight.

Crowe followed us out. "You're pissed," he said. "I get it. But you have no one to blame but yourself. And pulling something like that on Katrina in the first place? That was just shitty."

Alex set her hands on her hips. Her dark hair, caught by the wind, whipped around her shoulders. She looked fiery and dangerous. I loved her when she was like this, like a storm cloud threatening to rain hell. And I had no doubt she could pull it off, if raining hell was what she wanted.

"Why do you care so much about Katrina's feelings?" Alex challenged. "She's just one of four or five you're stringing along, am I right?"

Crowe ran his tongue along the inside of his bottom lip, and I took a step back.

Sometimes I wondered if there was more behind Crowe and Alex's animosity, some other discord between sister and brother that I wasn't privy to, that Alex stoked by defending me. Crowe seemed to have an ongoing feud with everyone right now. Or at least everyone who wasn't his subordinate. The Devils' League members were in his good graces because they took his orders without question. Alex and me, not so much.

Finally, Crowe shifted, moving away from his sister, and the friction dissipated. He started to leave, but not before leaning into me and saying, in a low, throaty voice, "You really need her to fight your battles for you?"

Bitterness flared inside me. "This isn't my battle at all. Who you sleep with has absolutely nothing to do with me."

For a moment, he was completely still, like his own magic had locked all his muscles and bones into place. "You don't understand at all," he finally said, very quietly. And then he left, the sledgehammer hoisted over his shoulder like it weighed nothing at all.

Alex and I ambled through the paths created by the lines of tents. I wasn't sure where we were headed, but it seemed like Alex was. I caught a glimpse of Katrina coming out of the Niklos tent, wearing a lace tank and looking confident and undeniably gorgeous. It only served to remind me of what had happened at the mall, and how Alex targeted Katrina in part out of loyalty to me.

"Crowe was right—I do let you fight my battles. Does sticking up for me bother you?" I asked, anxiety trickling in and threatening to extinguish the pleasant buzz from my Jack-infused coffee. I tossed the empty cup in a trash bin that had been set up next to the path. "I'm sorry if—"

"You don't have to apologize. I'm just happy you put up with my antics." She gave my arm a little shove. "And I'd punch the pope if he looked at you funny. You know that."

More likely, she'd curse him, as long as her magic wasn't bound. "I do know. I just wish…" I wished I could use my power like she did. I wished for once that every time I was around magic, it didn't make me feel like I was going insane. I craned my neck, looking for the beer tent. I found it right down the lane, radiating music and magic that hung in the air like a shattered rainbow.

Alex followed the line of my gaze. "You know I'm the biggest partier there is, so I'm not judging, okay? But I'm worried about you. I'm not going to be an asshole about it like Crowe is, but I needed to say that."

I closed my eyes so I wouldn't have to look at her—or the magic. "Just to take the edge off."

"The edge of *what*, Jem? You're among family. You belong here."

I opened my eyes and met her gaze. "Do I?"

"Of course you do. And if you'd actually use your powers like you did last night, you might realize that." She threw an arm around my shoulders. "If you ever want to practice on me, let me know."

I should totally take her up on her offer. She'd never laugh at me. Maybe I could even tell her about my weird reaction to magic. But I knew I wouldn't. As much as I thought about leaving the kindled world, I didn't want to be pushed out of it. If Alex knew magic made me feel sick, she probably wouldn't want to go to the Schoolhouse with me. She probably wouldn't even want to be here with me right now. She'd want to protect me, just like she always did. Maybe, though...

"You know what? Yeah," I said. "Tomorrow? No promises, but I'll give it a try—right after I unbind your magic."

I sounded a lot braver than I felt, and Alex rewarded me with a grin. "It's a date, and if you stand me up, well, I've got another smelly charm tucked away for a special occasion."

With a spring in her step, she started walking again, tugging me inside a red tent, the flap embroidered with golden filigree. A hand-painted sign staked into the ground read WARES. Because the festival wasn't really yet open for business, we had the place to ourselves, though Lori already had it all set up. Two long rows of tables dominated the space, with cuts organized for sale on the tabletops. Even if they hadn't been labeled, I would have known what they were by their scents alone, if not by the telltale wisps that rose from their intricately carved surfaces. But none of them was too strong, so I breathed through my mouth and cautiously walked deeper into the tent.

There was a table for almost every kindled power here. Not every family was represented in person—my mom's family, the Cabreras, were scarce in the States and based in Brazil, and the Kitsamuras were based in Japan. However, there were other kindled who, through our tangled family trees, had inherited the powers associated with those family names. Apart from the Medicis, who had their own trading space, the only one not represented was the Croft family. Their *tollat* magic had been both famous and despised in the kindled world—it included the ability to siphon others' magic and use it as one's own. But the Croft family had died out in the late nineteenth century, and to my knowledge, no one had turned up with those powers in the past fifty years or so, with one notorious exception.

Henry Delacroix, the former president of the Deathstalkers. With his death, it appeared the *tollat* magic had gone extinct. Our kindled world had lost a slice of its vibrancy and variation, but no one thought it was a bad thing.

I spotted the Niklos table and headed for it. They possessed *animalia* magic—the ability to talk to animals, control animals, sometimes shape-shift into them. I'd never met my grandmother Niklos on my mom's side—she'd died before I was born—but I'd always been interested in her magic. Talking to animals seemed like a very useful ability. Katrina was a Niklos and apparently had that power, but she was nowhere in sight anymore, thank God.

Alex wandered over to the Stoneking table and fingered a cut with a swirling silver design on the front.

"Let me ask you something," she said.

"Okay."

"Do you think it's possible to bind another family's magic to your own?"

I thought about that. "I heard that if you mix your blood with another kindled, you get temporary access to their power and a sort of rush." Blood magic was severely frowned upon in the kindled community. My dad had once told me it led down a dangerous path, but he wouldn't explain much more than that. I'd only been about ten at the time. "I've heard that it's addictive. Is that what you're talking about?"

She bit her lip. "I'm thinking about a lot more than mixing your blood with someone else's. But blood is the key, right?"

I gestured at all the cuts around us. "That's how you

make these. It's the only way to share power. A measure of blood plus a specific incantation or rune combination to trigger the magic."

"Yeah, of course, but that's using your own magic. I'm talking about stealing someone's power for good. Getting it directly from blood instead of a cut."

My eyebrows rose. "Are you planning to—?"

"No!" She glanced at the entrance to the tent as if she was worried someone was listening. "I'm just wondering about something called blood power, and how dangerous it is."

"Why?"

She bit her lip, apparently not yet ready to spill.

I let it slide for the moment. "The only way I've ever heard of taking another person's power without a cut *is* doing blood magic—but that's more about combining and mixing power, isn't it? Oh, and there's *tollat* magic. Siphoning someone else's power."

"That's only temporary, too, though. Right?"

I ran my fingers through a hanging display of cuts strung up on leather cording, sneezing as the scents mixed and hit my nose. "I guess we'll never know. But you're talking about something permanent? What's up?"

She shoved her sunglasses up on the top of her head and looked over at me. "That thing I wanted to tell you…

I found something of my dad's, some notes he was keeping before he died and—"

The tent flap rustled as someone entered, cutting Alex off. We both turned to the newcomer.

Darek stood in the doorway. He looked from me to Alex and pulled back a step. "Hey."

A flutter of excitement burst open in my chest, along with a stab of anxiety.

Alex tossed a *terra* charm back to its table. Her earlier seriousness disappeared, replaced by a flirtatious smile and a batting of her eyes. "And who are you?"

"Darek. Delacroix." He grinned, stepped past me, and offered his hand to Alex. "Alex, right? We actually met briefly at last year's festival. I guess I'm not that memorable."

She blinked at him. "I must have been trashed. I can't imagine forgetting that face."

He gave me a quick glance, still smiling. "Fair warning—I'm a Deathstalker. I know we're mortal enemies, but I can't help but appreciate beautiful girls when I see them."

She narrowed her eyes, but I could see the half-smitten smile creeping across her lips.

I suddenly felt a little sick.

"Is that right?" She shook his hand. "I suppose lines can be blurred for one day. This is my friend Jemmie."

111

Darek gave my hand a brief shake and turned so he faced us both. He'd showered and changed recently, his blond hair still damp and raked back from his forehead. He was now wearing ripped black jeans and a white T-shirt, a pair of sunglasses hanging from the collar.

"Were you looking for something in particular?" Alex asked. Her eyes flicked to me, speaking our unspoken language. *This one is cute*, the look said. *See, you should have worn short shorts!*

If only she knew.

Outside, the roar of motorcycles sounded in the distance. Alex let out a breath, disrupting a lock of hair that hung along her face. "That's my cue. Jem, I'll catch up with you in a bit. Nice meeting you, Darek. I hope my brother doesn't kill you." Alex side-eyed me, and waggled her eyebrows, before slipping outside.

When I was sure she was out of earshot, I whisper-shouted at Darek. "What are you doing?"

Darek frowned. "I'm sorry, do I know you?"

"She can't find out we know each other. You heard what she said—Crowe is looking for the slightest excuse to crush bones. Especially Deathstalker bones. Remember—he thinks Deathstalkers killed his dad."

"I asked some of the guys about that earlier. Michael Medici died in a motorcycle accident out on Bayou Road."

I nodded. "But Crowe said it looked like his *venemon* magic had been turned on him. Is that something Killian could have done?"

Darek laughed. "You met him last year, right?"

"Yeah, but just a handshake at a mixer. It's not like we're pals. He doesn't really—"

"Look like the leader of a gang?"

"I guess not." He looked more like an accountant, actually. "But come on. I've heard talk."

"It's true, Killian is a badass. And I guess he could manipulate someone into using their own magic against themselves if he wanted to, but trust me, the guy is determined to keep our club straight. I would bet my life he didn't harm a hair on Michael Medici's head. Unless he was bald. Was he bald? I never met him."

"Stop." I grew serious. "A lot of people around here are still grieving his death."

The smile melted off Darek's face. "I'm a jerk. I'm sorry." He reached out and touched my arm, and I sighed at the warmth of his fingers, wanting to relax into him again. "Forgive me?"

I laughed. "Okay. Just this once. But be careful about what you say around here. Promise?"

"Will do. Now…" He wrapped an arm around my neck and pulled me into his side. The cigarette-and-mint smell of him was heavier than it had been before. "Alex likes me. I'm a likable guy. What say we stop Romeo and Julietting around and take this public? It would be the talk of the festival."

"Absolutely not." I couldn't quite meet his eyes. He'd kept his voice light, but there had been a note of hope there, and I still wasn't quite sure it would be fair to him to start something.

He laughed and pulled me closer into a half hug. His mouth pressed against my temple. "It's okay, Jem. I mean, you're breaking my heart here, but I can try to withstand the pain a little longer."

"I have to go," I said, and pulled away.

Darek grabbed me around the waist and tugged me back.

"Why?" he asked.

"Because if Crowe walked in right now, one of us would be gutted. Probably me."

"Damn. Abusive much? You know that's what you're supposed to call that behavior, right?" Now he looked pissed. His fists were clenched. Crap. With the Harleys parked, the Devils could be heard shouting and laughing outside, and fear pulled me taut.

"I was exaggerating. He'd never hurt me." Not physically, anyway. He'd already hurt me emotionally, too many times to count.

"Don't make excuses for him," he whispered in my ear. "In fact, don't think about him at all." Darek's fingers found their way beneath my shirt, to the sensitive skin at the small of my back. His fingers were ghosts, his touch light but somehow far-reaching, too, so that I felt it all the way down to my toes.

I wanted him to stop.

I didn't want him to let go.

My knees threatened to buckle. The minty bite of my magic was all around me, clinging to him where our skin connected like it didn't want to let him go, either. I closed my eyes just long enough to summon an ounce of self-control. Darek's hands withdrew, and he stepped away.

"I'll see you later, then? At the house?" he asked.

I blinked. "Um...sure."

He started for the door.

"Wait." I brushed past him. "Let me go first. Just in case."

He nodded and waited in the shadows of the tent as I ducked outside into the stark light of day, suddenly blinded.

SEVEN

I LOST ALEX FOR A FEW HOURS AFTER SHE'D LEFT ME WITH Darek. I spent most of that time wandering the grounds, greeting and chatting with a few people I hadn't seen since last year in New Orleans, talking about their journeys to Hawthorne and their plans for the summer. I finally ran into my best friend near the beer tent. By then, the sun had started to slip lower in the sky, the branches of the surrounding woods reaching to swallow it entirely. People had started to arrive in greater numbers, and the makeshift parking lot at the eastern end of the property quickly filled up. The scent of magic all mixed together blended into a heavy funk that made my stomach churn and my vision blurry. My happy Jack Daniel's buzz had pretty much worn off, and beer was going to be a necessity.

"I've been looking everywhere for you!" Alex said, and grabbed me by the hand. She tried to pull me away from the beer tent, but I planted my feet.

"I've been looking for you, too," I said. "You were about to tell me something when Darek walked in and—"

"Calling him by his first name now, are you?"

"What else would I call him?"

"Hot Stuff, maybe."

I sighed. "So what were you going to tell me? Something you found of your dad's?"

"Later. First, we are on a mission," she said triumphantly, as if we were setting off to save the world. But I knew Alex well enough that I was immediately on guard. Her missions usually led to trouble. Actually, everything Alex did led to trouble.

"What sort of mission? And can I have a drink first?"

"Operation: Eavesdrop. And no, you can't." She tugged my arm, clearly willing to put up a fight.

With a whine, I started walking. "Who are we eavesdropping on?"

"My brother."

A few kindled I didn't recognize hurried down the path ahead of us, lighting lanterns suspended from curved iron hooks. Two of the kindled used conventional grill lighters. The third used her outstretched hand and a breath of shimmering pink air. The wick inside the lantern caught quickly, the tip of the flame crackling with magic. It reminded me of fireworks—a snap and sparkle, along with the earth-and-flowers scent of *terra* magic.

Alex led me to an unmarked tent that sat on the edge of the large clearing, far enough away from the festival entrance that no one had managed to stumble their way back here yet, and if Crowe had his way, no one would.

Shhh, Alex mouthed, and pressed a finger against her lips.

I rolled my eyes, because obviously I knew the finer points of eavesdropping.

The lanterns here hadn't been lit yet, and the shadows had gathered in wide swaths, giving us enough darkness to disappear. Suddenly I was eight years old again, and listening in on our parents as they drank and practiced and talked about the old days.

Adult conversations had always been their own kind of magic, and although Crowe wasn't much older than we were, club business—business we weren't technically privy to—was just as exciting to listen in on. Plus, the fog of magic was a little lighter here with fewer kindled and cuts around, so I could breathe and see a little easier.

We crept around to the back of the tent and got as close to the canvas as we dared.

I could hear the shuffle of boots over dry grass as someone circled the inside of the tent.

"Jane warned me something might go down tonight," Crowe was saying. "You all know we've made a lot of enemies. The Deathstalkers are here and shouldn't be underestimated, even if their numbers are small. And I'll be honest—I'm not sure if the Sixes and the Kings consider our beef settled from earlier this year—"

"I'm thinking you served that beef to them pretty well-done, Crowe," Boone said. A ripple of laughter went through the tent.

"I did what I had to do to discourage further patch-over attempts. Now, I know this is supposed to be a celebration, but it's also an opportunity for someone to make a move. We're all here in one place and half of us will be drunk by midnight."

A few of them whistled and clapped.

"I want our people safe," Crowe continued, and the tent fell silent again. "And we need to protect those who can't protect themselves for whatever reason. Brooke, keep an eye on Old Lady Jane. She might not be a Devil, but she's important and valuable."

"And old," said Brooke, laughter in her voice. "And weird as shit."

"Be careful about saying any of that to her face," said Crowe. "Unless you want her to tell you when you're going to die."

"She wouldn't!"

"She would," said Crowe. "She's done it before, and she's never been wrong." He sounded solemn now. And miserable.

Next to me, Alex's eyebrows rose in question.

"Boone," Crowe went on, "I want you on Alex. She's bound and powerless for the time being. Kent, keep an eye on my mother. She can hold her own, but you can't be too careful. Hardy, I want you on Jemmie."

I let out a surprised gasp. He was willing to waste one of his best men on shadowing me?

Alex scowled at me and I clamped my mouth shut.

From the crunch of his footsteps in the dried grass, I could tell Crowe was moving through the gang as he gave each of them their assignments. The light inside threw his shadow against the canvas as he approached, and he was now just feet away, a thin flap of fabric the only thing between us. I held my breath, hoping he hadn't heard me. I wasn't sure what he'd do if he caught us listening in on a conversation we definitely should not be listening in on.

"Flynn, keep an eye on the Stalkers," he went on. "They

have eight full-patch members here who you all know, plus a prospect. Darwin or Derwood or something."

Alex stifled a snort.

"I think his name is Drake," offered Hardy.

"Nah, it's Drew," said Flynn. "I ran into him near the outhouses earlier. He *definitely* looked like he was about to shit his pants." He had altered his voice with his *inlusio* magic, deepening it so that it echoed inside the flimsy tent. Puffs of his power wafted from within, and I inhaled the cigar scent of it.

Crowe chuckled. "Well, I'm guessing if none of us have heard of him and he hasn't drawn enough attention for us to even remember his name, he's not a major threat. I'd know if he had a rep."

I let out a breath of relief—Darek would have been stung to hear the Devils dismiss him like that, I was sure, but it was the safest thing.

Alex arched an eyebrow at me. I tried really hard to keep my face blank, but it felt like I was biting back a smile.

Crowe doled out a few more orders before dismissing everyone. When the tent was empty save for him and Hardy, Hardy said, "You really think they'll make a move tonight?"

"I don't know." A chair groaned as one of them sat

down. There was silence for a minute. I couldn't see him, but I could picture Crowe scrubbing at his face, revealing just a sliver of his worry to the one person he was okay showing it to. Hardy was his best friend, his brother in all things but blood. "Jane doesn't have anything concrete. She hasn't had anything concrete in the year or so she's been advising me. Doesn't mean we shouldn't be vigilant. She's seemed more on edge lately."

"You think she's holding back?"

"Don't know why she would. She might be a little strange, but she doesn't want anyone to get hurt. She's the one who came to me when she got a sense something would happen at the festival."

"Doesn't she know exactly what's going down?"

"She said it's too big to wrap her head around. It involves too many people at once, too many loose threads as she calls them. And...I think she worries that her predictions might actually shape the future in a bad way." He muttered something else I couldn't make out.

"People with *omnias* magic usually need to be touching someone to see their specific individual future anyway, right?" Hardy grunted. "Would you let her touch you, even if that meant she'd know when you're going to die?"

Even through the canvas, I could feel the weight of Crowe's sigh. "She already told me she wouldn't touch me—said she doesn't want to know. Honestly, I don't want to know, either. I have to be able to do whatever's necessary to keep everyone safe, and if I hesitate or hold back, I won't be effective."

"Yeah, brother. I know. We're all grateful you stepped up after we lost Michael."

"I can't let anything distract me from this or slow me down," said Crowe, his voice steely. "Speaking of—go find Jemmie and keep her out of trouble, will you?"

My eyes were probably the size of dinner plates. What the heck did that mean?

Hardy's voice was full of laughter as he asked, "Well, is she here yet? You seen her tonight?"

Crowe snorted. "She's here, all right. Check the beer tent first."

My face went from cool to blazing in the space of a second.

Crowe's phone went off. "I gotta take this. I'll catch up to you later." He answered the call as he left the tent, headed in the opposite direction of our hiding spot.

We waited a beat for Hardy to clear out, too, before creeping around the tent perimeter and back to the path that would lead to the bonfire. "What a jerk," I muttered.

"Well, you *were* headed in there when I found you," Alex reminded me.

"Screw you. We were going to party, weren't we? Should we do that in the kiddie tent?" Lori had actually set one up. It was flying a flag with a pink unicorn on it.

"Actually, I am in the mood for some face painting," she said with a wink.

"Where do you think you two are going?" Hardy said, and Alex and I both shrieked.

"Hardy!" Alex whacked him on the arm. "You scared the shit out of us."

"How long were you there?" he asked.

I tried acting innocent. "How long were we where?"

"Don't play me for a fool. I'm a Warwick, remember? Spidey-sense upgrade. I already know how long you were there. I could hear you two mouth breathers for miles. You're lucky I didn't tell Crowe."

Alex and I both cringed. "Then why did you ask?" I said.

"So I could catch you in a lie." Hardy pulled his cell phone out of his back pocket, selected a number, and hit the Call button. "Hey," he said when someone picked up on the other end. "If you're looking for Alex I'm staring at her right now."

Alex groaned.

"Over by the meeting tent," Hardy said.

Alex turned to leave, but Hardy stopped her with a strong arm around her midsection, hooking her like a shepherd hooking sheep. Looking relaxed as Alex struggled hopelessly against his iron-muscled arm, Hardy ended the call and said, "Boone is on his way over."

"And here I am," Boone said, appearing out of the dim light. Boone was the quintessential biker. Long gray hair tamed into a braid. He wore a blue bandanna around his head and the front of his Devil vest was covered in random patches, everything from a peace sign to a Grateful Dead skull.

"Little banshee," Boone said, his voice gravelly from smoking far too many cigarettes. "I was just headed for the beer tent. Care to join me?"

"No."

"She wanted to get her face painted," I said, not even cracking a smile.

He held his arms out. "Well, that sounds utterly wholesome. After you, then."

"I don't even know why I bothered coming tonight," Alex whined. "This is the least amount of fun I've ever had. I don't need a babysitter, you know."

"Then think of me as a bodyguard," Boone said. "Someone messes with the little banshee, they'll get shot in the ass!" He held up two finger guns, and tiny lightning bolts shot from his fingertips. "Bam! Bam!" He laughed, his beer belly chuckling with him as my nose itched with the scent of his *terra* magic, fresh-cut greenery and marigolds.

"Oh my God," Alex said, but she was smiling now. "Fine. Face paint. But you're getting a flower on each cheek. Jemmie?"

"Actually, the beer tent sounds awesome." I didn't want to give Crowe the satisfaction, but if I headed back into the thick of the festival without something to dull my senses, I already knew things were going to get ugly.

Hardy gave me a questioning look, but I could tell the call of the beer tent was strong for him, too. "Okay, fine. We could make a quick stop."

I nodded solemnly. "What happens in the beer tent stays in the beer tent."

Alex, who was in the middle of being dragged up the path by Boone, called, "I'll meet up with you later?"

"Definitely. Can't wait to see your face art!"

When they were gone, Hardy and I headed for our destination. Rock music pulsed through the earth beneath us and echoed off the forest surrounding us. This was a festival hosted by the Devils' League after all, and rock music was their anthem. And judging by the din accompanying the music, the festivalgoers were enjoying it, too.

The closer we came to the beer tent and the bonfire, the more crowded it became. The first night of the festival was always the party night, when people reunited after months of not seeing each other, sometimes years, depending on whether they had attended the previous celebration. The second day was for recovery and trading. Those who had spent the night before partying too hard sought out Medici charms for hangovers. And those who had erred on the side of caution shopped for the cuts they'd need throughout the next year. For a lot of people, those cuts were Medici healing ones anyway. It was why the Medicis had their own wares tent, separate from the red tent Alex and I had visited earlier. The demand for Medici cuts was too large to keep to one small table in the main tent.

Once hangovers were nursed and deals were struck, people started to relax, so the third day of the festival was for more partying and lots of reminiscing.

"Hey, Hardy," one of the lantern girls called as she passed. She gave Hardy an appreciative look, almost setting her hair on fire in the process. A flame skittered along her palm before she squeezed her hand shut and the flame died in a puff of smoke, her dignity right along with it.

If the girl knew a thing about anything, she would have known Hardy rarely swung her way. He'd had two girlfriends in the time I'd known him, which was forever. And seven boyfriends. Or maybe that was eight. He and Crowe were a lot alike in the romance department, save for their choice in departments.

Of course, if she was like most girls, she knew what Hardy's type was and didn't give a shit. Sometimes Hardy didn't, either.

We'd neared the beer tent, where people had started to gather. Headlights swept into the east field as new arrivals searched for parking spots. It was a dizzying, blinding dance of light and sound. Dense and smelling of steel and earth and fire, powerful magic crackled at the edges of my vision, threatening to close me in. I quickened my steps, sliding past groups of people in the hope of reaching my relief.

I ducked inside the beer tent, and Hardy followed. We wended our way through the tables quickly filling with people. Magic was so thick in here that I could barely see.

At the bar, Hardy ordered a shot of whiskey and I ordered a shot of tequila, because why not. The bartender, a Niklos by the smell of him, poured the shots and slid them our way. "Enjoy," he said, and tipped his head to both of us.

"Cheers," Hardy said, but by the time he raised his

glass, I'd already downed mine. He let out a low whistle. "Damn."

"It's medicinal," I said quickly, waving for another.

"Fine, but then you take a little break, all right?"

"You're the boss."

He grunted. "Obviously."

I slung my second shot back just as I caught sight of my dad entering the tent. "Great," I muttered. "My night is complete."

Hardy leaned back, propping his elbow on the bar top. "What? Oh. Never mind. I see him."

"Owen!" someone shouted, and waved Dad over to their table. Others followed his progress with a mixture of disdain and fear. He might have a few fans here, but joining the Syndicate had earned my dad a lot of enemies, too.

Hardy let me order a beer, maybe feeling sorry for me, and we watched the crowd swell over the next half hour. My limbs had taken on a pleasant tingle. The magic was still filling my nose and fogging my vision, but I no longer cared all that much.

"Huh. Didn't expect to see her here," Hardy commented, and I turned to look, craning my neck.

Old Lady Jane sat on a chair at the far end of the tent, surrounded by people gathered at her feet. Brooke, the Devils' League member assigned to guard Jane, was positioned in the corner, her eyes scanning the crowd. She inclined her head when she saw Hardy at the bar, and he did the same. A few other, older kindled were also in chairs near Jane, and one of them, a man with a stringy steel-gray ponytail and neck tattoos, was standing up, gesturing as he spoke.

"Let's go check it out," I said. "I'm bored."

Before Hardy could issue an opinion on the matter, I got up and staggered a little as I made my way over to the lawn-sitters. Once there, I plopped down next to a few girls wearing Curse King colors—orange and black.

"—and when she woke up to find the sun shining, she thought she had broken the curse!" the old guy was saying. "But then she ran back to her village and discovered that only a few houses were standing. The rest were overgrown with weeds, thatch caved in." He glanced back at Jane. "With *time*."

"That's why you never cross a Vetrov," said Jane with a tiny, dry smile. "Some of us can steal minutes, days, even years."

"Not the only reason you never cross a Vetrov, from what I understand," the man said, smiling. "But that's what it was. The crone had stolen forty years from the girl! Her sisters were old women and her parents were dead. The girl was crushed. She went to go find the old woman whose bread she'd stolen, but of course she was gone, too. So the girl wandered for the rest of her days, calling for her lost years, unable to bear the burden of the future."

"How fucking depressing," Hardy muttered as he scooted in behind me. "Do I really have to listen to this?"

Old Lady Jane stood up. "Time to hear the tale of the girl who bound the devil," she said, and Hardy shut up fast.

Jane's long white hair swished as she turned her head slowly and took in each person in her audience. "This one is a part of our ancient heritage, and it was told to me by my grandmother, whose grandmother told it to her. She begged me not to ever let it die. She promised me that if I told this tale at our gatherings, the magic of it would live forever. So here I stand." She paused to sip her beer, then raised her cup. "And here's to Granny Vetrov!"

Several people raised their cups and drank with her. I drained my own cup and set it in my lap.

"The tale is this," Jane continued. "Centuries ago, in Scotland, the devil came to call in the village of Dunkeld. The moon hid its face from him, and so did the sun, and the whole town fell into the deepest kind of darkness. No lantern or torch could stand against it. No one in the village could see, and they stumbled about, crying out in fear. None of them could feel him creeping closer—until it was too late. And when he put his arms around one of them, they clung to him, so glad they weren't alone anymore.

They thought he was a hero, come to save them." Her eyes met mine, and a chill slid right down my spine.

The corner of Jane's mouth twitched, maybe with amusement. "So he took each of his victims in his red embrace, and none of them could escape his hold once he had them. No matter what power they had on this earth, he knew how to turn it against them. One by one, they fell. And that devil, he loved every minute of it. He wanted to devour the world."

I rubbed my arms, trying to smooth sudden goose bumps even though the air was warm.

"Is she always this freaky?" Hardy whispered.

"Shut up," I whispered back.

"But there was one villager who wasn't caught in the darkness," Jane continued, now lost in her story. So lost, in fact, that she wasn't holding her cup upright anymore. It hung from her fingers, dripping beer onto her scuffed motorcycle boots, but everyone was too rapt to call her attention to it. "Her name was Nora, and she had been banished from this village by the sea for stealing crabs from the fishermen's nets. The people of Dunkeld wouldn't stand for such thievery, and they'd cut off her hands and sent her into the forest to starve."

Old Lady Jane was wearing a big smile now, and it was straight out of a freaking horror movie. "But Nora did not starve. She was a willful girl who refused to relinquish her life, and she lured little beasts with her singing and then caught them in her teeth."

"The fuck?" muttered Hardy.

"Shhh." I glared at him over my shoulder.

Jane's teeth were bared, yellowed by years of chain-smoking. "As the sun rose, she saw that a strange darkness had fallen over the little town that the light couldn't pierce, but instead of staying put or running away, she walked right toward it. And there was the devil, sitting in the village square with his victims laid out in a circle."

"How could she see him, if it was so dark in the village?" asked one of the Curse King girls with a smirk, clearly thinking she was poking holes in Jane's story.

"She could see through that dark," Jane answered. "Nora was aware of the murk around her, but her eyes were especially keen. Too keen. She saw the devil for what he was. She saw the trails of love and hate and lust and power dangling from his mouth, and she knew she'd caught him at his breakfast." Her eyes met mine again. "He was eating their souls, you see."

My stomach turned.

"Nora had been horribly mistreated by these villagers, and the devil knew it. He invited her to join him at his feast. And because she had no hands, he even offered to feed her."

Now the silence around Jane was complete, and her cup was empty. It fell from her knobby fingers and landed on the grass next to her boot. "Nora was tempted. These were the people who turned her out to die. These were the people who had cut off her hands. They had hurt her. But she knew the devil was no hero. She could see him eyeing her dreams and her will and her bravery and her rage like a starving man. She could see that he would eat her soul, too. She could also see there was no escape, for he was well fed and fast on his feet. So she did the only thing that was left to her."

Here, Jane paused, and as she turned I caught the glittering silver wisps of her magic, slowly swirling around her head. I could smell it, too—the scent of iron fresh from the forge. I shuddered. Jane seemed to catch the movement and tilted her head, her gaze on me once again. "Do you know what she did, Jemmie Carmichael?"

Heads turned toward me. "No," I said, shrinking from the sudden attention.

"She gathered up the strands of those souls in her arms, and she used them to bind herself to that devil. She had no fingers to tie knots, so she twisted and turned and wound them tight around her body and his. Then she hurled herself into the sea and dragged him with her."

"Did she survive?" I asked.

134

"What a question," said Jane. "Of course she didn't."

For some reason, I felt like I'd been punched in the gut.

"And that's the story. There's magic in it, my grandmother told me. It lives as long as the story does."

After a few moments of hush, someone started clapping, and then a few others did. The elderly guy scooped Jane's beer cup from the grass and shouted to the bartender to fetch her another. My ears were ringing as I pushed myself off the ground and headed for the exit.

"I need some fresh air," I managed to tell Hardy as I stumbled forward without waiting for him. It felt a little like being underwater, breathless, and clawing desperately for the surface. Just as I could see my escape through the crack between the tent flaps, they were pulled aside, and I found myself face-to-face with Killian Delacroix, president of the Deathstalkers.

His eyes searched my face, and then he smiled. "Speak of the devil," he said quietly. "And she shall appear."

EIGHT

"WHAT—" I BEGAN, LOOKING OVER HIS SHOULDER TO THE open air outside. A few hulking Deathstalkers stood just beyond the tent flaps.

"Someone told me you were here," Killian said blandly.

"Who?" I asked. Was it Darek? And if so, how much had he said? My cheeks flared with heat.

Killian said nothing, thereby amplifying my curiosity and my fear. If he said something about me and Darek in front of Hardy—

"Excuse me, Killian." I started to edge past him, wanting to escape, but he put a hand on my arm.

"Wait."

"Get your fucking hands off her," snapped Hardy, who'd caught up with me. His eyes narrowed with promised violence.

Fingers still circled around the crook of my elbow, Killian said, "I mean no harm," in his sweet, honeyed Louisiana drawl. My nose filled with the scent of copper and salt as crimson ribbons of magic unfurled around him and licked at Hardy's cheeks.

"Okay," said Hardy. "Fine." He didn't sound happy, but he no longer looked like he was ready to throw Killian into orbit.

The worst thing about Killian, if you asked me, was that he didn't look formidable on the outside. He was wearing his vest that marked him as a Deathstalker, but he seemed small and meek and forgettable. Close-fitting jeans underscored how skinny he was. Round, tortoiseshell glasses sat on the bridge of a nose that seemed just a tad too small to hold them. His dark brown hair was combed over to the side, tamed by hair product with a slight sheen. More nerd than badass—except he'd just stopped Hardy in his tracks with a mere thought.

"I was just about to go greet your father," Killian said to me. "Would you like to join us?"

Out of the corner of my eye, I saw my father on his feet, watching us. The room had gone silent. The air, stagnant.

Outside, I could hear kids playing, screeching and laughing, unaware of the tension growing in the tent. What I wouldn't give to be a child again, oblivious to this world we lived in. Instead, I was stuck between Hardy and Killian, watching Killian's power slide toward me, knowing I was about to accept an invitation I was desperate to reject.

There was a brief scuffling sound outside, and then someone entered the tent on my left. The tent flaps fell shut, blocking out the noise and diffused light of the night.

I could smell Crowe's magic before I could see him.

Killian released me. "Thank you for hosting this fine event, Crowe," Killian said, and offered his hand. "Looks like you all have done a great job."

Crowe stepped to my side. His fingers clamped over my shoulder, making me jump. Staring coldly at Killian, he raised his other hand and curled it into a fist while muttering under his breath.

Smoky-sweet skeins of *venemon* magic wended through the room, and everyone slumped in their chairs, their eyes closed. The only people still standing were Killian, Crowe, Hardy, and me. Even my father had succumbed to the spell.

Venemon magic could manipulate the human body, but I'd never seen anyone put an entire room to sleep. If Crowe had wanted to, he could have done it to me, too. I wasn't sure why he hadn't. And looking back and forth between the presidents of these two rival motorcycle clubs, I sort of wished he had. The tension was almost painful, and the sight and smell of their magic turned my stomach into knots.

"You think you can put me on the spot in public?" Crowe's lip curled. "Think again."

Killian clasped his hands behind his back. "I do believe this is entirely against the rules. Even if it is an impressive display of power."

"So is mind-fucking one of my Devils," Crowe said, jerking his head toward Hardy. "Would you like me to let him show you *his* magic?"

"He means no harm, Crowe," Hardy said, but as he did, Killian's magic shrank away from him. Hardy blinked. "But I could tear off his head and use it as a basketball if you want."

"Touch him again with your power and I'll let him," Crowe said to Killian.

Killian gave Crowe a small, cold smile. "I was trying to be sociable. Just ask Jemmie."

"Leave me out of this," I grumbled.

"Oh," said Killian, eyeing Crowe's hand on my shoulder, "I think it's too late for that."

Crowe let go of me. He took a step forward, putting half his body in front of mine like a shield. "What the fuck do you want?"

"I was just inviting Jemmie to have a conversation with her father and me. In fact, you should all join us." His eyes scanned the room. "My *omnias* seer, Ilya Vetrov, warned me that something was afoot. She didn't say what, but she did say it would transpire at the festival."

Crowe and Hardy exchanged looks over my head. "So you thought you'd come in here and stir shit up?" Hardy asked. "Make the prediction come true?"

Killian watched Crowe. "Should I be worried? The Deathstalkers are here for a peaceful gathering, just like almost everyone else. We have absolutely no desire to go to war with the Devils or any of the clubs—we came with the best of intentions, hoping to continue to mend fences and forge new alliances." He gestured at the tentful of sleeping people. "But now I'm wondering if you lured us here to finish what the Devils started seven years ago when your father's club nearly wiped us out of existence."

Crowe's gaze could have cut diamonds. "Don't play the innocent with me. We both know what you did to my father last year."

"My condolences on the loss of your father," Killian said. "But I had nothing to do with it, as I explained to Agent Carmichael when he interviewed me last year."

My eyebrows shot up. "What?"

"Your father was assigned to investigate the allegations that Michael Medici's death was foul play," Killian explained. "He closed it for lack of evidence. Didn't he tell you?"

I looked over at Dad, who was slumped over a table, snoring softly. "No," I murmured. Because he never told me anything. Then again, we rarely spoke at all.

"Or maybe you screwed with his head a little," Crowe snarled. "That's what you love to do, isn't it?"

"If you're trying to provoke a fight, it's not going to work," Killian said. "The Deathstalkers are straight, and we're not here to seek revenge. It took us years to rebuild, and I'm not going to endanger my people."

"You're so full of shit," Crowe muttered. "And if any of you put even a toe out of line over the next three days, you will answer to the Devils."

"I'll do what's necessary to protect my club." Killian's voice was harder now, and he looked bigger, more dangerous. "If you're planning something, we'll be ready."

The air was charged, like lightning might strike at any moment. My nose burned with barely restrained magic, including the minty sting of my own. I put a hand on my stomach as Crowe leaned forward and Killian stood up straighter, both prepared to meet the other's power with wrath. "Please," I whispered, though I wasn't sure what I was actually asking for.

The tent flaps opened again, and Darek walked in. The sight of him standing next to Crowe made me feel like I was walking a tightrope across the Grand Canyon.

"Whoa," he said, looking around the room. "Did someone spike the punch?"

"Who the hell are you?" asked Crowe.

"That's Derwood," said Hardy at the same time Killian said, "Darek."

"Derwood?" Darek asked. "Ouch."

"Darek," Killian continued without taking his eyes off Crowe, "go tell Ford, Ren, and Quincy that we're meeting an hour earlier, and I'm sure you'll find Brenda, Dallas, and Armand right outside."

"Yeah," said Darek, giving Crowe a nervous look. "Out cold."

Killian's lips pursed in apparent annoyance. "Get them back to our tent as well, as soon as Mr. Medici here sees fit to rouse them."

"Sure thing, boss," Darek said, his eyes meeting mine for a brief moment before flicking away.

It didn't escape Crowe's attention, though. His eyes narrowed as he watched Darek slip back through the tent flaps.

"Remember that the Syndicate is watching you, hmm?" said Killian. "What would they think of what you're doing right now? Wake the babes, Crowe, and let them drink. It seems we have nothing more to say to each other."

Crowe scowled, stuck his hand through the tent flaps, presumably to wake the Deathstalkers he'd sedated outside, then turned to the room and broke the spell with a simple flick of his fingers. People's heads snapped up, shaking off the effects of the magic. Murmurs swept through the tent as everyone tried to figure out what had happened.

Crowe leaned in to Hardy. "Spread a rumor. I don't care what it is. Just make the suspicion go away so people stop asking questions." To me he said, "You're coming with me."

He grabbed my hand and yanked me out of the tent, shoving past Killian and into the cool night air. Three members of the Devils' League stood at the tent entrance, watching Darek and the other Deathstalkers march up the path toward their tent in the northern section of the field.

"Jackson, come. The rest of you, stay," was all Crowe said to his men, and they obeyed.

In the amount of time I'd been inside the beer tent, the festival numbers had swelled. Magic hovered in the air like a dust cloud, sparking and glittering. My head swam and my nose itched. Alcohol buzzed in my veins, dulling the intensity but also making it hard to discern one type of power from another.

Maybe it was the added heat of the night, or the escalating tension, but right now I felt like I was about to explode with too much stimulation. Or maybe it was Crowe's hand in mine, turning my insides out. *Venemon* blood had the ability to amplify a kindled person's own magic, but did skin-to-skin contact have the same effect?

Crowe dragged me to the parking area, away from the gathering. We wove through the parked cars, to the back of the field, where a second driveway was hidden in the trees. Crowe's car sat parked beneath an oak tree, facing the exit, prepared for a quick escape should he need one.

He dug the keys from his pants pocket and tossed them at Jackson, who caught them. "Drive Jemmie home."

"What?" I wrenched my hand out of his grip as Jackson unlocked the car and slid into the driver's seat. Probably knowing we didn't want to be overheard, he shut himself inside.

"You're in no condition to drive, but it's time for you to go home," Crowe said as soon as the car door closed. "I'll make sure Owen knows you're safe."

"You're not the boss of me, Crowe."

He closed the distance between us with one stride and towered over me. "Go *home*. You're drunk. Count yourself lucky that I'm not going to make sure Owen knows that, too."

"I'm not drunk," I lied. If Dad knew, he'd probably use it as an excuse to put a containment barrier spell around the house—his version of grounding. "I had two drinks, for God's sake." Or was it three...?

"You were drunk when you got here," he snapped. "You're fooling *no one*, Jemmie. You're a mess, and you can't protect yourself. You have no business being here at all."

"What the hell?" I tried to shove him away, but he didn't budge. "Half the people here are already drunk, Crowe. It's a freaking party! And you're not in charge of me." My eyes were stinging with the humiliation. "I'm not a child, and I can stay if I want."

"No, you can't," said Crowe. "You heard Killian—he's up to something—"

"*You're* the only one who was making threats in there!"

"He murdered my father," Crowe thundered.

"Or maybe it was an accident," I shouted back. "And maybe you just want an excuse to burn down the world."

Crowe staggered back like my shove hit him a minute late. His shoulders heaved and his fists clenched. "Jane predicted something significant would happen at this festival. And Killian—"

"He said his seer made the same call. Why would he say that if he was planning something himself?"

"Because he's a twisted asshole who likes to play with people's minds," said Crowe. "And I needed him to know—"

"Why did you keep me awake when you put almost everyone else to sleep?" I blurted out.

Crowe ran his tongue along his bottom lip. "You need to understand the threat."

"And that threat is you?"

"Jemmie, go home. Just go home. I have too many people to protect, and you're a liability. Sober up, figure yourself out, and practice your magic, because you have no place here if you don't."

"You don't understand," I mumbled. "I can't just—"

"If you can't do it, then maybe you should get the hell out of Hawthorne," he said roughly. "You're only going to get hurt if you stay."

I blinked fast, fighting tears I was *not* going to shed in front of him. "That's what you want?"

His breath shuddered from his chest, and he looked away. "Yeah."

"All because I had a few drinks. All because I won't do magic on command."

"How about both?"

"Why do you even care?"

As he brought his eyes to mine again, his voice was

slightly gentler. "No one drinks like you do unless they're hiding from something, and I think you're hiding from your magic."

I sighed. "That's not how it is."

"Bullshit. Is it your dad? You stopped practicing right around the time he left. I remember Alex telling our mom." His voice had lost its sharp edges, but his words still packed a punch. "There's no shame in having the same kind of magic he does. There's no shame in using it."

"Quit trying to psychoanalyze me. You suck at it."

"Am I wrong? I've known you your whole life, Jemmie Carmichael, and you've never been chickenshit about anything except your own power."

"It's none of your business." I bit back a bitter comment about how he had made sure of that when he started kissing other girls right in front of me.

"It is my business when it affects the Devils—we have to protect you because you can't protect yourself. You can't help protect Alex, either, and Lord knows she needs it sometimes."

For a moment, we just stared at each other, and I remembered what Crowe had said to Hardy while I eavesdropped, about how I was a distraction, something that would slow him down. Shame wound so tightly around me that I couldn't breathe. Crowe was right: I didn't belong here. I was a disappointment to everyone. I was failing my best friend. And suddenly I wanted to be a million miles away.

Maybe living in a dreck world, far away from Hawthorne and the kindled community, was exactly where I belonged. Sometimes, when I thought about it, when I *really* considered it, it seemed like a welcome relief.

I let out a breath. "Fine. I'll go home. But Alex—"

"Boone is with her, and he'll be taking her home soon."

"And you? What are you going to do?"

He smirked, the seriousness suddenly gone. "Now you care whether I live or die?"

I've always cared, you idiot. I turned away and looked at the car, where Jackson waited inside, his head bowed over his phone. "Just don't go around picking fights."

He snorted. "I'll try. Think about what I said, all right? Stop hiding and face whatever you're scared of. Whatever it is, I'm guessing you're strong enough to deal with it."

My back still to him, I rolled my eyes. Then I climbed into his car and Jackson turned the engine over, the roar of it like a jet plane in the intimate press of the forest.

As Jackson drove away, I checked the side mirror and was disappointed to see the reflection on the glass empty save for the silvery paint of moonlight on the trees.

NINE

WHEN I GOT HOME, I IMMEDIATELY TRIED CALLING DAREK, but he didn't answer. I tried Alex, but hers went straight to voice mail.

I paced the house. Watched TV. Took a shower. Watched more TV. No one called me back. No one texted.

It was like all of them had forgotten that I existed. They had enough to deal with already, and couldn't bother with me. Or maybe they were having so much fun that I just didn't cross their minds.

Sometime after three in the morning I lay down and somehow managed to fall asleep, despite the ongoing silence from my friends. In some distant corner of my dreams, I heard the rumble of a Harley as it tore down my street and parked in front of my house. But it wasn't until Crowe was at my bedside, shaking me, that I came fully awake.

It was still dark out, the moon only a phantom light behind my bedroom curtains. Crowe was hidden in darkness, but I knew it was him by the honeyed, smoky smell of him and the feel of his hands on my skin.

"What is it?" I croaked, and sat up on an elbow. "How did you get in here?" Dad was right—the barrier around our house was obviously shot.

"You weren't answering your phone."

"I was sleeping."

He flicked the bedside lamp on and I winced.

"Have you heard from Alex?" he asked, an unfamiliar edge in his voice.

"What? No. Is she not home?" I grabbed my phone from the table and activated the screen. Five AM. Four missed calls from Crowe. There was nothing from Alex. Not even a text.

"I haven't seen her since this afternoon." He said *this afternoon* like it was still the same day, like he hadn't slept at all yet. "She managed to slip away from Boone in the crowd."

I kicked the blankets off. Crowe started to pace. "And

you searched all over the festival?" I asked. "Even in the woods? Sometimes she—"

"Yes. I searched." He ran a hand through his hair. "I searched the whole place."

"Okay. So." I scrubbed at my face, trying to knock the sleep from my eyes. "Someone has to have seen her. She kind of stands out."

"Jackson didn't see her after he got back from dropping you off. Hardy got too plastered to know the difference between a girl and a lamppost. Boone came up with nothing. Gunnar is still hiding from me. Brooke said she thought she saw Alex heading off to the parking lot with my mom, but Mom hadn't seen her in hours. Not since we were all in the tent during setup, and Alex isn't at home."

"Was her car still in the lot?"

Crowe shook his head.

"What about Flynn? Did he see her?"

"I tried his phone before I came here, but he didn't answer."

I slid from the bed and grabbed a pair of jeans off the floor, realizing as I tugged them on that I wasn't wearing anything at all other than an old T-shirt. Crowe went still, watching me in that unreadable way of his.

"Turn around," I said, so he did, and I quickly slipped

on a bra. Once my shoes were in my hands, and my bag on my shoulder, I said, "Let's start with Flynn's house; he's always putting up strays. We'll find her, okay? She's probably just passed out somewhere." I wasn't that worried—Alex and I had plans to practice magic today, and I knew how long she'd been wanting me to cast. "It's also possible she doesn't want to be found right now, especially by you. She was pretty pissed about what you did at the Schoolhouse."

He didn't reply, but the grit of his teeth and the sharp nod of his head implied that it would be better for all of us if Alex was found sooner rather than later. Otherwise I feared the world might crumble around us, crushed by Crowe's devastating magic.

Crowe didn't bother knocking on Flynn's front door, and he knew the invocation to open it. Once he grunted the word out, the door creaked open and Crowe strolled inside.

"Flynn has a barrier spell on his house?"

Crowe glanced at me over a shoulder. "Yeah. We had to buy them at a premium because your dad bailed on us." His look said it all—he thought I could do this kind of magic if I practiced...and he clearly thought I owed my allegiance to the Devils. He didn't seem the slightest bit put off by my scowl. "Speaking of, you should strengthen your perimeter protection and change the invocation. The barrier at your place is weak, and I knew the password on the first guess."

I rolled my eyes. "Did you and my dad compare notes?"

Crowe ignored me and stepped into the living room. I ran right into his back when he pulled up short.

"What is it?" I said, and followed him through the doorway.

As soon as the heavy cigar smoke and autumn leaves scene hit me, I knew. Slowly, I leaned around Crowe.

From the entryway, the room had looked like a normal living room. Couch. Coffee table. Empty beer cans on the floor. A TV on the wall.

Now we were standing in the middle of the woods, surrounded by wolves.

"Crap," I whispered.

"Yep," Crowe said.

We both knew it was an illusion. We were standing inside Flynn's house, after all, and half the time you just couldn't trust your senses around the guy. But while illusions weren't real, and even less real when you knew they were there, they could still feel real. If the wolves were so inclined to eat us alive, we'd feel every bit of that pain.

"Don't move," Crowe said.

The pines rustled as the wind kicked up. The scent of the

sap on the air and the earth beneath my feet overwhelmed the smell of the magic itself. I could smell the muskiness of the wolves, hear the vibration of their snarls in the backs of their throats.

Crowe stretched a hand out, then snapped it closed, and the wolf closest to us crumbled into a whimpering heap. Three more wolves took its place. Crowe took out another, and another three wolves appeared.

"Okay, so don't kill the wolves," I said.

"Goddamn it, Flynn!" Crowe shouted.

A giant gray wolf crept closer, its lips pulled back, baring its fangs. It snarled, tensed, and leapt.

Crowe lunged in front of me and the wolf clamped down on his forearm, sinking its fangs into his flesh. Blood splattered the speckled gray fur at the wolf's throat and Crowe hissed. A black wolf charged toward me, but I pivoted at the last second and it barreled past me.

A third wolf—a roan female—nipped at Crowe's free arm while he struggled to free himself from the gray.

"Barrier, Jemmie!" he shouted.

"What?" I scanned the woods, looking for something to use as a weapon.

"Use a goddamn barrier spell!"

The desperation in his voice sliced my fear at the seams. Relying on reflex and instinct, I dropped to one knee and slammed my hand into the dirt. The magic left me like a great wave crashing over stone, spreading out in all the spaces in between. The barrier mushroomed up and around us, blue and glittering like a firecracker. I nearly choked on the astringent fumes of it. I could barely see through its sapphire ribbons twisting in the air around my body.

Sweat beaded on my forehead, and sudden dizziness made me pitch forward. Crowe was next to me in an instant, his hands on my shoulders, keeping my face from hitting the floor. Just beyond our little bubble of protection, the curse-wolves snapped and snarled.

A light flicked on overhead. The wolves disappeared. The woods faded into the walls of the living room and Flynn stood over us, blinking against the light.

"What the hell are you two doing on the floor?"

Crowe examined his arm. The skin was still whole, the flesh unmarred. All the blood that had covered him a second ago was gone.

Crowe closed his eyes, panting. "You asshole."

"What?" Flynn said, and shrugged. He dropped into his easy chair and lit a cigarette. "You said we needed extra precautions, what with all these other clubs in town. So," he spread his hands out, "extra precautions."

Crowe held his arm to his chest, like it still ached from the phantom bite. "I could kill you right now."

155

"It'll fade in a few minutes."

"I could still kill you."

Flynn laughed. "But you won't. It's six in the morning. Who wants to take care of a body at six in the morning? Not I, I tell you. Of course, I'd be the body in question, so..."

I stood up and held out a hand to Crowe. He ignored it and climbed to his feet.

"What's this about anyway?" Flynn took a hit off his cigarette. Smoke curled in the air.

"Can't find Alex, and she's not returning anyone's calls or texts." Crowe perched himself on the arm of the couch and leaned forward, hands on his knees.

"Well, she *was* pretty pissed at you—"

"I *know*. And I don't care. Have you seen her?"

"Not since last night."

"When?"

"She left the festival around ten with that boy, you know?"

Crowe gritted his teeth. "No, I don't know. If I knew, I wouldn't be here."

"Ahhh..." Flynn snapped his fingers. "That boy, the son of the bartender at the Schoolhouse?"

"Dara's son, Stephen?" I said.

"That's the one." Flynn flicked ash into an empty tuna fish can. "He seems harmless enough."

"Yeah, but Alex would never leave the festival with him," I said. She had always been kind to him, but he was gangly and awkward, his face covered in acne. Dara hooked up with one of the Devils seventeen years ago and got pregnant. When Stephen started showing signs of having inherited his father's power, Stoneking *terra* magic, he'd been taken under the wing of the Devils' League. He wasn't a member and wouldn't be eligible for years, but people looked out for him. He *was* harmless.

I glanced at Crowe. "This is all wrong."

Crowe nodded and hung his head.

"What's wrong?" Flynn asked.

"Brooke said she saw Alex leave with her mom," I said.

"And you saw her leave with Stephen around the same time," Crowe said.

Flynn took another drag from his cigarette. "Well, that's not good. Think it was an illusion?"

"Alex couldn't cast, even using a cut," I said. "Her magic is bound." I remembered the look on her face when she'd told me it was still gone, and guilt sat heavy in my gut.

"Someone else could have cast it," said Crowe.

"I didn't do it," Flynn said, like he needed to defend himself. "I swear it." He was serious now.

"I believe you." Crowe stood up and fished out his cell phone. He dialed someone's number, and when they picked up on the other end, he said, "Meet me at the Schoolhouse in fifteen minutes." He hung up without a good-bye.

"Get dressed," he told Flynn. "You're coming, too."

Flynn nodded and disappeared down a hallway.

"And me?" I said.

"You too. I'm going to need you."

Mom texted me as I pulled into the Schoolhouse parking lot. Where are you?

Nothing to do but tell the truth. With Crowe. I have the car. Alex took off and we're looking for her.

Should I be worried?

No. I'm fine. She's probably fine, too. At least, I hoped so.

And Crowe?

I glanced up as Flynn and Crowe arrived on their bikes. Worried about Alex, I texted.

Working the lunch shift today. Will I see you later?

I let her know I'd check in with her when I knew about Alex, and she seemed fine with that. I got out and walked across the lot to meet Flynn and Crowe, noting from the cars and bikes around me that Lori Medici and most of the Devils' League must already be inside. Crowe took the steps up two at a time and held the door for me so I could enter ahead of him. Lori met us in the hallway.

"No one has any news," she told Crowe.

Crowe squeezed her shoulder as he walked past. I followed them down the hall to the bar area.

Boone and Jackson sat in one of the booths along the wall. Flynn went over and joined them. Hardy sat, propped on a barstool, looking like he might still be slightly drunk from the night before.

Crowe went behind the bar, poured himself a shot of whiskey, and slung it back. When he was finished, he slammed the glass on the bar top. Dark circles ringed his eyes. It was now nearly seven and he hadn't been to bed yet.

In a terse voice, he relayed the news that Alex was missing, and that someone had cast an illusion to conceal who she left with.

"Was Stephen even at the festival?" Boone asked.

"Yeah," Hardy said. "Saw him not long after Jemmie left."

"Was Dara there, too?"

Only a few drecks were allowed at the festival. Only those who knew the world, and Dara knew a lot about it. She would have been invited, since her son was still a minor.

"I saw her," Jackson said. "She was playing tag with the kids in the field near the parking lot."

"Then I need to talk to her," said Crowe.

"What's Dara got to do with it?" I asked. "We already agreed Stephen didn't actually leave with Alex."

Crowe dug his cell phone from his pocket. "Think. Why did people see Alex leave with two different people?"

Flynn said, "A complete illusion will be seen and felt by all. An unstable one will produce varied results."

Lori clutched a coffee cup in both hands. "Not enough power to cast a complete illusion. The caster would have to be selective about who it would affect."

"Exactly." Crowe scrolled through his contacts. "The illusion was probably only for the people likely to stop Alex from leaving—the Devils. Whoever it was would have been interested in only one thing: getting Alex out. Dara isn't a Devil, and we know she was by the lot. She could have seen the real guy."

Once he'd found Dara in his phone, he made the call and put it on speaker. She answered with a sleepy voice.

"Did you see Alex leave the festival last night?" Crowe asked, skipping a greeting altogether.

"Yeah. Just after ten, I think."

Crowe spread his arms out, hands propped on the bar top as he hunched closer to the phone. "On her own—or with somebody?"

"She was with a guy." Dara sounded a little nervous.

"I need you to tell us as much about this guy as you can. What did he look like?" Crowe asked.

"He was young. Looked a little older than Stephen, but not by much. He was six foot, maybe? Blond hair. He was wearing a white T-shirt and those god-awful skinny jeans."

My throat closed up. Her description sounded an awful lot like Darek.

We all looked at one another.

Dara must have read into the silence, because she asked, "Why? Is something wrong with Alex?"

Crowe ignored her question. "If you think of anything else, call me, yeah?"

"Sure, of course."

With the call ended, Hardy let out a sigh and scrubbed at his eyes. "That description sounds an awful lot like that Deathstalker prospect kid."

"I don't know what it is about that guy, but he pisses me off," Crowe said, his fingers curling into fists.

I cringed internally. I knew he'd noticed Darek last night, but I hadn't realized he'd taken such an instant disliking to him.

Crowe straightened abruptly and ran a hand through his hair. "Fucking Deathstalkers! I should have killed that kid when I had the chance. Killian probably ordered him to take Alex. God only knows what he's done with her."

161

"Crowe," Lori said, clearly trying to calm her son, "I'm worried, too, but it's dangerous to jump to conclusions."

"I know, Ma, but can you blame me?" He came around the bar and started to pace, his hands on his hips. No one said anything. Inside, I felt like my guts had been knotted a hundred different ways. Had Darek really left the festival with Alex? Where had they gone? Why hadn't he called me back last night? Or texted me?

I checked my phone again and found nothing.

"Jemmie," Crowe said, finally turning his attention to me. He opened his mouth to speak, glanced around, then said, "Can I talk to you in the hallway?"

Frowning, I followed him out of the bar area. Did he know I knew Darek? "What's up?"

"You think you can cast a locator spell?"

Relief rolled through me. My secret was still safe. But it wasn't just that—a glow of gratitude warmed my cold thoughts. He'd asked me privately about the magic, instead of putting me on the spot in front of everyone. Except...the look in his eyes was so intense that, even here, with just the two of us, that's exactly where I was.

I sighed. Could I really say no? He was so desperate to find her.

And I was desperate to know why she and Darek had left together.

"I can try."

Crowe nodded. "Let's go to the house and find something of Alex's to strengthen the spell."

For a second, I watched him as he walked ahead of me to the door. I couldn't help but notice the heaviness in his shoulders, as if he was having a hard time keeping himself upright.

"You should get some rest, Crowe," I said.

He barely glanced at me as he replied, "I'll get some rest when I know my sister is safe."

TEN

As Crowe and I cut across the Schoolhouse parking lot, clouds rolled in, blocking out the early light of day. The air had turned chilly and brisk. A storm definitely seemed imminent.

Several paces ahead of me, Crowe threw on his Devils' League vest. He glanced at me over a shoulder when he reached his motorcycle, the wind tousling his hair into a perfect mess.

"You want to ride together or meet me there?" he asked.

"What do you think?"

He didn't answer, just slid on his black helmet, flipping the tinted visor closed with a definitive snap. While most of the Devils rode traditional Harleys with chrome everything, Crowe owned a 1960s model that he'd customized himself. The frame was matte black from rear to front, and so was just about everything else on it.

Though I knew very little about Harleys, I had to admit Crowe's was practically a work of art. No one knew their way around a bike quite like he did. In fact, he had an annoying talent for fixing just about anything. Except our relationship, apparently.

Without waiting for me, he started the bike up and tore out of the lot, the roar of the engine echoing through the neighborhood. The sound of his bike used to make my heart do funny things. Now it just irritated me.

The Medici house was on the north side of town, tucked into the center of dense woods, and as I wound my way down the mile-long drive, I tried to prepare myself for what was about to happen. It wasn't just that I was going to try to do magic on purpose, that I would have to brace myself for the smell and the sight and the feeling that was about to crush me like a tsunami. It was also the first time I would be alone in the Medici house with Crowe since the night we'd kissed.

When the trees finally gave way to the house and I saw Crowe's bike sitting in front, I inhaled and exhaled three measured breaths. I'd read somewhere that doing so helped with anxiety and stress. Turns out it didn't help me at all.

I parked and climbed out of the car. I entered one of the open garage bays and was greeted by the familiar scent of grease and gasoline. The Medici garage was not used for parking; it was used for wrenching. Several bikes were torn apart, their pieces strewn around in what looked like a non-sensical mess but was actually Crowe's version of order.

The door to the house squeaked open, and Crowe handed me a bottle of water when I met him on the steps.

"Thanks," I said, taking the offering.

Crowe passed the staircase and headed for the screened-in porch on the other side of the house. I hesitated in the living room, unsure if I should follow him or leave him be.

A glutton for punishment, I went to the porch, my heart pounding erratically in my chest.

A little over a year ago, I'd crashed with Alex after a night out to celebrate my seventeenth birthday. But when I couldn't sleep, I'd gone to the kitchen to get a glass of water and noticed someone on the porch.

I'd found Crowe sitting out there alone in the dark, drinking straight from a bottle of Jack Daniel's. He'd never told me what propelled him from his own bed that night, and at the time, I hadn't cared. The sight of him there was too thrilling, too tempting.

The older we got, the less time Crowe spent with Alex and me. By that point, I was starving for his attention, trying to remember what it was like before, when the thing I needed was plentiful, when I took it for granted.

He'd offered me the Jack and smiled a lazy smile. "Wanna join me?"

I did.

We drank and talked. We laughed at the stupid things we did when we were kids. In that late, first hour together, we'd closed the space between us on the couch until I was sitting right next to him, my knee touching his. I wasn't sure when my feelings toward him had changed, when I'd stopped looking at him like an annoying older brother and started looking at him like something more. It had happened gradually, but by then I had been aware of it for at least a couple of years. And suddenly he was close and the air was warm, and I was drunk on something other than the Jack.

"I miss this," I'd told him that night. "I miss you."

He'd glanced at me, his stupidly handsome face painted in the glow of the moon. I'd recognized that glint in his eyes right away because I felt it, too. I even had a name for it: *hunger.*

"Oh, Jemmie Carmichael," he'd said, and then he kissed me, hard and fast, his hands ghosting over my skin.

When he pulled away, just enough to get a breath, lick his already wet lips, I shivered and tangled my fingers in his hair, pulling him back in.

I'm not sure how far it would have gone if we'd been given the chance. But the sun had started to come up and footsteps thudded down the stairs, and Crowe and I lurched away from each other like we were on fire.

Lori had poked her head into the porch and given us the kind of look you give someone when they've been caught doing something they shouldn't.

As we'd prepared to leave for the festival in New Orleans, I'd floated in a state of near-constant euphoria. Stupidly, I'd wondered whether Crowe would spend time with me there. I'd imagined us walking through the grounds, hand in hand. And then, the first night of the festival, I'd seen him with Katrina Niklos. He saw me, too. Looked me right in the eye. Then he'd pulled Katrina to him and kissed her on the mouth. He'd walked away with his arm around her waist, and I'd ended up drunk in a swamp. If it hadn't been for Darek, I might have been eaten by a giant reptile.

Now Darek might be doing the same thing Crowe had done to me—only with my best friend, who had no idea Darek was my... actually, I didn't know what he was. I didn't know what I wanted from him. All I knew was that the memory of kissing Crowe was like an eclipse, blocking out the light that could have allowed any other feelings to grow.

Now here I was, back at the scene where it had all begun, rain pattering softly against the porch roof, and I couldn't help but feel an impending sense of déjà vu. I realized, with startling, sickening clarity, that I wanted to kiss him again. For some insane, foolish reason, I wanted his hands on me and his lips on mine and I wanted the darkness crowding in around us, the outside world nothing but a smudge against the night.

I had to get out of there.

"I'm going to Alex's room," I said quickly. "You'll wait here?"

Crowe dropped into a chair in the corner, avoiding the couch, as if he, too, was suffering from memories better left forgotten.

"I'll be here," he promised.

I nodded, rushed out the doorway and up the stairs, putting as much distance between us as I could.

Alex's room reminded me a little of the Medici garage, complete and utter chaos organized in a way that only Alex understood. Clothing was piled in a chair beneath the window and on the end of her bed. Makeup and lotion bottles cluttered the top of her dresser. Shoes peppered the carpeting, not a single match in sight.

With a sigh, I scanned the mess, trying to decide what was best used in a locator spell. And then it hit me: cuts created by Alex that she'd been intending to sell. They'd contain her blood.

Alex's room was large by my standards, with a lot of places to hide important things, but I knew exactly where she kept her casting kit and her unused cuts.

I went to her top dresser drawer and pulled it open, shoving aside a fair number of bras and tank tops. Finally reaching the bottom, I popped the false plank out and peered into the hiding spot, already able to smell the magic inside. There were a handful of Flynn's cuts, and a few I knew were made by Crowe's hand. Even though any person with *venemon* magic could have made them, as soon as my skin grazed the wood I could detect the subtle, masculine scent of Crowe. In fact, all of the *venemon* cuts were his. I couldn't find a single one made by Alex.

I kept digging until my fingers brushed over a little leather notebook. I pulled it out, thinking perhaps it was Alex's diary, or maybe a spell book.

But when I pushed open the cover, I didn't immediately recognize the handwriting. It was small and slanted. Alex's handwriting was big and looping.

I scanned a few pages, not wanting to infringe on anyone's privacy, but it quickly became apparent that I was reading a dead man's journal.

The notebook belonged to Michael Medici.

This must have been what Alex was trying to tell me about yesterday.

I dropped onto the corner of the bed and flipped to the last page.

Henry Delacroix had more secrets than we ever knew, and I'm about to expose the biggest. I have to make sure the threat is gone. I'm not going to let anyone get close to that kind of blood power ever again. The cost has been way too high.

Blood power...Alex had mentioned that exact phrase.

The date at the top of the page was from a week before Michael Medici died—and a chill ran down my spine as I realized it was the day before Crowe and I had kissed. I ran my fingers over that page and felt tiny ridges, so I flipped it to look at the back. There, in dark ink, like he'd been pressing the pen deep into the page, it read,

I don't know if I regret convincing Old Lady Jane to touch me or not. The good news is I know exactly how much time I have left. I can say good-bye without really saying it. I can make sure the succession is planned. And even if it's the last thing I ever do, I'm going to expose the truth and end the threat before anyone else is hurt.

My heart ached as I read his final words. Suddenly, I wondered if that was what Crowe had been brooding about the night I'd found him. Had his father been somehow trying to tell him good-bye and prepare him to take over?

It was almost too tragic to contemplate, but that wasn't all—there was this secret that Michael had discovered. Had it led directly to his death?

"Did you find anything?"

The sound of Crowe's voice made me jump a mile, and the notebook slid out of my lap. I retrieved it from the floor and handed it over. "Not yet. But look at the last page."

He flipped to the back and locked his jaw, brows furrowed deeply.

"This is my dad's handwriting."

"I know. Turn the page."

He did. When the words settled in, he collapsed on the end of the bed next to me, his arms heavy in his lap, the notebook flopping open on his knee. "The other day, Jane told me what he'd done, how he fooled her into touching him so he'd know when he was going to die. It made so much sense." He ran a hand through his hair. "He was acting so strange before last year's festival. Right before we left, he told me I was about to be made president." He swallowed and looked out the window. "He told me I'd have to do whatever it took to protect the club."

"But he didn't tell you..."

"That he was about to die?" Crowe shook his head. "I

thought he was going to leave like your dad did or something. I was so angry at him. But I was also determined to do as he said, for the sake of the Devils." He turned and met my gaze. "I couldn't afford to think of anything else," he added quietly.

And that was it. The explanation for what happened between us. No apology, no request for forgiveness, but I understood it. This was why he'd pushed me away. No time for distractions.

Apparently, that's all I was. "Did he tell you what Henry Delacroix's secret was?" I asked in a husky voice.

"No. He didn't even mention it. But I'll bet his little brother Killian was right at the center of it."

We sat there in silence for a few long moments. "What now?" I finally asked.

"Do you have what you need to cast the spell?"

"No. I found that first."

He got to his feet, scanned the room, and grabbed the little stuffed bear propped against Alex's pillows. "Use this." He looked at the notebook lying discarded on the bed. "Now I'm even more worried about what Killian is up to. He must be behind Alex's disappearance."

"And if I find her?"

"If you find her, then we'll go get her. And if someone took her by force, I'll murder them. Not with magic. With my bare hands."

"What if she's just...holed up with someone?"

His eyes narrowed. "Like that prospect?"

I swallowed hard. "No idea." I wasn't sure what to think. I was imagining Darek and Alex wrapped around each other, and although it didn't make me happy, it also didn't fill me with jealous rage the way seeing Crowe with Katrina had.

I wasn't sure whether that was a good thing or not.

"Jemmie," Crowe said impatiently. "Sometime today, please."

I slid from the bed to the floor and sat cross-legged, the stuffed animal in my lap. My dad had tried to teach me a locator spell when I was little, and of course the magic had overwhelmed my senses. I understood the mechanics of the spell, but I'd never successfully cast one. It should be easy for someone with my kind of magic, but here I was, my upper lip beaded with sweat, my gut rolling with anxiety over what was about to happen.

A warm hand closed over mine, and I looked up to see Crowe on the floor next to me. "When my dad first taught me to cast, I didn't want to," he said. "I was scared. I had so much *venemon* inside of me that it was almost like it was trying to tear its way out."

I knew Crowe was crazy-powerful, but I'd never considered what it must have felt like as a child, to discover that power, to know what a great burden and responsibility it was to possess it.

"How did you get over it?" I asked.

"I accepted it. And then I practiced."

I groaned. "You make it sound so easy."

"It wasn't. My hands used to shake so badly that I couldn't control what was happening. One time I accidentally broke my mom's leg because she was hanging laundry nearby. My dad healed her, but..." He shook his head at the memory. "All I'm trying to say is that you can learn to do this if you just work at it."

"You don't understand," I whispered.

"Then make me."

I hung my head. "It would change everything." He'd push harder to convince me to move away from Hawthorne. He'd—

His fingers tipped my chin up. "Try me, Jem. I know we haven't been close lately, but that doesn't mean I don't know you. Whatever's holding you back, you *can* overcome it. And I'll help however you need me to."

I looked up into his dark eyes, and I felt his gaze inside me, picking the locks I'd clamped onto all my secrets. Could he really help? Or, at least, understand? "I...can feel magic."

His brow furrowed. "We can all feel it."

"No, that's not what I'm talking about. When I'm around magic, I just…I can smell it. And see it. The magic itself, not the effects of it." I huffed. "I don't know how to explain it."

"Try. Because I don't—"

"*Venemon* magic is gold. It loops out of you so thick sometimes that I can't see past it. It smells like—" My gaze flicked to his and away. "Wood smoke. Honey. Yours is muskier than Alex's. Deeper. It hangs in the air around you like glitter sometimes. Even when you're not casting."

He was so quiet that I glanced at him again and found him staring. "No shit?" he whispered.

"No shit," I said ruefully. "Hardy's *invictus* magic is orange and smells like cloves. *Terra* magic is pinkish. Cinnamon, flowers, grass, depending on the person and the charm. Do I need to go on?"

"Why wouldn't you tell anyone about this? That kind of power would be useful. It makes you invaluable."

"Yeah, well, it also makes me dizzy and sick, especially when I'm around a lot of kindled. Sometimes I feel like it's suffocating me." I swallowed hard. "Sometimes I feel like it's driving me crazy. It's too much. I can't take it. It's like an illness with no cure."

"And that's why you drink. You're trying to self-medicate."

I winced and bowed my head.

"I still don't get why you've kept this a secret. You're close to your mom—why haven't you told her?"

"That's complicated," I said. "But mostly I don't want to give her one more thing to worry about." Or to feel helpless about. I didn't want to rub her face in her own powerlessness, not after what Dad had put her through.

"What about your dad, though? Haven't you—"

"I can't believe you're even asking me about him. He *left* me, Crowe."

"But Alex. She loves you—"

"Exactly!" I threw my hands up and let them fall into my lap. "But there's nothing she or anyone can do, so why make her worry about it? It would change the way she looks at me, and that would only feel worse."

"So you've shut out the people who love you most."

"Because I keep hoping it'll go away! Because no one else has this problem. I just want to be a part of our community, Crowe. But I don't fit, and I hate it." Tears stung my eyes. "I just want to be normal. And you said it yourself last night—I *don't* belong."

He cursed under his breath. "I was angry. And worried about you. I didn't understand any of this. In my defense, that's because you're damn good at keeping a secret."

"I don't want people to look at me like I'm defective."

I let out a shuddery sigh and laid myself bare. "Especially you."

"Look me in the eye." His voice was so authoritative that I obeyed. His eyes captured mine and refused to let go. "We've all got problems, Jemmie. We've all got sore spots and flaws and shit from our past and mistakes we're still dealing with. You want me to tell you you're perfect? I can't. But I can tell you this: You're brave enough to push through this. You're strong enough not to let it hold you back. And that's what actually matters."

He said this with complete certainty, and it reminded me of Alex. But while her faith in me was warm and comforting, his was both exhilarating and terrifying. It felt like flying. And I was afraid of crashing and burning. "Please keep this between us."

"It's not my story to tell. You'll do it when you're ready."

"Thanks."

He sighed. "But I need you to help me find Alex. You know she'd risk anything for you without even thinking." He grunted. "Though the not-thinking part is always kind of worrisome." He offered me a tentative smile laced with all the complexity of the last few minutes. "Please?"

He was right again—Alex would dive into hell to save me. What kind of crappy friend was I if I wasn't willing to risk the same for her? "Okay. I'm going to try this."

He withdrew to sit on the bed again, and the only sound in the room was my own heartbeat thundering in my ears. I closed my eyes and inhaled, picking up the very faint whiff of *venemon* magic in the room. In the next moment, my own magic rushed forward and overtook it. My nose stung with it, and when I opened my eyes, sapphire ribbons danced before me, awaiting my command. Fighting the urge to cough or try to contain it, I clutched harder to the teddy bear. I pictured the Medici house, the driveway, the woods around it, and flung my magic outward. The ribbons pulled taut, stretching beyond the house, reaching for Alex.

When the tug came, I gasped. "Oh my God."

The bed squeaked as Crowe stood. "What is it? Did you find her?" He seemed a little breathless, anxious, hopeful. But most of all scared.

I smiled as I felt another vague pull at the thin thread of my magic—the essence of Alex fizzed faintly along the connection, shimmering gold. "I think I did."

ELEVEN

CROWE DROVE MY CAR WHILE I GAVE DIRECTIONS WITH my eyes closed, still focusing on the magic, on the weak, unsteady tug at the line I'd cast. I was terrified of losing my grip on it. My fingers were clutched around the teddy bear and the edge of my seat, and my lungs burned with a minty sting, but Crowe had been right—I was getting used to it. I could stand it, and taking this risk was worth the look on his face and the relief in his voice.

"To our left," I muttered, and felt Crowe turn a moment later.

"We're headed back to the festival grounds," he said after a while.

I cracked one eye open. "The pull is still really weak. It's like having bad reception on a phone. I'm sorry. I'm not that good at this."

"Bullshit," he said. "You're doing just fine."

I went back to focusing on Alex, on the fleeting pull of her, but the more time passed, the more frustrating it got. "It's like she's fading in and out."

"We're here," he said. I opened my eyes again to see that he was backing into his spot in the hidden driveway near the festival grounds. "Can you keep it going here?"

I glanced up the path toward the distant domes of tents, where I could already see the heavy haze of magic blocking out my view of the midday sky beyond it. Most groups were probably tucked away in their family or club tents for lunch or to escape the heat, so the grounds probably wouldn't be crowded, and when I opened the car door the scents were strong but not overwhelming. "I'll try."

We got out of the car, and Crowe tossed me my keys. I hooked the ring around my middle finger, the metal clacking together as I fidgeted.

Crowe came around and met me at the passenger-side door. He grabbed my free hand, lacing our fingers together. "If you want to close your eyes and focus again, I'll make sure you don't fall."

Too late, my thoughts responded as I felt the warm press

of his palm against mine. "Um. Okay." I bit my lip and let my eyes fall shut. His grip on my hand tightened. "To the right."

Pine needles crunched softly beneath our feet as we walked forward. Crowe was silent, but I could feel his tension, his hope, his fear. I could tell there were a million questions he wanted to ask, but that he was afraid of pulling my focus from Alex.

I was afraid of the same thing. One moment I could feel her pull and see the faint amber glow of her in my mind's eye, and the next I was plunged into a numbing darkness. My stomach would drop with dread until she flickered back. I didn't really know what a locator spell was supposed to feel like and could only hope I was doing it right. My embarrassment at my lack of skill kept fraying my concentration.

"To the right," I murmured. "Wait, no." I opened my eyes as she disappeared from my magical radar again. "Shit." I looked around. We had skirted the main festival grounds and were at the far northwestern end of the clearing, beyond which were dense woods.

We were near the Deathstalker tent. Crowe was glaring at their scorpion flag as if he'd like to set fire to it. "Is that where you were leading us?" he asked.

"I...don't know," I said. "I just lost her again." I took in our direction, the place I'd been heading before my sense of her had vanished. "We were heading away from their tent."

"But you said the signal was weak, right? And that you haven't done a locator spell before." He was still staring daggers at their tent. "You got us pretty damn close."

"Let me try to find her again." My magic wreathed around me like a blue ribbon, and my nose became full of the stinging scent of my own power. With her teddy bear clutched under my other arm, fingers digging into its plush body, I focused on my best friend.

And found nothing.

"What the fuck are you doing here?"

Crowe whipped around, releasing my hand. I staggered a little and turned. Six Deathstalkers were coming toward us, the long grass parting to form a path for them. The smell of *terra* magic reached me a second later, and I could see the telltale pink haze of it coming from a guy with broad shoulders and a scorpion tattoo on his chest, visible as his leather vest gaped open. "He's probably a Stoneking," I whispered, nodding toward the guy.

Crowe gave me a sidelong glance and nodded, his hair blowing in the breeze the Deathstalker had conjured. "We're looking for my sister," he said to the group as they came to a stop at the edge of the woods, about twenty feet from where we stood.

They fanned out quickly, hemming us in. Crowe put up his hands—which were completely steady. "If you've got her," he continued in a low voice, "the best thing to do is to let her go."

"Yeah?" said a Deathstalker with full-sleeve tattoos and a scar across her forehead. "How about you give up our prospect first?" This one was emanating faint wisps of crimson—*animus* magic, like Killian's.

"She might be trying to influence you," I murmured to Crowe, whose eyes narrowed.

"We don't have your prospect," Crowe said to the woman. "But I'd like to know where he is, too. He was the last one seen with my sister."

"Uh-huh," said a third. He had buzzed black hair and a long beard. Glimmers of sapphire hung in the air around him. He had the same magic I had, but either he was holding it close or he didn't have nearly as much as my dad.

"*Locant*," I whispered.

Crowe gave me another look, this time with an arched eyebrow, before returning his focus to our current predicament. "Where's Killian, Ren?"

"None of your fucking business," said a fourth Death-stalker, the one apparently named Ren. She had dreads pulled back in a red bandanna and intense pale green eyes that contrasted with her dark skin. "And we're gonna have to ask you to clear out now. We're having a meeting."

"Without your president?" Crowe asked. His fingers, still held up to show he meant no harm, twitched. A faint amber glow, one I knew only I could see, flared off his fingertips.

"Get back to your clubhouse, Crowe," said the bearded guy, cracking his knuckles.

"I want my sister. If Killian has her somewhere on these grounds, I'm going to find her. And if she's hurt, I'm going to have to find some way to work out my *extreme* disappointment." His fingers curled, and shimmering, undulating threads of *venemon* began to stretch from their source.

"And if you've hurt Darek—" Ren began.

"I don't give a fuck about Darek," Crowe snapped. He took a step forward, and all six Deathstalkers had their hands out in front of them, fingers spread, power fogging and slithering in the air as the scent of all of it rolled toward me. It was coming from all sides, closing us in.

And then I smelled something new, something terrible, like stale cigarettes and burning meat. It was a magic scent I'd never come up against. My head swam with it, and I swayed as my stomach threatened to revolt.

"Crowe..." I licked my lips and peered through the

cloud to try to find the source of the unfamiliar odor. To our far right, several yards into the woods, someone tall ran between trees, too fast for me to recognize. The person was emitting strands of pale yellow and crimson streaked with black. "Someone is..."

Crowe took a step in front of me, his arms spreading, his magic billowing from him.

"Watch out," Ren shouted. "He's going to cast!"

"Crowe!" shouted a familiar male voice. Hardy, who must have seen us and come on the run. *Thank God.* But whatever he shouted next was lost as a fierce wind whipped my hair. Crowe stumbled into me, and we both went down. Branches cracked over our heads as curses flew from all sides. My ears were ringing and I could barely breathe—I was choking on magic, on the bitter, burning stench of it.

Crowe's hands were on my waist and his voice was in my ear. "Can you run?"

My breath came out of me in a strangled wheeze. "Crowe," I tried to say as amber *venemon* burst from his palm and rocketed wildly into the murky fog around us. He could probably see clearly, but I was almost blind from all the magic swimming around and overwhelming my senses.

A sharp wind slammed into us again, sending twigs and leaves scraping against my cheeks and forehead. My mouth filled with grit as I struggled to my feet. Crowe shouted something I couldn't make out in the storm of air and people and magic around me.

"I can't—" My next words were stolen from me as I staggered back from a sudden impact. Heartbeat pounding at my temples, I looked down at my shoulder to see the hilt of a knife protruding from my shirt. The pain hit me a beat later, a racing, pounding lance of agony arching out across my shoulder like a net of needles. My knees gave out.

"Jemmie!" Crowe shouted. Two people ran by in the shadows. We were in the middle of a full-on kindled brawl, shouts and grunts and gasps punctuating the fight. More of the Devils' League must have found us because we'd initially been surrounded by Deathstalkers, but now people had spread out, seeking safe places from which to hurl their curses. Their voices were coming from all sides.

Another knife whistled through the air, a glint of steel in a ray of sun, piercing the blanket of thick fog around me. Crowe ducked out of the way as he landed at my side, and the blade skimmed past his face, leaving a long, bloody gash across his jaw.

I tried pulling myself into a sitting position, but every inch of my body throbbed with pain, as if the knife had pierced not just my flesh but every nerve in my body, sending electric shocks down to my toes. Was this real or an illusion? I put my tingling fingers up to the wound and felt blood streaming across my palm. As I became dizzy with shock, I squinted at another person moving between tree trunks nearby, palms open toward us, giving off puffs of purple magic mixed with red and black. Confusion filled me. Was that who it looked like?

Crowe wrenched me toward him before I could get my eyes to focus, and I inhaled the smoke-and-honey scent of his power as he muttered a healing incantation. But then he groaned and clutched at his middle. Only a few dozen feet away, the person I had spotted smiled a beautiful, evil smile as the *animalia* curse took hold. Crowe doubled over at my side, vomiting centipedes and beetles and spiders and black moths, and this was no illusion. A great, writhing mass of insects grew into a puddle around him, and no matter how much he retched, more just kept coming. This curse was going to kill him.

And I knew exactly who had hurled it. I just couldn't understand why she would do such a thing.

My vision pulsed with blackness. Blood loss threatened to pull me into unconsciousness. And even if I could put up a barrier around us, it wouldn't help Crowe now. Whatever was wrong was already inside him.

So I did the only thing left to me, something my father had once told me I should never do.

"Crowe," I said in a choked voice, and stretched out my bloodied hand, hoping he'd understand what I was offering.

Blood.

He didn't hesitate—he frantically swiped the blood dripping from the gash on his face and clamped his hand in mine.

Medici blood met Carmichael blood. *Venemon* and *locant*.

Tingling spread through me, hot where our hands met, warm everywhere else. I wondered if Crowe was feeling the same. My heart thumped in my head and in my toes, pumping magic through every inch of me. Crowe's grip on my hand was iron—he had taken control of our combined power, and I would have given him anything in that moment. Ribbons of blue and gold surrounded us, braiding together, taking on a color I'd never seen before, indescribable and vibrant and entirely new. It was neither *venemon* nor *locant*. It was…*more*. A sigh escaped me. Everything inside of me felt like it'd been touched by the sun. It was the first time in my entire life that magic had felt like this.

Still holding on to me to keep our blood mixed, Crowe pressed his fingers against his throat with his other hand, squeezing till his veins bulged. Bugs squirmed behind his black-stained teeth, gnashed together. He was beyond speaking, but I swear I could hear his thoughts whisper an incantation. Somehow, he was casting using this new magic we'd created through our connection, and the effect was instantaneous. The tendons in his neck stood out in stark relief as a growl vibrated in the back of his throat, and the growl swelled to a roar as he finally opened his mouth. The insects scuttled past his teeth and over his lips, vaporizing when they hit the air, burning off into curling ribbons of black smoke.

When the lethal curse was extinguished beneath Crowe's healing hands and the alchemy of our mixed blood, he looked down at me, and I sucked in a startled breath.

The whites of his eyes were gone, bled completely to black. "This is amazing," he said, giving me an eerie grin. Even though the pain from my wound was gnawing at my ecstasy, I grinned back, knowing my eyes probably looked the same but unable to worry about it.

Heavy footsteps thudded toward us. Every single one was like a nail pounding into my skull. Crowe dropped my hand and scooted away from me, blinking fast and shaking his head as if to clear it. The warmth I'd felt seconds ago faded instantly, leaving me trembling and raw.

"Jemmie!"

"Dad?" I wheezed as he crouched over me. His gaze didn't focus on my eyes, so I could only assume they looked normal again. The fog of blood magic had certainly dissipated, but so had my vision in general. My heart stumbled and skipped. My breath was wet and unsteady.

I was pretty sure I was dying.

"This is the Syndicate," my dad shouted to the woods around us. He spread his arms and threw out a massive, glittering barrier. "Anyone caught showing further aggression will be sentenced to binding!"

"They're running," said Hardy, who had appeared next to Crowe and was helping him to his feet.

My mouth opened and closed as I tried and failed to gather the strength and volume to tell them who I'd seen in the woods, who had used such evil magic against Crowe.

My dad pressed a hand to my shoulder and I made a guttural, inhuman sound. My vision flashed to pure white. "Hang in there, Mo."

Don't call me that. . . . Words were out of my reach.

"Crowe, she needs you right now!"

I've needed him for a lot longer than that, I thought, my brain a tangle of dream and memory and now, fraying and unraveling before dissolving to pinpoint flashes of light, then fading to nothing.

There was no more magic, not now. All I had was darkness.

TWELVE

My sense of smell returned first, bringing me the scent of *venemon* magic, of Crowe, smoke and honey. Then sound. His voice, commanding and fierce.

"Dammit, Jemmie, open your eyes."

I obeyed, squinting at slivers of sunlight shining through the canopy of leaves above me. Crowe blocked the view a moment later. "You're fine," he said tersely, pulling his hand away from my shoulder. My shirt was torn and covered in drying blood, but my wound was gone.

"Your eyes," I whispered.

They were dark green once again. "Shhh," he said.

Voices from behind him told me my dad, Hardy, Jackson, and Boone were talking about what had just happened.

"—better that we just let people cool down before we jump to any conclusions," Dad was saying.

"Are you shitting me?" Hardy snapped. "Those bastards nearly killed them both without any provocation!"

"It wasn't Deathstalkers," I muttered, "not all of it, at least." I'd seen two people with that black-streaked magic in the woods—the tall, fast-moving shadow I'd spotted just before the knife had hit me, and the other...I still couldn't believe it, but she definitely wasn't a Stalker.

Crowe gave me a look that said he was holding back a lot of questions, but then stood up and helped me do the same. I swayed as I tried to get my legs to hold me up. The feel of his arm around me was scary and comforting at the same time, and for a moment I leaned into him, not wanting to let go.

Then I remembered he wasn't mine—and that I didn't want him to be. I wriggled away from him and ended up facing the others, who were gathered around us several paces into the woods. Over their shoulders, I could see the scorpion flag whipping in the wind above the Deathstalker tent, all of it within a faint blue bubble of *locant* magic.

"Where did they go?" I asked.

"I closed 'em up in there for the time being," Dad said. "For their protection and ours."

"What the hell happened, Crowe?" Hardy asked.

Crowe glanced at me out of the corner of his eye. "We were looking for Alex." He leaned over and scooped her teddy bear from the ground. His jaw clenched as he took in the splotches of blood that now marked its fuzzy head and limbs. "Jemmie did a locator spell."

Dad's eyebrows rose. "You did?" A hint of a smile played at his lips.

"I tried." Was that all he cared about? Whether I could do magic? "I lost the connection, though."

"Right here?" asked Brooke, her face flushed from the fight, her curly hair, usually tamed by a black bandanna, loose and wild. She scowled at the Deathstalker tent.

"I don't think they have her," I said. "They seemed focused on finding Darek." I stumbled a little over his name. "He's their prospect. And they thought we had him."

"If that's true, why did they attack you?" asked Boone. "Or did you attack them?"

Crowe's gaze scanned the woods around us. "I didn't have a chance to hurl much of anything—Jemmie got hit and I was trying to help her. Then I got slammed with…" He shook his head. "It could have killed me." His eyes flicked to mine as he left everything else unsaid. We'd done blood magic together—we'd mixed our essences to enable him to break a killing curse. It had been desperate and necessary but was technically illegal.

"Which of them hurled the lethal hexes?" Dad asked. "It's one thing to brawl, but what happened to both Jemmie and Crowe was attempted murder."

"Jemmie's had to have been someone with *arma*," said Boone. "That knife in her shoulder turned to dried leaves when Crowe tried to pull it out."

I rolled my formerly wounded shoulder, wincing. "Glad I wasn't awake for that."

"Yeah, you were too busy scaring the shit out of me," Crowe muttered. "But if the person who sent hex knives in our direction was *arma*, it couldn't have been the same person who hurled the insect curse—that had to be *animalia*. Jemmie's right—I don't know all the Deathstalkers, but the ones I'm familiar with don't have those powers. And both curses were too strong to have been produced by cuts."

"We can dig deeper into which Deathstalkers might have *arma* or *animalia*, but I thought we had all the Stalkers on the run right before you got hit," said Hardy, rubbing the back of his head, leaving his dark hair mussed.

I thought back to what I'd seen, that red-and-black-streaked magic that smelled of ash and cinders, like stale cigarettes. "Like I said, it wasn't all Stalkers. I saw two people deep in the trees. I only got a good look at one of them. It was Katrina Niklos. I saw her hurl the curse at Crowe."

Hardy looked as if I'd hit him over the head with a two-by-four. "Katrina?" He turned to Crowe, who was frowning at the ground. "Um. I guess she didn't take it well?"

Take what *well?* It almost came out of my mouth.

Now we were all looking at Crowe, and my heart was pounding with hope and suspense. He shook his head. "But I wouldn't have expected her to do anything like this, and why would she step into the middle of a brawl between Stalkers and Devils? We've got no problem with the Sixes."

Boone chuckled. "Yeah, but Ronan ain't exactly a fan after you put his boys in the hospital last fall."

"I'm going to pretend I didn't hear that," Dad said.

Crowe rolled his eyes. "Ronan understands our kind of law. He sent his crew to my town because he thought we were weak. He thought *I* was weak."

"Oozing boils and uncontrollable puking, though," said Hardy. He whistled. "It was pretty gross."

"It was a deterrent," Crowe replied firmly.

"Let's get back to Katrina," Dad interjected. "That was a pretty serious curse—and accusation. Besides, although she might be able to conjure insects, she couldn't hurl an *arma* hex, and as far as I know, none of the Sixes have *arma*." He tilted his head. "Are you absolutely sure she cursed Crowe, Jemmie? Or maybe…"

Anger rose up in me. "Yeah, Dad. I know what I saw. I'm not lying."

He put up his hands. "I can certainly ask her a few questions," he said. "In fact, what if we all head over to the Sixes tent now?"

"Yeah, because it's going to go real well when we show up with a Syndicate agent in tow," grumbled Brooke.

Dad shrugged. "I didn't ask you to be happy about it. But it might be good to put space between you guys and the Stalkers, especially if Killian shows up."

"Yeah, where is that guy?" asked Hardy.

"If he has Alex, I'm going to kill him, Owen," Crowe said. "You won't be able to stop me. He's not going to take another member of my family away from me."

"We have no evidence that Killian Delacroix has done anything wrong," my dad replied. "Then or now."

Crowe muttered something hostile under his breath before turning away. The clench of his long fingers around that little teddy bear made my heart ache.

"Crowe, wait," I said. "Before we go, maybe my dad could try a locator spell…?" We'd come here to find Alex, and I didn't want to leave if she was close. "He's a lot better at them than I am."

Dad smiled, looking relieved. "I'd be happy to, Crowe. It's the least I can do considering you just saved Jemmie's life. I owe you."

I wasn't quite sure how to feel about that. On the one hand, I wanted to stay mad at my dad—it hurt less than opening myself up to disappointment yet again. On the other, I remembered the desperate look in his eyes as he hunched over my bleeding body, and the wrenching sound of his voice as he begged Crowe to save me.

Dad accepted the stuffed animal from Crowe and closed his eyes. My nostrils flared as the stinging scent invaded. Blue tendrils sprouted from my father's body like vines, slithering along the forest floor, winding up tree trunks and into the canopy above. I watched in awe as his magic expanded so easily, so controlled. But then it shrank back just as quickly, and Dad frowned. "There's nothing," he said quietly.

"What do you mean?" asked Crowe. "Jemmie sensed her. She led us to this spot."

"I'm sorry, Crowe," Dad said. "I'm just not picking anything up, and if she's anywhere within a hundred miles from here, I should be able to."

"I probably got it wrong," I said miserably. "Crowe, I'm so—"

"No," he snapped. "You sensed her, and you know it. Don't get scared now. Own it."

I stepped back, stung. "I warned you I might not be able to do it." I couldn't escape his gaze, hard and full of challenge.

"Crowe," my dad said quietly, "Alex isn't a *locant*, so she couldn't hide herself from me."

Crowe's eyes narrowed. "Then maybe someone with *locant* took her."

"Okay," Dad said cautiously, "but the number of people with enough *locant* to completely conceal a life spark from someone like me is so small that—"

"My sister is not dead!" shouted Crowe.

Dad took a step back. "That's not what I'm saying. We'll all help you search. But maybe we should talk to Ronan and the Sixes first. If Katrina is looking to punish you, that might be the best place to start."

"Fine, let's go talk to them," Crowe said. His lip curled as he gazed at the Stalkers' tent. "I need to get out of here anyway, before I change my mind and curse all of them with explosive diarrhea."

"Never thought I'd say this, but thank God Owen put

up that shield around them," said Brooke. "Because we don't have nearly enough toilets for that."

The Devils fell into step just behind Crowe as he stalked off down the path toward a tent flying the emblem of the Rolling Sixes, some type of crouching demon with ragged wings clutching a human leg bone with its clawed fingers. Wind ruffled my hair and dried my sweaty face as I followed. Dad made his way to my side and caught me by the elbow when I tripped over a clump of grass. "You might be healed, but you lost a fair amount of blood before he got that wound closed," he said.

"I'm fine. I just want to figure out what's going on, and I want to get Alex back."

"I didn't mean to make you look bad back there, Mo. I think it's great that you tried to do a locator spell."

I stared stonily at the path ahead. "I'm not a child, Dad. You don't have to talk to me like one." It wasn't his fault I was freaking incompetent. I could have sworn, though, that I did it right. My own magic had flared out just like his— but unlike his, I had connected with Alex, however briefly. "I know I found her. I just...didn't get a good sense of the location quickly enough."

"Crowe was right—she could have been cloaked," he said. "But it would take someone with *locant* magic even more powerful than mine."

"One of the Stalkers has that kind of magic."

"Ford? He can barely cloak himself, let alone someone else. He's always been resentful because he doesn't have much power and can't do much with what he has."

"So you don't think the Deathstalkers could have been responsible for kidnapping Alex?"

"Do we know she was kidnapped? She's been gone less than twenty-four hours, and from what I hear, she's grown up to be quite the wild child."

"Alex can be wild, yeah, and she can be tough when she's mad," I said. "But I don't think she would deliberately make the people who love her worry like this. I mean, Crowe, maybe. He's the one who bound her magic, but—"

"Wait, Crowe did that?"

"No, I did, but—"

"So you *are* using your magic," he said, looking pleased.

"Yeah." I offered him a bitter smile. "Now that you know I'm not a reject, are you gonna come home?"

Dad's face went from tan to ashen in the space of a few seconds. "You think I left...because of you?"

I scowled and kept walking.

He grabbed my arm and pulled me to a stop. "Jemmie, it killed me to leave you."

"Uh-huh."

His eyes shone with emotion. "You have no idea what

we did. I had to go, to try to make it right." His voice was husky. On the verge of breaking.

"What who did?"

"Me and Michael. At the time it seemed like we had no choice, and I went along with it. But it was wrong, Jemmie, and I couldn't live with it."

"What the hell are you talking about?"

Dad looked past me, back at the Deathstalkers' tent. "When we took down Henry Delacroix and every single one of his officers." He winced, as if he was seeing something horrific in his mind's eye. "I helped Michael kill six men that night, Jemmie."

Crowe and the Devils were way ahead of us now, and though I wanted to know why Katrina had attacked us, I needed to know this. "It was *just* you and Michael? Why did you two have to kill all of them?"

"The officers were following the orders of their president," Dad said, his tone soaked with regret. "But Henry— he was about to do something that would have changed our world forever. Have you ever heard of the cruori spell?" When I shook my head, he went on. "It's blood magic. The worst of the worst."

My cheeks bloomed with heat as I thought about the blood magic between Crowe and me. A thrill of his power still ran through my veins, my heart beating with it. "I didn't know there were levels of badness when it came to that type of magic."

Dad shrugged. "It's never good. Blood incantations involve taking someone else's essence into your body, or losing it to another person, and you can never know how it's going to affect either the taker or the giver."

"What if it's sort of...mutual?" Crowe had used my magic, but I was the one who offered it.

"You still can't predict how it might change you," he said sternly. "But the cruori spell is on a different level. It involves stealing kindled life forces so you can permanently possess every type of magic."

"Stealing life forces?"

"It is what it sounds like—you have to kill the person, or come close enough to absorb all their magic."

"But...you'd have to kill a lot of kindled! There are eleven known types."

"Well, now there are ten. The Crofts and their *tollat* magic..."

"The family line ended, but didn't Henry have that *tollat* power to siphon that the Crofts were known for?"

He nodded. "He must have had Croft blood way back in his family tree, because that power hadn't been seen in years before he came on the scene, and he was the last person to have it. But to complete the cruori spell, you have to completely drain kindled of their various abilities. That's what Henry was trying to do, Jemmie. That's why we had to stop him. If he'd succeeded, he would have been all-powerful. He could have ruled our world. Or ended it."

I shuddered. "But you stopped him."

"We got wind of what he was doing after Paul Medici turned up dead, blood drained."

Paul had been Michael's cousin. I'd met him once at a summer barbecue when I was eight or nine. He'd let me sit on his bike and wear his helmet, and I cried when Mom told me he had died. "Did Henry get his power?"

Dad shook his head. "Not permanently. There's something about all the magics combining that binds them to the spell caster and amplifies each one. We think Henry was just experimenting with Paul. But after his murder, it was personal for Michael. I rode with him down to Nola. We didn't let anyone know we were going."

"The guys would have backed you up."

"We wanted to keep it quiet, and the whole club on the road would have let them know we were coming. No, we needed to sneak up on the bastard. And we did. We watched him snatch a Cabrera—one of your mother's relatives, actually—from a bar. The boy was one of the few remaining *merata* kindled. He was a friend of Killian's. Visiting from Brazil."

"Did Killian have anything to do with Henry's plans?"

"He was eighteen at the time, Jemmie. I don't think he had a clue."

I thought about that. Crowe had been nineteen when his father died, and he seemed the opposite of clueless. "You stopped Henry from hurting the Cabrera, right?"

Dad grimaced. "Normally, the kid should have been invincible—that's the essence of *merata* magic. But he would have had to summon it, and they slipped something in his drink, just to knock him out. Then Henry and his sergeant at arms took the kid to a warehouse out in Algiers. We followed him and snuck in. He already had four others with their magic bound, all chained up and waiting for the slaughter." Dad's expression had gone dark and dangerous. "We didn't plan to kill him. I didn't want to kill anyone."

"What happened?" I whispered. We were standing in the middle of the field in broad daylight, beneath the mid-summer sun, and I still felt a chill run up my back.

"I trapped them all inside the building with a barrier," he said. "Henry realized we were there—and he had his officers each run to one of the chosen victims. He ordered them to kill, just to keep them from being rescued."

"You had to stop them."

"Yeah," Dad said quietly. "I got a bubble around all but one. I wasn't fast enough to protect Carlos Cabrera. Kyle

Horst—the Deathstalker vice president who was the meanest *invictus* kindled I ever met, cut his throat. And the kid—he never regained consciousness, so he had no chance to protect himself. Michael couldn't stand for it. He snapped Kyle's spine with a mere thought, and then he just kept going. Before I could stop him, the officers were dead and only Henry was left. He tried to run." Dad bowed his head. "But Michael shouted for my help, and I couldn't let him down. I bound Henry's siphoning magic, rendering him powerless, and then I basically delivered him to Michael on a silver platter—I immobilized him with a vault hex. And Michael..." He sighed. "He turned Henry inside out, Jemmie. Literally. He pulled him apart and left ten pieces of him scattered across that warehouse floor, a message to anyone who would ever even think about trying the cruori spell."

"Pieces?" I said weakly.

"It got out of control, and I couldn't stop it." He ran a hand through his hair. "We should have called in the Syndicate, and instead we took the law into our own hands."

"But Henry was in the process of doing something terrible."

"That doesn't mean we had to become like him to take him down." He raised his head. "That's why I left, Jemmie. It had nothing to do with you, except that I was too ashamed to look at you afterward, too afraid of what I had turned into. I couldn't stand to think that I had that much blood on my hands. I had to atone."

"So you left us," I said in a dead voice.

He sighed. "I'm not saying I did the right thing. I just did what I had to do to be able to look at myself in the mirror again. It took a long time to feel like I wasn't staring at a killer. Truth is, I haven't felt worthy of being your father for years. Haven't felt worthy of being a husband or a real friend, either."

In that moment, standing with my father in the middle of that field, I finally realized how alone he had been. "Did you ever talk to Michael after that night?"

"He tried to talk to me. He kept saying he'd done what he had to do." Dad stared at Crowe's distant form. "But if you become a monster to kill a monster..." He shifted his attention to me. "Doesn't change the fact that you're a monster. And I get the feeling that Crowe is a lot like his father, Jemmie. He's got more power than he knows what to do with, and more rage than Michael ever did."

I swallowed the lump in my throat. "You're here for him, aren't you?"

"I'm here to make sure history doesn't repeat itself."

"And you think Crowe's going to kill more Deathstalkers?"

"I think he's just looking for an excuse. Part of me wouldn't be surprised if he's got Alex hiding somewhere."

"Just to pin the blame on the Stalkers?" I gaped at him in disgust. "Do you have any idea how worried Crowe is about her? He's sick with it. And you—" I turned and started walking after Crowe. "If you want to make up for whatever you did, and if you want to make sure Crowe doesn't take matters into his own hands, help him find his sister!"

"I asked for this assignment, Jemmie. I asked because if it hadn't been me, the Syndicate would have sent others, and they don't care about this club the way I do. They think the Devils are outlaws and would love to take the entire club down. But I know these people. I grew up with them. I watched some of them, like Hardy and Jackson and Brooke, take their first rides. I don't want innocents to get hurt, and I don't want anyone caught in the crossfire, including you."

"But you don't give a shit about Michael Medici's son!" I yelled, my voice cracking. "You're here, looking for any excuse to bind him and take him in, just to make yourself feel better for what *you* did!"

"In the last year, Crowe Medici has shown that he's more than willing to hurt other people to make a point."

"He was protecting his club."

"He's going to take it too far someday, Jemmie. He reminds me so much of Michael."

"So you've already tried him and found him guilty. Sounds fair." I headed off, needing to put distance between us.

"Wait, Mo, I need you to understand—"

"I think I understand perfectly well," I shouted back. "If a person can be judged on the basis of who their father is, then I need to get the hell away from *you.*"

I cut between the Warwick and Flynn family tents, past the kiddie tent, past the beer tent, all the way to the tent of the Rolling Sixes, where I found Crowe and Hardy and a few other Devils facing off with Ronan Niklos and what looked to be half his full-patch members. My throat was instantly coated with a funky mixture of *venemon* and *animalia* magic, and my vision clouded with amber-purple haze. A fierce growl drew my eyes to the enormous Doberman hulking at Ronan's side, teeth bared and eyes fixed on Crowe, as if he'd already been given a target.

"You know I didn't," Crowe was saying. "I had no reason to hurt her."

"You've got a history of breaking people who so much as look at you funny," Ronan said through gritted teeth. He towered over most of his fellow Sixes—he had to be six eight, and most of him was covered in tattoos of hellhounds dragging lost souls into the flames of damnation. His clenched fists were huge, and it looked like he was ready to use them.

Hardy glanced over his shoulder and spotted me, then poked Crowe and whispered something to him. Crowe turned, and his eyes locked with mine. "Jemmie. Tell Ronan what you saw when we were attacked."

Suddenly aware that I'd become the center of attention, I sucked in a deep breath, then coughed as the heavy scent of magic burned in my nose and mouth. "I—I saw Katrina. In the trees just past the Deathstalker tent. She hurled a curse that hit Crowe. It could have killed him."

Ronan's eyes narrowed. "I know who you are. My niece said you were out to get her. That you and that little Medici bitch cursed her in the middle of a mall."

I crossed my arms over my chest as the Doberman turned its head and snarled at me. Ronan was controlling it—I could see the purple loops of his power around the animal's body and head. "I stand by what I saw. I'm telling the truth."

Ronan snorted and spit on the ground. "That's what I think of your truth, little girl. You have as much reason to lie as Crowe does."

"Then ask Katrina," I said. "Maybe we can have Old Lady Jane question her. Doesn't she know when someone's lying to her?"

"He can't," said Crowe, very quietly.

"Why not?" my father asked, moving to stand next to me.

"'Cause Katrina's missing," Ronan barked. "No one's seen her since early this morning—but Fang here did sniff this out." He held up a torn scrap of fabric that looked a whole lot like the lacy top I'd seen Katrina in the night before. "Found it at the edge of the grounds. There's blood on it."

I stared at a red-brown stain on the dangling scrap. "Oh." My mind spun with questions, like whether she might have done this on purpose to frame Crowe. But with the Sixes, half of whom were her cousins or brothers or uncles, all glaring murder at us, I didn't think now was the time to question it. "Have you tried a locator spell?"

"You think we're idiots?" This came from a Six who looked to be in her twenties and was wreathed in *locant* magic. "There's no sign of her anywhere."

Ronan nodded. "So I'm actually glad you stopped by, Crowe. *Now* we've got a problem."

"Why? I'm not trying to start anything, Ronan. I just want to find my sister."

"And I want to find my niece!" roared Ronan.

"Maybe the same person took—"

Ronan shook his head. "Don't give me that bullshit,

Crowe Medici. I've been asking around all day. And you know what people told me?"

The skeins of purple *animalia* tightened, and the Doberman refocused on Crowe. Its hackles rose, and a low, deep growl rolled from its throat. Ronan leaned forward and dropped the scrap of Katrina's shirt at Crowe's feet. "You were the last person to be seen with her."

THIRTEEN

My stomach dropped as amber skeins of magic unfurled around Crowe—he was preparing to defend himself in the only way he knew, and it would make things worse.

"There are three people missing right now," I said loudly, shoving forward to stand next to Crowe, ready to do my best to throw out a barrier around us if it came to that. It might not work, but I had to do something. "Alex Medici, Katrina Niklos, and Darek Delacroix. The Devils, the Sixes, and the Deathstalkers are each looking for someone."

"Gunnar Reyes went missing two days ago," Crowe added. "Still hasn't been found. So we're missing two."

Ronan's eyes narrowed. "Your point being?"

"What if they're all being taken by the same person?" I asked. I wasn't sure I believed that—it was still possible Darek and Alex were holed up somewhere together. I *knew* I had seen Katrina hurl a curse at us less than an hour earlier, and Gunnar was known for disappearing for days on end. Except...the other person I had seen in the woods seemed to have some kind of screwed-up *arma* power—I had seen the swirls of pale yellow mixed with black and red as he ran between the trees. Could that have been Gunnar? If it was, why would he hurl a hex knife at me? I shook off the thought. Right now, I just wanted to make sure we didn't start another brawl. "What if we get all the clubs together and try to figure out what the hell is happening?"

Crowe said nothing, but the amber ribbons of his magic slithered back into his fingertips, and I stood up a little straighter.

"It's a reasonable suggestion, Ronan," my dad said, trying to keep the peace, like any of this shit mattered to him. "If you want to find Katrina, convening the officers of each club seems like the best plan."

Ronan was still glaring daggers at Crowe, but his magic was pulling away from the dog at his side, and the animal whined and sat, leaning its head on the enormous man's thigh. "All right, *Agent* Carmichael. But if I get even a hint that Crowe's behind this, I won't hold back."

"Same," Crowe said in a hard voice. "Ronan, I propose you and I go talk to the Stalkers and the Kings. If everyone agrees, we can meet in the gathering tent after dinner—around eight. It's neutral ground." Without waiting for an answer, he turned to me. "Will you go get Jane for me? I want to talk to her before we all meet. She's camped out—didn't want to make the trip back and forth from her cabin—so she should be in the south field."

Circles had formed under his eyes, and I was once again reminded that he hadn't slept in nearly a day and a half. "Yeah," I said. "On one condition."

His eyebrows rose.

"You get a few hours of sleep before tonight," I whispered. I held up my hand when he opened his mouth to argue. "You have to be sharp to pull this all together, Crowe, and you're human. You nearly died less than an hour ago. You have to rest."

For a moment, he simply looked down at me, and every nerve in my body thrummed with awareness of him. "Okay. Once I get this set up and check in with Jane, I will." He touched my arm as I turned. "And, Jemmie? Thank you," he murmured. "I mean it." He trudged away and joined a knot of Devils who had gathered between the tents.

Without looking at my father, I turned and marched toward the camper grounds. People who didn't have large family groups, or who simply preferred a little more solitude, were allowed to pitch tents or park their RVs in a wide-open area at the south end of the festival fields. Jane Vetrov sat on a ratty lawn chair outside a rusty old Airstream. Her knobby knees stuck out through tears in her jeans. A Harley T-shirt hung loose on her body and a half-empty bottle of Jack dangled from her fingers. Despite that, her gaze was sharp as she caught sight of me marching toward her. I braced myself as the silver threads of her *omnias* magic stretched toward me like a giant spiderweb.

"Trouble?" she asked when I got close enough.

"Yeah. Four people are missing and everybody wants to blame someone else."

Jane looked unsurprised. "And they want me to come tell them what the hell is happening."

I nodded. "Will you? They're meeting in the gathering tent around eight, but Crowe said he needed to talk to you before that. We still can't find Alex or Gunnar. The Sixes want to blame Crowe for Katrina Niklos's disappearance, and the Stalkers seem to think he might have kidnapped one of their prospects. It's kind of a mess."

Jane grunted and slowly stood up. "That boy's a magnet for trouble," she muttered.

"He didn't do it."

Her pale eyes met mine. "You sound awfully sure, Jemmie Carmichael."

Her magic smelled like steel and machine oil as it caressed the sides of my face. I shuddered and pulled back, and Jane tilted her head, peering at me with sharp curiosity. "You were always a funny child."

"Um. Thanks?"

"Sometimes your parents and the others would come out to my property to drink and cast and talk about the future. They'd bring you along, and while the other kids were playing tag and hide-and-seek in the woods out back, I'd always see you squatting behind a chair or near the wood pile, watching."

"I guess I was interested in what the adults were doing."

She chuckled. "That's what your parents said. Nosy little Jemmie. But that wasn't what it looked like to me. You weren't watching them. You were watching the air around them."

I swallowed and rubbed at my arms. "If you say so."

"You used to enjoy being around all of it, but after you hit six, maybe seven, your mom told me you started asking to stay home with a babysitter. She said you'd have a screaming fit if they tried to bring you."

It had all gotten to be too much. The older I got, the

more the magic overwhelmed me. "Well, I'm here now. Wondering why you're telling me this. Can we go?"

Jane didn't budge. "You're here now, all right. Only half-in, though. Your energy is split right down the middle."

I suddenly thought of Darek, out there somewhere, maybe with Alex, maybe in trouble, and then I thought of Crowe, trying to find his missing people and make sure this festival didn't end in a gang war. "Can you see my future?"

She moved a step closer to me, and I inhaled her metallic essence. "Yours in particular? Not unless I touch you, and I don't think you want me to do that."

"It might be nice to have some answers," I said quietly. "And if you know what's happening, what's going to happen, shouldn't you tell us? People's lives are on the line."

"People's lives are always on the line, little girl." She clucked her tongue. "And they always come to me, wanting answers, and then they can't handle what I see. Sometimes *I* can't handle what I see. Sometimes this gift feels more like a curse." After a long pull from her bottle of Jack, she capped it and tossed it into the long grass by her chair. For a moment, I thought about asking her for a swig, then realized...I didn't really need it.

Jane started to walk slowly toward the festival grounds. "Lots of Vetrovs go crazy, you know. You dip your toes in the Undercurrent even once and you can hear it whispering, and we can't help but go back again and again."

From the haunted look on her face, it seemed like she might be listening to its call right now. "Is that why some *omnias* kindled can supposedly raise the dead?" I asked. "You know how to pull them from the Undercurrent?"

She clucked her tongue. "Takes more strength and power than I have to do something like that, but yes. Comes with consequences, though. *Omnias* always does. Soon as we come into the power, no matter how old we are when it happens, we know the day we're going to die without even trying. You can't get close to people, because if you touch them, you know how it all ends. Imagine how that would feel. It's why so many of us prefer to be alone."

Suddenly, my situation didn't seem quite so bad. "Does it ever feel good?"

"Why does it need to?" she asked, an edge in her voice. "Life isn't about feeling good. Magic isn't about feeling good. You have it, you respect it. You use it the best way you can. Or...you don't. You whine about it, you abuse it, you avoid it, whatever. But it's always your choice."

I was glad we were walking, because I didn't want to be facing her, letting her look at me and watch me squirm. I didn't know if she was talking about herself or me, but I knew which one I wanted it to be. "But you met with Crowe and warned him that something would happen at this festival. You help people sometimes."

"Is that what I do?"

I bit my lip, remembering what I'd read in that old journal. "Michael Medici asked for your help, didn't he?"

"Did Crowe tell you that?" She grunted. "And how do you think Michael felt when I told him he'd celebrated his final birthday? How do you think he felt when I told him the exact day he'd leave this life?"

"Did you see how it would happen?"

"I've already explained this to Crowe. I don't get to see exactly how someone dies, just a certainty about when it will happen. Seeing the future isn't like watching a movie on a screen, girl. It isn't like some tapestry hanging in a museum. It's more like shreds and scraps scattered across the ground. It takes experience and practice to interpret it correctly, and even then it's fragmented. But I always recognize certain pieces—they tend to stand out."

"Was Michael scared when you told him he was going to die?"

"Ha! No. He was pissed as hell. And he was determined to prove me wrong." Her pale eyes stared into the distance, at the Medici flag flying over the family tent. "That's one thing I'm never wrong about, though."

I shifted my weight, edging a little farther from her so a careless step wouldn't bring our skin into contact. "You can predict the future without touching someone, though."

"Touch or not, it's still threads that have to come together to weave a complete future. Now that you're next to me, I can tell you're one of those threads, Jemmie. Dangling in the wind. Not sure which way you'll blow, what you'll tangle around." She arched an eyebrow. "Who you'll mesh with."

A warm breeze blew across the field, bringing hints of smoke and honey, along with a confusing mixture of a dozen other things, all magic. "I'm really a part of all this?"

She stopped. "You've always been a part of it, Jemmie Carmichael. You can run as far as you want, but that won't change."

My heart skipped. I'd never actually spent time talking to Jane, and it was for this reason exactly. Mom had told me she always knew just a hair too much. "I'm not going anywhere."

"If you're here, better make sure you're all here."

I sighed. "Okay?"

She leaned in, and I took a step back. "I saw you at the Schoolhouse that night. I saw you practically peeing your pants in fright over a simple binding. I saw you acting like you were terrified of your own magic. If you want to save the Devils and the people you love, I'm thinking you'd better get over that."

I scowled at her. "I'm working on it."

"Uh-huh." She resumed her hike toward the gathering tent and said, over a shoulder, "Maybe you should work a little harder."

I stayed where I was. Crowe had said all the clubs would meet after dinner. And Crowe hadn't actually invited me to come—he'd sent me to fetch Jane while he rounded up the officers of the Stalkers and the Kings. I wasn't officially a Devil. And I'd avoided being formally affiliated with them, because that meant they could ask me to contribute my magic for the good of the club, and I'd always been too scared.

But today, I'd done a halfway decent locator spell. I'd been ready to protect Crowe with a barrier spell. And I hadn't had one drink, or even craved one, to help tamp down the sensations that came with being around this much magic. Crowe had told me to push through it, and I had— because Alex needed me.

Jane was right. I had been only half here. And if I wanted to find my missing friends, I needed to do better than that.

I ran into Brooke on the path to the parking lot, carrying a couple of kegs as if they weighed nothing. "Hey—did the Curse Kings and the Deathstalkers agree to talk?"

"As far as I know," she said. "Crowe's got his hands full, though. Everyone's pointing fingers."

Most of them at Crowe. Protectiveness surged inside me. I needed to practice a few spells and make a few cuts if I wanted to watch his back. That meant I needed my casting kit, which had been buried at the bottom of my closet for seven years. Practice would also help me to get away from the overwhelming magic of the festival grounds. I might be able to tolerate it for now, but I had only been here for an hour or two, and my concentration was fraying at the edges. I hadn't been craving a drink, but the more I thought about it, the more it sounded kind of appealing. I wanted to be here—but I needed to pull myself together.

"Who's watching out for Crowe right now?" I asked.

"He said he was headed to the Medici tent to catch a little shut-eye, with Hardy to watch his back." She gave me a sly smile. "You worried about our pres, Jemmie?"

I twirled my keys around my finger, trying to look casual. "I just know he's worried about his sister and Gunnar. He's trying to take care of everyone. He hadn't slept in a day and a half."

"Uh-huh."

We stood in awkward silence for a few seconds before I pointed stupidly at my car. "Um. I'm just heading home. Thanks for the update." I started to step around her.

"Hey, Jemmie?" Brooke bit the inside of her cheek, looking conflicted. "We're all hoping Katrina's okay and all that, but I don't think she ever meant all that much to Crowe."

I suppressed a smile. "Why are you telling me this?"

Brooke's cheeks flushed. "No particular reason. See you later?"

"Yeah." I fought the urge to grab her by the shoulders and ask her more, but she'd probably end up hitting me in the head with both kegs. "I'll be there after everyone meets."

She nodded and continued her march back to the festival fields.

I drove home, and as I approached the house I realized more fully that Dad and Crowe had been right about the perimeter protection—it had gone soft. I hoped maybe I could replace it myself instead of asking Dad to do it, but for now I needed to save my energy for more urgent things. I called out for my mom as I walked through the living room, but then realized she probably hadn't gotten back from working the lunch shift at Denny's. Thinking about personal barrier spells and vault hexes, I entered my room and turned toward my closet.

Hands snaked around my waist and pulled me back. With a shriek, I jabbed at my attacker with my elbow and stomped down, hoping to crush a few toes.

"Ow!" he said, and let me go.

I whirled around, and my mouth dropped open. The minty scent of my own magic filled my nose, probably caused by my surprise. "Darek?"

"Yeah," he said weakly, rubbing at his abs. "Sorry for startling you."

"Where the hell have you been?"

He gingerly pulled off his aviator sunglasses, revealing two black eyes and a gash across his left eyebrow that had been closed with three stitches. "Hospital."

"What happened?"

He winced at the shrill sound of my voice and then gestured to the bed. "Do you mind?"

I watched as he collapsed on the bed and then sat on the edge of it. It looked like every part of him hurt. "I've been worried about you. Why didn't you answer my texts? And do you know where Alex is? A few people saw her leave the festival with you last night, and she hasn't been seen since."

His brow furrowed. "Really?" He frowned. "That's messed up."

"No kidding. But *did* you see her?"

"Yeah. I walked her to her car. But then she drove off,

and that was the last time I saw her." With a grimace, he turned onto his back and laid his arm over his eyes to block out the sunlight streaming through my window.

I probably should have been relieved that my best friend hadn't shacked up with my...honestly I didn't know what Darek was. I only knew that if she hadn't been with him, she was still missing. "Hey—how did you end up in the hospital?"

"Oh, thanks for your concern," he said drily. Then he let out a pained chuckle. "You haven't talked to Crowe?"

"Huh?"

"I figured he would have told everyone. But I guess maybe he wanted to keep it between us."

"Darek, just tell me what happened."

He lifted his arm off his face. "Crowe saw my connection with you. I thought he kind of looked at us funny when I came into the beer tent last night."

I thought back. "I guess he might have."

"Oh, trust me. After I walked Alex to her car, I was taking a shortcut from the parking lot to the Stalkers tent when he stepped out from behind a tree. Blocked the path. Dude is big."

"Crowe was hiding in the woods, waiting for *you*?"

"Who knows if he was waiting for me? Maybe he was spying or looking out for someone else. Whatever. He took the opportunity when it wandered up the path like a clueless idiot." There was a bitter twist to his voice. "He told me I didn't belong there. At first I thought he meant on that part of the land, and I apologized. Then he made it clear what he really meant." Darek's blue eyes were stark. "He told me to stay away from you."

My stomach dropped. "Oh."

"I told him to fuck off." Darek let out a weary sigh. "He didn't take it well."

"He beat you up?"

"He told me he could kick my ass with a simple blink of his eyes, but he preferred to do it the old-fashioned way." Darek rubbed at his jaw, which was bruised and swollen. "He did a damn good job, if you ask me."

"That doesn't sound like Crowe. I know he has a temper, but—"

"I'm a Deathstalker, Jemmie," Darek snapped. "And I was a little too obviously interested in you, I guess."

Everything inside me wanted to argue. Surely Crowe wouldn't have... but the tiniest whisper of doubt crept in. Suddenly I remembered what Crowe had said about him this morning, how Darek just pissed him off, how he should have killed him when he had the chance. Was this what he meant? Had he actually used *me* as an excuse to beat on Darek? "Does Killian know?"

Darek pulled several small objects from his pocket and

dropped them on my bedspread. I peered at the shattered remains of Darek's phone. "Honestly, I'm not sure what happened after the fifth or sixth time he hit me. I woke up in a ditch at the side of Highway Ten just over the city limit. When I crawled out, a passing driver stopped and called an ambulance. I've been in the ER getting stitched up. I hitched a ride here when they let me out. I thought you..." He looked away. "I hoped you would be worried." He held his hand out, palm up.

I slipped my hand into his, and he squeezed my fingers. "I don't know what to say, except that I'm sorry if I played a part in this."

"Did you tell the president of the Devils to go after me?"

"I think you know the answer to that."

"Then this isn't your fault at all. Just...I don't want to cause trouble, Jemmie. Killian made it clear to all of us before we rode up here that he wanted us to behave. He's worked for years to resurrect this club after what happened to Henry and the others, and I'd say he's just about done it. So the last thing I want to do is start some kind of war."

"Letting Killian know you're safe is probably the best thing you can do, then."

He let go of my hand. "I guess I will. It's just..."

"What?"

"It's so fucking humiliating, Jem. I try to have a good

attitude. I've tried for years. But sometimes it feels like more than I can bear."

"Having so little magic, you mean?"

"I wanted to fight back. I *want* to fight back. I'm not weak."

"I know you're not, Darek." My heart ached for him, for the tortured look on his face. "I know it's hard."

"You can't know how it feels," he whispered. "And I've had to do this alone. I've always been alone. At least your dad is still *alive*."

"I'm sorry. I know you miss your parents a lot."

"You know, it's funny. My dad died on the same stretch of road that took out Michael Medici. Quite the coincidence."

"I didn't know."

He shrugged. "Didn't seem worth mentioning. Killian knew my dad really well—they were raised together. So he got a nice couple to take me in. Used to come visit me from time to time." He chuckled. "I guess he wanted to keep an eye on me. Make sure I was brought up right." His sad smile faded. "But like I've told you, they were drecks, Jem. They didn't understand me. Sometimes I wondered if he did that on purpose."

"Because he knew you didn't have a dominant power?"

"You said it, not me," he grumbled. "It took a lot of

convincing to get him to let me prospect. I finally talked him into it, though. I'm gonna prove myself to him."

"You will. And I'm not saying I know how you feel, but I do know what it's like to feel alone, and to be different from others around you. I know it sucks."

He sat up, not meeting my gaze. "Since I can't text Killian, I guess I'd better get back to the grounds."

"Are you going to confront Crowe?" I knew Crowe was tough, and I knew he hated the Deathstalkers and suspected they had a hand in Michael's death, but Darek was no threat to him. His only crime had been looking at me.

I wouldn't have thought Crowe cared about that. He thought I was a distraction and nothing more.

"The last thing I want is to play a part in starting another war between the Stalkers and the Devils," Darek said. "It's the opposite of what my club needs, and I pledged to protect my club. A man's got to be able to take a beating, and that's one thing I can do." He smiled, then winced as it pulled at a cut on his cheek. "Pretty well, at least."

Anger ran hot through my veins. "This is wrong, Darek. Crowe needs to face what he did."

"I'm not the one to make him. I'll tell them I drank too much and walked into a tree or something." He got to his feet with a groan, then tugged my hand and pulled me up next to him. "I'm sorry Alex is missing. She's a tough, smart girl, and I'm sure she's fine. She was awfully pissed at her brother, though. Maybe she decided to remind him of the importance of family or something."

"Yeah," I murmured. "Maybe." But it was now late afternoon, and my friend was nowhere to be found. Untraceable even with *locant* magic. "I won't feel good until we find her, though."

"You're an amazing friend, Jemmie." He ran his fingertip along my cheek. "I'm glad you're one of mine."

I looked up at him. "And I'm glad you're okay." I took in the cuts and bruises on his face. "Mostly okay, at least."

His hand slid around my waist. "Right now I'm feeling pretty damn good." He lowered his head and pressed his lips to mine, and I blinked in surprise. It felt...it felt like a kiss. Soft and gentle, warm and minty from his breath, along with a hint of stale cigarette. If I had planned to kiss him regularly, I would have told him to quit that nasty habit, but...

He lifted his head and gave me a smile. "I've been wanting to do that for about a year now."

I smiled back, though my insides were squirming. "And?"

"Amazing," he whispered. He cupped the back of my head and crushed his lips to mine. My thoughts flew in a thousand directions as I felt his tongue skim my bottom lip.

Did I want this? Darek was so sweet, and so nice, and so hot, but for some reason, being this close to him didn't light up my insides like being next to Crowe did. Which sucked, because if Darek was telling the truth, Crowe wasn't the man I'd begun to believe him to be. He was more like the man everyone else thought he was, and that was a man I didn't like all that much.

"Choose me, Jemmie," Darek murmured against my mouth. "I want you so much." His tongue slid between my lips, and his arms tightened around me, and all of a sudden my head was swimming with dizziness, light exploding behind my closed eyelids, my heart pattering unsteadily as my tongue captured a hint of bitterness from his last smoke. Darek sensed me swaying and lowered his face to my neck. "You feel it, don't you?"

With the room spinning, I clutched at his shoulders to keep myself upright. "I...have to think about this. I don't want to move too fast."

I braced for him to resist, but his hands dropped away from me, and he kissed my forehead. As I opened my eyes, I could see my own *locant* magic winding around us, like I'd lost control of it in the heat of the moment. I took a step away from Darek and turned to lean against the wall. "There's just a lot going on right now, okay?"

"Okay," he said quietly. "I don't want to push you. But I

need you to know where I stand. I'm in love with you, Jemmie." His voice broke over the words. "I'm tired of being alone."

I squeezed my eyes shut. "We'll talk later, all right? I'm so glad you're okay."

He touched my shoulder as I inhaled the minty scent. "Later. Be careful tonight."

"You too."

I listened to the sound of his footsteps through the house, the click of the front door closing. I could offer to drive him back to the festival, but I needed space. I needed time. I needed to figure myself out. I dragged myself over to the bed and collapsed on it, feeling like all my plans and energy and strength had just swirled down the drain, along with my understanding of Crowe.

Alex was still missing, and that had to be the priority. Old Lady Jane was still predicting something would happen at the festival, and she'd told me I was part of it. She'd said I was a thread dangling in the wind, and she didn't know where I'd end up, who I'd end up with.

I closed my eyes and tried to summon the will to face it all, but right then, all I really wanted was a nap.

FOURTEEN

I JERKED AWAKE WITH A START TO THE SOUND OF MY MOM coming in the front door, keys jangling. Blinking in the darkness, I pulled my clock over and peered at it. "Shit," I whispered. It was after eight. I'd slept for four hours.

"Jemmie?"

"Yeah," I croaked. My mom was in the doorway and flicking on the lights as I swung my legs off the bed.

"You all right?"

"I'm fine. Just needed a nap."

She pulled the tie from her dark hair and it cascaded messily over her shoulders. "I smell like french fry grease.

I'm gonna take a shower and put some dinner on. You want to stay in and watch a movie with me?"

"I was actually going to head back to the festival. We still haven't found Alex."

Mom's brows drew together. "Did anyone try a locator spell?"

"We've tried a lot of things." I didn't want to get into it right now—all I could do was hope that she'd magically be there when I got back to the festival. "I'll keep you posted."

She nodded. "Did you catch up with Darek today?"

"Um." I played with the frayed edge of my bedspread. "Very briefly."

"What about Crowe?"

I sighed. "No comment. But I don't think either thing is going anywhere. They're both wrong for me."

"Doesn't always mean it won't go anywhere," she said, and it was to her credit that she only sounded mildly bitter.

"Mom, did you know why Dad left?"

"I knew he'd done some things he regretted and had a falling-out with Michael. But our relationship was coming apart before that. So it was really the combination of the two. I know it was hard for you."

I shrugged one shoulder. "I wish one of you had explained it to me. I thought he left because he was disappointed in me.

I know that sounds totally childish, but it made sense at the time. In some ways it still does. The thing about me he's most interested in is magic, and whether I'm doing it."

"He loves you, Jem. Might not always be good at showing it, but he does. Magic is the thing he thought he had in common with you. When it looked like you might be a little more like me..." She raised her arms from her sides to show off how absolutely unmagical she was, but I knew she had a bit of it in there. In fact, there was the faintest of pearlescent glows around her in this light.

"I'm not like either of you." I had magic. And I had this other thing, the sensitivity to it. Somehow, I had to figure out how to manage both in order to do what Jane said, to play my part. "But I'm trying to figure out where I belong."

"You will. And...I'm sorry about Darek. Less sorry about Crowe."

I rolled my eyes miserably. "Yeah, me too."

She left me then, and a moment later I heard the shower start to run. Stretching, I stood up, ran a brush through my tangled hair, and paused in front of the closet, thinking of all my plans for my casting kit, the spells I wanted to practice.

Then I remembered that the man I'd wanted to protect had beaten up a guy just for looking at me funny. "Seems like he can protect himself," I muttered, then grabbed my keys and headed out. I wanted to know if Alex or Katrina had shown up. If they had, the festival was the place they'd be.

I paused at the front door, remembering the bottle of Jack behind my bed. Should I try to dull myself down to get through the night? My fingers tightened on the doorjamb.

"No," I whispered. This was something I needed to face. Crowe had been right about that—I had to be brave enough to push through it, and I wanted to be sharp in case I needed my actual magic. Decision made, I walked out of the house and left the bottle behind.

The lot was packed when I arrived back at the festival, and people were streaming onto the grounds for the second night. As I got out of the car, magic hung above the tents like a pollution haze, and the scents danced in the air, flickering through my awareness. I took a deep breath and forced myself to focus, mentally tallying what I detected, pulling each color and smell apart.

Venemon. Animalia. Animus. Invictus. Inlusio. Locant. Arma. Terra. Omnias. I had run into each one and could now distinguish them if I was paying close enough attention. None of them smelled like the terrible smoldering stench I had detected just before Crowe and I were hit with lethal hexes. I wished I knew what it was—but I was also glad I couldn't pick it up nearby.

"I can do this," I whispered, shuddering. Without the benefit of alcohol, it all felt sharper and brighter, but, I admit, I also felt slightly more in control of it. I headed up the path slowly, behind crowds of people. Some were gossiping about Katrina and Alex disappearing, and some were whispering about the tension between the clubs. I quickened my steps, heading for the Medici tent. I didn't really want to talk to Crowe, but I thought maybe Lori would be able to give me an update.

I pushed through the hanging flaps over the entrance to the tent and ran face-first into Crowe's chest. He caught my arms and looked down at me, smiling. "Where have you been?"

I pulled myself out of his grasp. "Home. I was tired."

He frowned. "Are you okay?"

"Fine. Did the meeting go well? Any leads?"

"No leads. Killian didn't even bother to show up, and his people claim they don't know where he is—they're grumbling that maybe he's missing, too, but I'm not buying it." His expression had gone dark and dangerous. "Especially since it turns out his prospect wasn't missing after all."

"Oh, really?"

He went on, seemingly too wrapped up in what had happened to detect the suspicion in my voice. "I haven't been able to reach Flynn for the past few hours, either. I've got Jackson and Brooke out hunting for him. I met with the leaders of the other clubs. Ronan, Terrence, and Ren volunteered members to guard the perimeter, and I did as well. Everyone works in teams. No one goes it alone. Assuming we manage not to kill each other, it seems like the best way."

"True," I said. "Walking through the woods by oneself seems like a great way to get beat up."

Crowe arched an eyebrow. "Yeah," he said, drawing out the word. "I guess so."

I looked at him steadily. "Did Darek say what happened to him?"

Crowe tilted his head to the side and looked at me through narrowed eyes. "He said he got drunk and ended up in a ditch, basically."

"And everyone believed that?"

"I wanted to question him about my sister, but he insists she drove off alone. Not sure I believe him, but I can't push it right now, not with Katrina missing and Ronan stomping around about it. I've got Hardy keeping an eye on him, though. If he has done something to them—"

"He was the one who was hurt, Crowe."

"That's what he wants everyone to believe, sure."

"Ugh." I turned and stalked away, but Crowe grabbed my arm and wheeled me around.

"What's wrong with you tonight?" he asked. "I was worried about you this evening. Jane said she spoke to you. I wondered if maybe she said something, or—"

"What's wrong with me? I thought I knew you, and then I come to find out that you're the type of person who beats up innocent people!"

"What the fuck are you talking about?"

"Darek," I shouted. "You jumped him in the woods!"

"Who told you that?" Crowe's face went from confused to grim in a fraction of a second. "Oh, I get it. I saw the look he gave you in the tent last night and wondered about you guys. I mean, I knew you two hooked up last year, but—"

"Hooked up? He was my friend!" I yelled. "And believe me, I really needed one."

Crowe held his hands up, but no magic was coming from them now. "You think I beat up your *friend*? That's the kind of guy you think I am?"

"You don't exactly have a history of hashing things out nonviolently."

Crowe ran his tongue along his bottom lip, and my stomach tightened. "At least I know what you think of me now. Did your dad help convince you? He came to town just looking for an excuse to bind me. Meanwhile no one's taking a close look at Killian Delacroix, who can plant thoughts in people's heads and make them do stuff they aren't even aware of. Everyone's forgotten who his brother was and what he did. That guy needs to be taken off the street, Jemmie. He's dangerous."

I stared at him. "So are you, Crowe."

"Yes, I am. I won't apologize for that. I took responsibility for this club and everything that came with it. I'll defend it to the death if I have to." His jaw clenched, and he looked around. Then he pulled me off the path, heading for a more isolated spot at the bottom of a low hill. "I think Killian is trying to finish what his brother started. I think that's why he's here. He's good at messing with people's minds, so no one would suspect. He could have even used Katrina to attack us this morning—that's exactly the kind of thing he could do."

I thought back to this morning. I hadn't sensed much *animus* magic, crimson and coppery, during that brawl, though there had been red streaks mixed with black around the two people who had cursed us. "Killian seems to want peace more than almost anyone else," I said, thinking back to what he'd said in the beer tent, maybe trying to convince myself.

"All he wants is to gather one kindled for each type of magic," Crowe explained, his eyes bright with fierce hope.

"Think about it—Alex, *venemon*. Gunnar, *arma*. Katrina, *animalia*. If he's got Flynn now, that's *inlusio*. Darek doesn't have a dominant power, right? So he didn't fit my theory, but the others do. And it turns out Darek was never missing to begin with."

"Crowe—"

Crowe's mouth snapped shut around whatever he'd been planning to say next. "You don't believe me."

"I don't know," I said quietly. "He'd have to kidnap a lot of people, and this isn't exactly familiar ground for him. Why would he risk it here? If he wanted to do something like the cruori spell, why not try last year, on his home turf?"

"*Because* it was his home turf," he said in a flat voice.

"I hope you can get more evidence before you take this theory public—because tensions are high already."

"I'm not stupid, Jem," he said. "But Jane said something big was going to happen, and someone doing the cruori would certainly count as big."

And she'd said I was a part of it. I just wish I knew how. "Did she say anything else this afternoon?"

"She sure did." Crowe's nostrils flared as he let out an exasperated breath. "She said that by this time tomorrow, someone would be dead. She wouldn't say more than that."

"Great. Really helpful." I rubbed the sudden goose bumps that had rippled across my arms.

"In the way only Jane can manage." Crowe pulled out his cell phone and typed out a text. "I have to go take a shift with Ren and a few others. Boone will keep an eye on you. Make sure you're safe."

"I don't need—"

"Yes," Crowe said, his voice rising. "You do."

"I'm not going to fight with you." Looking at his face was painful. Was he lying about hurting Darek, or was Darek the liar? Or…could Killian have made Darek believe that he'd been beaten up by Crowe? Could he have manipulated Crowe into beating up Darek or hurting Katrina? I rubbed my hands over my face, wishing I could figure all this out.

Wishing I had Alex with me, to talk it through like we always did.

"Ho! Just got done hanging out with three big hairy men," Boone called as he crested the rise and headed down to us. "Time to hang out with a pretty girl."

I waved at Boone before returning my attention to Crowe. "Is my dad helping with the perimeter guard?"

Crowe nodded. "He's with my group. You know, to make sure I don't beat up powerless kids in the woods."

I hung my head back. "Look—"

"I won't defend myself to you, Jemmie. I shouldn't have to." He leaned in, and I inhaled his smoke-and-honey scent. Having his face this close to mine made it feel like the ground had just dropped out from beneath my feet. "You know me better than that," he murmured. Then he turned and walked away.

Boone clapped Crowe on the shoulder as they passed each other, then came to stand next to me. "Boy's got the weight of the world on his shoulders," he said quietly. "Not many are strong enough to carry it."

I watched Crowe disappear over the rise, just aching. His father had literally torn someone apart to avenge the death of a family member. Crowe had told Hardy he had to be ready to do anything to protect the people he was responsible for. Between Jane's prediction that death would find someone here at the festival and my own swirling sense that things were about to explode, I could barely contain my dread.

"Let's take a walk," said Boone. "You look like you're about to jump out of your skin."

I agreed gratefully, and we set out along the edge of the woods. Maybe a circuit of the entire huge field would clear my head enough to allow me to socialize in the beer tent without bowing to the temptation to drink myself into a place where my fear for Alex and Crowe and Darek and everyone else couldn't find me. "Boone, how much do you know about Michael's death?" I asked.

"The crash was pretty bad. Looked like he swerved to avoid something in the road, and that was it." He shook his head sadly. "Happened pretty quick. I never thought it would be so bad, if I went down that way."

"And he was alone when it happened?"

Boone nodded. "He'd told me and Crowe he had something he needed to check out. Wouldn't let either of us go with him."

He'd known he was going to die, though. "Why wouldn't he take you with him?"

"Said he had to deal with it on his own. We didn't know he was going out for the last time. I felt like shit—it took us two days to find him. Not much out there."

I thought about that. "Why does Crowe think he was murdered?"

He sighed. "The coroner's report said Michael's heart muscle was lacerated in an unusual way. She said it could have been trauma from the accident, but Crowe didn't buy it. He believes it could have been a curse."

"So either another kindled attacked him with *venemon* or someone used a cut against him?"

"No cut is that strong. Few kindled could do that kind of curse anyway." He blew out a long breath and tugged at his beard. "In fact, Crowe's the only one who might have been strong enough to do it."

"Or Michael himself," I said, thinking of my father's description of what they'd done to Henry Delacroix. "Crowe thinks someone turned Michael's magic around, made him attack himself."

Boone nodded. "But the only one who could have done that was Henry Delacroix, and he's resting in pieces, if you get my meaning."

I did. "So Michael went to 'check something out,' and he never came back. He was on Deathstalker turf." He'd written in his journal that he'd discovered something about Henry, about his secrets. My thoughts turned like slippery gears, unable to catch.

"Oh, thank God," said a gruff voice.

Boone and I turned toward the sound of thumping footsteps to see Flynn jogging through the woods, his face pale, his body emanating wisps of his *inlusio* magic. It was all around him, like he couldn't contain it.

"Hey, you jackass!" Boone pulled a flashlight from his pocket and ran the beam over Flynn's sweaty face. "Crowe's been looking for you. Where'd you get off to?"

"I found them," Flynn said, breathing hard. "Come on!" His eyes were wide as he beckoned for us to follow him. He snatched the flashlight from Boone's hand and ran back into the woods.

"You found Alex?" I asked, my voice shrill as I followed him. "Is she okay?"

"You have to see," said Flynn as Boone and I trailed

close behind him, trying to keep up as we zigged and zagged through the trees, heading deeper into the woods. "You just have to—"

Flynn pivoted on his heel and slammed the flashlight into the side of Boone's head. The older man went down like a bag of cement, groaning. Still radiating skeins of *inlusio*, Flynn brought the flashlight down on Boone's head again as I screamed, but before I could run he lunged for me. I landed on my back with him on top of me, crushing the air from my lungs with the impact. His hand clamped over my mouth.

"Quiet," he said, his voice unsteady and strange. "I'm trying to save your life. I'll explain everything, I promise. Will you give me a chance to do that?"

I nodded, if only so he would give me a chance to breathe and think. Boone lay bleeding in the dark just feet away from where Flynn was rising to his feet and helping me to mine. "Why?" I asked, my voice breaking.

"Come on," Flynn said. His voice wasn't even his own now—it was echoing and cracking like a bad radio. The scent of *inlusio* magic—cigar smoke and autumn leaves—was so dense that it was all I could do not to cough, but it was mixed with something else…a faint whiff of copper, and of bitter ash. Before I had a chance to think about it, he grabbed my hand and dragged me farther into the woods. I stared around me at the darkness, trying desperately to identify distinctive trees or hollows that would allow me to find my way back to Boone, who was breathing loudly and wetly as he lay unconscious on the forest floor. But it was hard to see anything past the tiny circle of light provided by the flashlight, especially with the thick funk of Flynn's magic swirling in the air around us—mixed with threads of red and black.

"Um...I think I should go back," I said, panting, my heart punching hard against my ribs.

His footsteps stuttered as he ground to a halt and slowly turned, shining the flashlight upward so I could see his face.

Except it wasn't his face. Killian stared down at me, sweaty and wild-eyed like Flynn had been, *inlusio* magic dissipating like a cloud under the heat of the sun. "Don't scream," he said quietly as those threads of crimson became thick ribbons emanating from his body, still shot through with darkness.

I pulled against his hand, trying to put space between us as the scent of copper and ash rolled over me, overwhelming everything else. "Please let me go."

His right eye twitched. "I will." Then his mouth pulled into a half snarl. "I won't."

"Did you do something to Flynn?" I asked in a strained voice as ribbons of his magic coiled around me, licking at my skin. As they did, a sense of peace came over me. He didn't want to hurt me. He wasn't going to hurt me.

"I had to warn you. You're important and you have to

be safe. He's not safe, and you have to stay away—" He grimaced and bowed his head.

"Where have you been?" I asked.

He let out a low, broken chuckle. "I never expected he would do anything like this."

"Did you take Alex?" I whispered. "Do you have Flynn and Gunnar, too?" Somehow, he'd had Flynn's magic all around him just now. A complete illusion. My throat constricted. "Can you steal other people's magic?"

Just like his brother had.

"You have to be careful. You can't trust him."

"Crowe?"

Killian raised his head, and his face was pulled into a terrible grimace. "He has to be stopped!" His *animus* magic wound more tightly around me, and the blood-and-ash scent of it made me feel like I was drowning. I leaned against him as it sapped every thought from my mind, and watched helplessly as it slid around him as well, across his sharp cheekbones and into his ears, his nostrils. As it did, the pungent ashy scent grew stronger, like the smell of a hundred stale cigarettes, and the light of the flashlight dimmed as magic as dark as the night wafted between us.

"Crowe has to be stopped," Killian said firmly. "He'll destroy everything." He clamped his eyes shut and shook his head, then groaned.

Images of Crowe, *venemon* snaking from his finger-tips, his eyes dark and forbidding, filled my head. He could rain destruction on the people in this festival if he wanted. He could curse us with plague. He could boil our blood in our veins. He could carve his initials on our hearts with the brush of his thoughts. Somewhere in a dark corner of my mind, a rebellious thought held its own, though. *No.*

"N-no," I mumbled.

Killian's grip on my hand tightened. "Stop him," he begged. "You're the only one who can."

I tore my hand from his, feeling like I was swimming through rapidly hardening cement. Every step was a chore. The crimson threads of Killian's magic were wrapped around my throat, my face, but now all I could smell was cinders and ash, not copper and salt. Killian made a desperate sound and bashed himself in the face with the flashlight. "Don't listen to me!" he shouted. As he staggered backward and dropped the light, the threads of *animus* fell away like he'd taken a pair of scissors to them.

I sucked in a breath—and I ran.

FIFTEEN

"No!" Killian shouted. The sound of thrashing and unsteady footsteps followed, but I was powered by pure terror. I practically flew through the forest, dodging trees, branches scraping against my arms and cheeks. I ran, blundering through the darkness with my hands out, my breath squeaking from me in desperate bursts, until my head spun and my side ached. Finally, I had the wherewithal to pull out my cell phone and use the flashlight app to light my way. But the farther I went, the more confused I was.

Killian, who had been nowhere to be found for most of the day, had just ambushed me while pretending to be Flynn. He'd told me that Crowe was going to destroy everything.

He'd also seemed completely unstable and insane. He'd beaten Boone and left him bleeding and unconscious. He'd hit *himself* in the face, too, for God's sake. All while exuding *animus* magic streaked with black. It definitely hadn't looked that way last night.

A chime from my phone brought me to a stop just as lights in the distance told me I was about to reach the festival grounds.

It was a text from my mom: **Come home. I need you.**

With trembling fingers, I replied. **What's wrong? Are you okay?**

Just come home.

I frowned. Mom was no alarmist, and if she needed me, it was probably serious.

But so was what had just happened. Either Killian was convinced Crowe was up to something terrible, or Killian himself was using other kindled powers, just like his brother had.

I recalled the scent of ash in the air. A kind of magic I'd never before sensed—until this morning when Katrina had been surrounded by it as she hurled a terrible curse at Crowe. Had Killian been behind that, too?

Nothing was making sense.

Using my cell phone light, I made my way back to the spot where Killian had attacked Boone, but Boone wasn't there. Blood on the leaves told me I was at the right spot, though. He must have gotten up and gone back to the festival, maybe to get Crowe. But a shaky mistrust filled my head when I thought of seeing Crowe, so I texted the one person who might be able to shed some light on what I'd just experienced with the president of the Deathstalkers—Darek.

Hey. Just saw your pres in the woods and he was acting super weird. Can we talk?

I had just hit Send when I remembered that Darek's phone had been destroyed. With a groan, I pulled my keys from my pocket and staggered to my car. Confusion ruled my thoughts, and all I wanted to do was make sure Mom was okay. Then I'd decide who to talk to first and figure out what the hell was happening. Dad was at the top of that list, considering figuring this out was literally his job, but I was too frazzled to deal with him at the moment.

Gravel popped under my tires as I sped down the road. I was home in less than ten minutes. Mom's car was there—but so was another, parked right next to it. Darek was leaning on its trunk as I pulled the car into the driveway.

"What are you doing here?" I asked as I got out, realizing as I did that there was a blue thread of magic wound around me, spiraling up into the sky like a beacon.

I knew immediately what that meant.

Darek was talking, his head hung, his eyes hidden behind aviator sunglasses despite the heaviness of the night. "I came to say good-bye and—"

"Someone is tracking me with a locator spell," I said, cutting him off. His words barely registered. "Have you seen my mom?" I peered behind him, at the house. Warm light glowed in the windows. "She just texted—"

A roar of motorcycle engines hit our ears.

"Shit. That must be Crowe." I couldn't see the riders yet, but I was guessing Crowe was at the front, leading the pack.

"When he catches me with you..." Darek started.

"I know. I know." I sighed and scrubbed at my face. Crowe had already done enough damage. I wasn't going to allow him to do more. "Come on," I said, and grabbed Darek by the hand, the minty scent of my magic immediately hitting my nose.

The drone of the engines grew louder, and headlights shone up the road toward my house. I yanked Darek toward the front door, fumbled at the doorknob for what seemed like too many minutes, and finally got the door open enough for us to slip inside.

Two Harleys swerved onto the front lawn as I ran into the living room, wondering if I could get away with hiding Darek in the coat closet.

Footsteps crashed through the garden, and the kitchen door banged open a bare second before Hardy charged into the living room and saw Darek and me frozen on the other side of the couch.

"Jemmie..." he and Darek said at the same time.

Footsteps in the kitchen and the smell of honey and smoke told me who was about to join us.

"Go!" I yelled, and pushed Darek down the hall.

Hardy leapt over the couch behind us.

Darek and I stumbled into my room, and I slammed the door shut. *Locant* magic burst from my palms in frenzied waves—a weak barrier spell.

"What now?" Darek asked.

"Window," I said, but as I turned toward it, more head-lights flashed outside.

Darek chuckled. "Hell is empty and all the Devils are here."

I spun on him as Hardy pounded a fist against my door, threatening to shatter the reflexive barrier I'd covered it with. "Come here." I held out my hand. Darek took it, and I gritted my teeth, calling on all my power and muttering an incantation my dad had made me practice all those years ago, when he still had hope for me.

The protective shield burst out in an orb around us, cascading down around Darek and me like glittering rain.

Mint stung my throat, my eyes, but I stood firm as Hardy tore my door off its hinges.

By the time he reached us, though, the bubble had closed. The hair on my arms rose on end, the air suddenly charged with electricity.

"Where is she?" Crowe yelled as he stormed down the hall. "Jemmie!"

Hardy stared at me through the fractured light of the barrier. "She's in here," he called, keeping his eyes locked on me, nostrils flaring.

Crowe barged into my room and froze when he caught sight of me, standing there inside a barrier bubble, Darek safely beside me.

"What the fuck is this?" shouted Crowe.

"I win," Darek said simply. "And you lose."

The calm, cold sound of his voice chilled me. I looked up at him as he slid the sunglasses off his face.

His perfect, unbruised face. He gave me a smile. "A little of your friend Flynn's *inlusio* goes a long way. And when you cloak it under *locant*? You don't even know it's there."

"Boone's gone," Hardy said to me. "We had your dad do a locator to find you. He said you were here."

"She came here because I asked her to," Darek said.

"Where's my mom?" My voice was so thin I'm surprised he heard me.

"Snug as a bug in a rug," he said with a wink.

"You're helping him," Crowe said to Darek, amber ropes of magic sliding over my barrier, looking for a way in. "You're helping Killian gather kindled to do the cruori."

Darek laughed. "Nah, you big idiot. You've got it all wrong." He set his hand on the back of my neck, his fingers curling around my throat. "Let me make it all perfectly clear."

A lance of pain shot up my spine. I cried out. Darek squeezed harder as the air left my lungs. Smoke and honey and ash filled my nose. Gold and black streaked my vision. *Venemon.* This was Alex's magic! Mixed with...

"Oh my God," I whispered.

Darek Delacroix wasn't powerless. Not at all.

My knees buckled. "Killian," Darek explained as he guided me to the floor, "is helping *me.*"

"Don't hurt her," Crowe pleaded, slamming his hands against the barrier.

"Then don't make me," said Darek.

I couldn't feel my feet. Not my arms. Or my hands. Not even the breath in my lungs. My mind felt fractured from the rest of me, separate from my body.

Hardy beat his fist against the shield. It held firm. No one except another *locant* kindled could break through it, I knew. I had put this one up with intention, and I was stronger than I'd believed. Maybe even as strong as Dad. Too bad I had discovered it at exactly the wrong time.

"I'll liquefy her insides if you don't back the hell up," Darek said.

I retched, and blood splattered on the floor. Whatever Darek was doing, I couldn't feel it, and I was suddenly grateful for the disconnect.

Crowe grabbed Hardy and the two of them backed away, holding up their hands. "Okay. Okay," said Crowe. "Please stop hurting her."

I reached for my magic, trying to pull the barrier down, but the more I tried to sense it inside me, the farther away it seemed, until I felt abandoned by it entirely. My pulse thumped wildly beneath Darek's fingers. He squeezed harder, and ashy black skeins of magic filled the barrier bubble, magic only I could see and smell.

"What are you doing to her?" Crowe said.

"Taking what I need," Darek replied. "It's kinda my thing." He crouched over me, bending low to kiss my cheek, his smug tone softening. "I didn't want to hurt you, but they made me do it. I love you, Jemmie. You never thought you had much magic, but you are so wrong. It's the reason I'm going to succeed." He set his forehead on mine. "I wanted to tell you. So many times. And I'm going to give you one last chance." His eyes glittered with emotion as he stroked my hair. "When this is finished, come to me. I'll give you everything. I'll never hurt you again—and I'll make sure no one else touches you." His gaze flicked to Crowe and back to me. "Just choose me. That's all I ask."

He stood up and reached out, tearing down my barrier as if it were a spiderweb. Crowe lunged for him, only to be blown off his feet by a stinging, blue-tinged wind. When Darek shifted, the light caught him and I saw the telltale sign of an impenetrable barrier hugging him close, like a second skin.

I'd never seen anything like it, even though it was my magic that had created it.

"I'm going to walk out of here," Darek said. "And you're going to let me."

"Where's my sister?" Crowe growled.

"You can have what's left of her back when I'm done with her." Darek stepped toward the door. "You Medicis. So tough. Think you run things in the kindled world. Your dad was the same." He rolled his eyes. "I gotta say, he really set me on this path when he came after me."

Crowe went very still. "You…"

"A life for a life," Darek said casually. "He killed my father. And I killed him."

We all stared at Darek, who was glowing with a swirl of blue and amber clouded only by an acrid stench of black magic.

His magic. *Tollat* magic. Power he'd been cloaking ever since we met by slowly siphoning my power and using it to hide—it was why no one at the festival could remember his name, why no one thought of him as a threat, why I had only detected my own magic and only hints of his. And he'd done it all with the magic he must have inherited from his father.

"You're Henry Delacroix's son, aren't you?"

"Uncle Killian hid me away as best he could," Darek said. "At first I was a good boy and did as he said. But the more I learned about who I was, the more I knew I was never meant to hide."

"My father found you," Crowe said. "He knew who you were."

Darek shrugged. "He figured he'd take me out and that would be that. A preemptive strike—no justice, no fairness. So I gave him what he deserved." He smiled. "He was pretty surprised when I carved my initials on his heart using his own magic."

Crowe let out a wrenching sound and dove for Darek

again, only to be slammed against the wall by the power of Darek's *locant* barrier.

"It was a messy job, I admit. I mean, I was just borrowing his power, after all. It never lasts as long as I want it to." He looked down at me. "It's why I have to recharge, Jemmie. But I'm working on a more permanent solution. I won't need to take your magic ever again."

"I won't let you do this," Crowe said, grimacing and bleeding from a cut on his cheek. He was on his hands and knees, trying to push himself off the floor.

Darek's smile was so bright, so beautiful. "Come at me, Crowe Medici. I want you to. Let's see who comes out on top."

He turned and walked for the doorway. Hardy stepped back, reluctantly allowing him through. There was no point fighting him anyway. He'd drained all the magic I had inside me, so for now, with a barrier like the one he'd conjured around himself, he was nearly invincible.

Hardy followed him out at a distance as Crowe scooped me off the floor and into his arms. "I'm sorry," I whispered. "I was so stupid."

He squeezed me. "Shut up. Focus on breathing." His fingers scrabbled at my shirt, pulling it up at the hem until his fingertips touched my skin. Warmth spread from that point of contact. I leaned my head on his shoulder as the healing spell wound along my limbs. A sigh escaped me. This felt better than I wanted it to.

"Good?" he asked, and I nodded. "On your feet." With his help, I managed to stand upright, feeling a little woozy but otherwise all right.

"He's got Flynn," I said, pulling my thoughts back to our current problems. "I'm sure of it. Killian was covered in *inlusio* magic when he was impersonating Flynn, then he tried to convince me...." I frowned. "Actually there was something wrong with him. I'm not sure he's helping Darek willingly. Killian had traces of Darek's *tollat* magic all over him—maybe Darek had siphoned Killian's *omnias* power and turned it against him, like he did to Michael."

"You heard Darek—Killian's the one who hid him away so no one would know the kid had the same power as his father."

"I get that, but it doesn't mean Killian wanted history to repeat itself."

"Crowe!" shouted Hardy from outside.

Crowe and I rushed to the front door. Using the magic he'd been born with, Hardy sprinted after Darek's car as it tore down the road. His fingers scrabbled at the trunk. "Gina!" he shouted.

A massive blue barrier exploded around the car, and

Hardy collided with it at top speed. He crumpled to the ground as Darek's car sped away. Crowe and I ran across the lawn to reach his injured best friend.

"I'm sorry, Jemmie," Hardy muttered, climbing back to his feet. "I'm really sorry."

My heartbeat was hollow as I took in the tortured look on his face. "What?"

"I heard thumping as he drove away," he said, gesturing to his ears to indicate his uber-sensitive hearing. "He has your mom in the trunk."

Crowe picked up a rock and hurled it down the street. It bounced off the shimmering blue barrier that spread so wide I couldn't see around it.

"Oh God." I covered my mouth with my hands. "He's going to try to use her for the spell," I said weakly.

Crowe's brows lowered. "I thought Gina had no dominant magic."

"She doesn't, not really, but she definitely has traces of *merata* in her blood. She never gets sick...."

"Remember when Owen had that accident while she was riding on the back?" Hardy asked Crowe. "Your dad had to heal Owen's broken leg and cracked ribs, but Gina—"

"Had only a few scratches despite hitting the pavement at thirty miles an hour," Crowe finished for him.

"*Merata* magic is rare. She's the only person in this area who has even a little bit of it," I said. Tears filled my eyes. "God, Crowe, we have to do *something*. He's going to kill them all."

"We will," he said, squeezing my hand.

"I'm so sorry I doubted you."

"I've given you more than enough reason to doubt me." His thumb slid over the back of my hand. "We'll stop him, Jem, and we'll get our people back and then we'll figure this out."

I shivered, feeling the heaviness of his words, the promise that came with it. I didn't know what the outcome of *figuring it out* would be, but I understood that we weren't done. We hadn't ever been done.

He let me go and said, "How long do you think it'll take you to get your magic back?"

"No idea," I said. My eyes skimmed the barrier Darek had created. "That thing is huge. I can't believe it came from me. There's a lot of magic there."

Hardy squinted. "Wait. You can actually see it?"

I blinked, realizing I'd just revealed a secret I'd been trying to keep for years. But somehow, it just felt right. It was time to stop hiding. "Yeah." Resolve filled the empty cavern inside me, the one that had been filled with my magic. "And I'm going to try to take it down."

Hardy looked back and forth between me and Crowe. "She can see her own magic?"

Crowe's eyes flicked to meet mine, and in them was something that I hadn't felt in a long time—respect. "She can see everybody's magic."

"Whoa," Hardy said. "And that wasn't drained when Darek stole your *locant*?"

I frowned, realizing that was true. "I don't think he knew it was there, so he didn't know to take it. I've never really told anyone about it. It's not a kind of magic anyway, or a power."

"The hell it isn't," said Crowe.

I smiled at the awe in his voice, realizing he was right. I'd been so focused on avoiding magic for so long that I hadn't really understood what I could do, or how useful it could be. I could see the magic people had. I could see when they were preparing to attack, or when a spell was wrapped around another person or thing. I could see all of it.

"Oh my God," I whispered as another realization struck. "We have to get back to the festival. We were looking for the wrong thing."

Crowe frowned. "What do you mean?"

"We were trying to locate the people who were missing, but Darek must have cloaked them using the magic he's been siphoning from me. That's why Alex disappeared from my radar, and why we couldn't find Katrina or anyone else. He's shielded them."

Hardy dusted himself off. "So, what do we do?"

"What do *I* do, you mean," I said, walking up to the barrier and placing my hands against it. "I'm going to take this down, and then we go back to the grounds." I looked over at Crowe. "And then I'm going to look for my own magic."

SIXTEEN

I APPROACHED THE BARRIER WALL, SHIMMERING SAPPHIRE under the starlight. My nose and throat stung with the sharp mint prickle of it, but I knew now that it couldn't hurt me if I didn't panic. For so many years, I'd done exactly that, running or drinking or doing whatever I could to avoid letting the sensations get too intense, all out of fear that I couldn't take it.

I wasn't afraid anymore.

My magical battery might be low in the aftermath of what Darek had done to me, but I could see the *locant* magic hanging in the air so easily, the threads of it braided together to form a kind of mesh across the road and far into the distance in the fields on either side, stretching high up into the air. It actually made me smile to know that my power had produced it, even if it had been controlled by Darek at the time. It meant I could do it if I tried.

I laid my palms on the barrier's firm surface, and light pulsed through it, reacting to my touch. To Crowe and Hardy, I was pressing my hands against empty air, but they were silent as I worked, and their faith added to my confidence.

I felt the warm throb of power against my skin, and I whispered an incantation to call it back to me, to let me through. I was glad that even though I hadn't ever practiced these things, I had studied them. Now I realized they came naturally once I stopped hiding from them. And being able to see the magic only made it better.

Feeling a bit of magic trickle from me, I pushed against the threads of the spell, feeling them start to fray. The net of *locant* magic began to wrap itself around me, and for a moment the burn of it in my lungs made my heart pound with anxiety. But I reminded myself that this power belonged to me. My fingers curled and dug in, boring holes through the barrier. With one last command, I tore through the thing, leaving a gaping hole, and then I ran my hand along the edges, widening it.

Smiling, I turned back to see Crowe and Hardy watching me warily.

"Is it done?" Hardy asked.

I looked back at the barrier wall, which now contained an archway the width of the road. "Yep."

Crowe walked over to me, and Hardy laughed. "You might want to put out your hands to keep from busting that pretty face of yours against the barrier if she's wrong," Hardy suggested.

Crowe gave me an assessing once-over. "Nah," he said, then strode confidently through the hole that only I could see. "She's got this."

The way he was looking at me made me feel like my bones were melting.

A few minutes later, I stood shivering in my driveway as Crowe primed his bike. I held his helmet in my arms, waiting. I had sworn I'd never ride with him again, but a little thrill ran through me when he kick-started the bike with a quick, downward thrust of his foot. The engine caught right away, the sound of it like rumbling thunder. When he gave it a little throttle and looked at me over his shoulder, the ram's skull patch on his vest almost glowing on his back, I knew I was a goner.

I'd spent so many months trying to forget him, trying to hate him. I'd thrown myself into my thing with Darek, pretending I could feel the same way for him that I'd once felt for Crowe. Pretending it was enough, pretending that it felt right. But there was no avoiding this now, just like there was no avoiding what I could do. I needed to face it.

Whether I was a distraction to him, only a friend, or anything else, it didn't matter. My heart knew the truth.

I wrapped my arms around his waist and held on tight as we raced back to the festival. The closer we got, the more real the challenge became. Jane had been right—I was a part of this, not just someone watching from the fringes. If I couldn't figure out where Darek had hidden Alex, my mom, and the others, they would all be dead. I could tell by the tension in Crowe's body that he was thinking about it, too. And when he rolled into the parking area at the festival and pulled off his helmet, the look on his face said he felt the same weight on his shoulders. "He gave himself a big head start," he said, frowning as he looked up the path toward the festival. "You really think he's here?"

"I think we should head for the spot near the Death-stalkers tent," I said. "That's where we were when I lost Alex's signal."

He nodded. "Hardy, go find Owen, Jane, and the rest of the Devils. See if Boone has turned up."

Hardy swung his long leg over his bike and left his helmet on the seat. "Should I alert Terrence and the Kings? What about the Sixes?"

"No. Not yet. We're missing the most people—their lives mean more to us than they do to any of the other clubs, and it's my responsibility to get them out. Besides, the more people we have chasing after Darek, the greater the chance is that we'll be found. We have to go in fast and quiet. Let's keep our numbers small."

"Copy that," Hardy said, and jogged up the path to the RVs.

Crowe and I headed for the woods. "Who is Darek missing for his spell? He has Alex, so that's *venemon*. Katrina is *animalia*."

"If he took Gunnar the night he got into town, that's *arma*," Crowe said. "Flynn is *inlusio*. And your mom would be *merata*. That's half of what he needs, and if he grabbed Boone tonight, he's got *terra*, too." He frowned. "But he left you at your house tonight after draining you. He didn't even try to take you, even though your *locant* magic is strong as hell."

"He must have someone else."

"That, and he's in love with you," Crowe said drily.

"But…" He cursed. "Owen is easily the most powerful *locant* here."

My heart lurched. "You just saw him, though, didn't you? And Darek was at my house grabbing my mom.…"

"He's not working alone, Jem." Crowe already had his phone against his ear. "I'm calling your dad now." He gritted his teeth together as the phone rang and rang. "Voice mail," he said, and jabbed at the screen.

Icy fear sat like a weight in my gut. "He might have both my parents."

"We'll get them back. He still needs *animus*, and I have a hard time believing he'd kill his uncle or one of the Death-stalkers to get it, and he also needs *omnias* and *invictus*.…"

The fear grew, pressing against my lungs and making it hard to breathe. "You just sent Hardy after Jane."

Crowe's only answer was to turn on his heel and set off at a dead sprint for the camper grounds. He had his phone at his ear again. "Goddamm it," he yelled a few seconds later when no one picked up.

I was about ten steps behind him as we took a back trail around the main festival gathering area. The mixed scents of leather and cloves, of lavender and mint, of cigar smoke and pungent greenery all found me at once. The scent of magic. It glowed in the air around the tents, and I squinted, trying to pull apart the threads to see each specific kind. My eyes ached and stung with the effort, and I didn't have time to focus because it was all I could do not to trip over my own feet on the uneven, dimly lit ground.

When we reached Jane's Airstream trailer a few minutes later, Crowe banged on the flimsy door, then tore it open to find no one inside. I could detect a hint of fire and steel in the air, though. "She's been here recently," I said to Crowe, sniffing as I walked around the camper. "Hardy has, too. And..." I swallowed as I caught a thread of mint on the wind. "My father."

"What the hell," Crowe said, turning in place.

I did the same. "They can't be more than a few minutes ahead of us. I just don't understand—" I paused as another scent hit me—ashy and bitter. "Darek was here." I scanned the festival grounds, the woods. "We're directly south of the Deathstalker tent—it's just on the other side of that patch of trees." I pointed to the north, where the forest bumped out into the field and obscured the view of the tent. And just beyond it... "Look," I whispered.

Crowe did, but then cleared his throat. "I can't see a thing, Jem."

I stared at the faint blue glow arcing over the woods about a mile away. "That's where he has them."

"Where?"

"The old logging mill. That has to be where they are—it's

the only thing that's there, right? There's a *locant* shield over it. I can see it over the trees."

"Maybe we can catch Darek before he gets back there." Magic ribboned out of Crowe's body as he started forward, and I knew he was aching to use it against Darek.

"Let me go first," I said, tugging at his arm. "You're blocking my view."

He moved to the side, and we ran along the path into the woods. He activated the light on his cell phone to guide our steps, and then reached out and slid his hand beneath my arm. "So you can focus on what's out there," he said quietly.

I relished the solid reassurance of his steely fingers wrapping around my elbow. We moved along the tree line as quietly as we could, strains of music from the festival reaching across the distance, reminding us that life was going on just a few hundred yards away. It seemed so fragile, especially as I remembered Jane's prediction that someone would lose their life tomorrow. I glanced anxiously at Crowe as Darek's challenge echoed in my head. "He wants you to come find him," I said, slowing to a stop. "Crowe—"

"You know I have to," he replied. "I'm strong enough to stop him."

Just like his dad had stopped Henry. "Darek has had years to think about revenge. And your father—"

274

"My father knew he was going to die," Crowe said in a hard voice. "He seemed resigned to it, even though he was probably hoping he could take Darek out before it happened. And I promise you, Jemmie, I am not resigned. If it's me who's supposed to go down, I'm going to drag him into hell with me."

My heart squeezed. Crowe's words reminded me of Jane's story about the girl who dragged the devil into the sea. I shuddered just as I had that night, and the faint scent of metal and ash tickled the back of my throat. "Wait." I peered deeper into the woods and gasped when I saw a silvery wisp of Jane's *omnias* magic in the air to our left. "That way."

Without waiting for the light of Crowe's cell phone, I took off in the direction of the magic, my hands out to help me avoid trees, frantically sniffing at the air to try to pick up what was ahead. Crowe was running parallel to me, and I could hear the rush of his breath with each step. Ribbons of orange *invictus* magic laced the air ahead of us. "Hardy's up there," I said, panting.

Crowe's light illuminated hunched forms at the base of a tree in a clearing a few dozen yards away. On Crowe's left side, thick blue reams of magic unfurled through the trees and slammed across the path in front of him. I wheeled around in time to see him crash face-first into them and fly backward. I shouted his name as the *locant* magic tried to block my path as well.

The moment I smelled it, I knew what had happened. Mint mixed with ash and copper. *Locant* and *tollat* and *animus* twined together. Darek had my dad under his control—using Killian's power to do it. And if my dad was trying to block us, that meant I needed to reach the people on the other side of the barrier—Hardy and Old Lady Jane. With clawed fingers and a forceful incantation, I tore through the barrier and saw crimson and orange tangled around each other. In the center of those ropes of magic were two struggling figures. Hardy was grappling with Killian on the forest floor, the moonlight reflected in the sheen of sweat on their faces. Normally, it shouldn't even be a fight; Hardy was ten times stronger than any normal person. But Killian had his influence wrapped around Hardy, so Hardy kept pulling his punches. He was moving like he was surrounded by thick gelatin. Still, he seemed to have caused Killian enough pain that the Deathstalker couldn't concentrate enough to end the fight, and so the two were locked in combat. Another figure lay curled up at the base of a tree behind them, silvery wisps of magic rising up around her.

"Jane!" I raced to her side and gave her a quick once-over. She had a raised welt on her forehead but seemed otherwise unhurt. "Thank God," I said. "What happened?"

"He grabbed me outta nowhere," she said, staring at Hardy and Killian as they wrestled. "And your father—"

We turned at the sound of a shout to find Crowe on the ground again. My dad was just a blue glow between the trees as he scrambled up the path, heading in the direction of the logging mill, leaving only the scent of ash and mint behind. "Darek is influencing him using Killian's magic," I said, my throat constricting.

Crowe was on his feet again, stalking toward his best friend and his known enemy, the promise of violence etched on his face. Shimmering amber magic snaked from his fingers, found its target, and wrapped around Killian's chest. His eyes bulged. "No," he gasped out.

Hardy punched Killian in the stomach, then rose to his feet as the Deathstalker rolled off him and lay writhing on the ground, in the grip of whatever horrible curse Crowe had just thrown down. Hardy turned to us. My eyes went wide as I saw the streaks of black and red through the orange haze around him. "Crowe, it's not Killian," I shouted as Hardy lunged for Jane.

"I have to take her to Darek," Hardy said. He grabbed the old woman around the waist.

I didn't think. I reached for Jane's grasping hands, my magic puffing around us, wispy and still weak. My fingers laced with hers, and silvery threads wrapped around our hands.

Jane's eyes went wide and her mouth dropped open. Her horrified gaze met mine.

"I'm so sorry, Jemmie. I'm so sorry," she whispered hoarsely. "It's going to be you."

Her prediction broke my concentration, and Hardy wrenched her away from me. Crowe tried to grab his friend's arm, but Hardy lashed out with a side kick that sent Crowe crashing into a tree six feet behind him. I sank to the ground as Hardy took off at superhuman speed with Jane in his arms, leaving a vapor trail of ash and cloves and steel behind him.

Trembling, I crawled over to Crowe, who lay on his side with bits of leaves in his hair and dirt on his face. A haze of blue misted around me as I helped him sit up.

He clutched at his middle. "I think he broke one of my ribs," he said with a wheeze. Amber and gold spread from his fingertips and across his torso as he healed himself. While he did, I sat with the realization of what Jane had told me.

It was going to be me. I was going to die.

A suffocating mixture of defiance, disbelief, and grief welled up inside me. Was this what Michael had felt like on that final day?

"Jemmie, you okay?" Crowe asked as he got to his feet and slowly approached Killian.

"Fine," I murmured. If I told him, he wouldn't let me

go with him to the mill. And I had to. I was part of this. It was going to be me. "Killian was trying to stop Hardy from taking Jane."

Crowe's magic pulled away from Killian's wracked body, and the Deathstalker president went limp, his eyelids fluttering. Crowe prodded him with his toe. "Does that mean I have to heal him?"

"If you want help getting all our people back alive," I said. "Hardy and my dad were under the influence of Killian's magic, but I smelled Darek's power as well. *Tollat* magic. I never knew what it smelled like before." I laughed bitterly at how stupid I'd been. "I bet that asshole didn't even smoke—it was his magic that smelled like ash and stale cigarettes. I was sensing his power the whole time and didn't even realize it."

"That's because he's the only one who has *tollat*—you had nothing to compare it to," Crowe said grimly, spitting blood on the ground. He knelt at Killian's side and pressed his palm to the man's chest.

Killian took a deep, shuddering breath, his face twisted into a grimace of pain. When Crowe lifted his hand, Killian abruptly rolled to his side and retched into the rotting leaves beneath him.

"Come on," said Crowe impatiently. "You're gonna be okay."

"Fuck you," whispered Killian, struggling to get to his hands and knees.

I bent over and hooked my hands under his armpits, then helped pull him to his feet. "Darek had you under his control earlier."

"Sort of," said Killian, wiping his mouth. "I was fighting as hard as I could. I was trying to warn you...."

"But Darek had sent you to convince me that Crowe was the bad guy."

Killian nodded, giving Crowe a bitter look. "It wasn't that much of a stretch."

Crowe's lip curled. "That's rich, considering you've been harboring a killer for years."

"He's family," snapped Killian. "My brother made me promise to keep him safe. I had no idea he had *tollat* magic. He kept it from everyone."

"You must have known something. You never let on that Henry had a son," Crowe said.

"Should I have, knowing you assholes would hunt him down? He was a kid!"

"He might have been siphoning your magic and using it against you for years," I said quietly. "Both Henry and Darek could have manipulated you into protecting him."

As Killian stared at me, I could almost hear his heart breaking. "But Darek is my nephew," he whispered.

"Darek is a psychopath," Crowe said. "And he murdered my father."

Killian blinked at him in genuine surprise. "I never would have condoned that."

Crowe looked away. If he had thought Killian was lying, he would have called him on it, but it was too painful for him to acknowledge that he believed a man he'd been so invested in hating. "Help us stop Darek now," Crowe finally said, "and you've got yourself a truce."

Killian ran his hand over his hair. His glasses were nowhere to be seen, probably a casualty of the fight. "He's got them at the logging mill," he said bleakly. "All of them."

"All of them?" I asked. "What about *animus*—who else besides you has that kind of power?"

"He said he has someone already," Killian said. "Which means if we don't get there fast, he's going to complete the spell."

"And then he's going to tear everyone I love apart," growled Crowe. His power pulsed around him as he started to run along the path Hardy had taken. I followed, with Killian just behind me, panting heavily.

I'm part of this, I told myself firmly. *There's no turning back now. It's going to happen no matter what.* And I was willing to risk anything to save Alex and my parents, so it didn't really matter whether I was ready to die or not.

I reminded myself of that over and over again as I ran, even though the rest of my mind was screaming to stop, to run, to go far away and hide from the truth that had been in Jane's horrified eyes.

It was going to be me. Somewhere beyond these woods lay my fate, but that fate wasn't in question anymore.

I was going to die. But maybe, just maybe, I could help save everyone else first.

SEVENTEEN

WE REACHED THE MASSIVE CLEARING OF THE LOGGING mill a few minutes to midnight. In the darkness, the decrepit building hulked like a beast surrounded by the bones of its victims. Stacked lumber and unprocessed logs had been left to rot under the rain and the sun, casualties of a failed business that had shut down a decade earlier. Crowe and his family owned this land now, but they'd never done anything with this part of it. The Sable River rushed along the eastern edge of the clearing, where the logs used to be sent downstream. The mill had been built right here on its banks, and the curve of the water hugged its edge, threatening to carry it away someday.

Light glowed from the windows on the second floor of the main structure. I pointed at it as Crowe crept in next to me. We were crouched behind a stack of damp, spongy wood. Killian stared up at the windows from his nearby hiding spot behind a rusted-out truck. "I tried to influence him when I realized what he was doing, but he's been siphoning *locant* magic and using it to conjure shields against me."

"Against all of us," Crowe muttered.

"I might be able to take it down," I said.

"He has other ways of defending himself. He can siphon any magic with a simple touch."

I met Crowe's gaze.

"I'll be able to warn you about what he's doing so you can defend yourself," I whispered. "I can try to conjure a shield, but..." I looked down at my hands. Pulling barriers apart was one thing, but Darek had completely drained my *locant* magic just over an hour ago, and I wasn't sure I could actually conjure one that would be effective.

"Hey, they're over there!" someone shouted from our right. We'd been found. From between piles of lumber, a twist of green magic wafted into the sky.

"It might be a trick," I whispered as footsteps sounded off nearby. "I can see *inlusio*."

"Or it could be Flynn, under the influence of Killian's stolen magic," Crowe said, rising to his feet.

"Got 'em," shouted another voice, from our left.

"We're surrounded." Crowe grabbed my hand and dragged me along first one aisle of lumber, then another. We ended up in a muddy area with piles of wooden disks, cross sections of trunks, some of which were large enough to serve as tabletops. Looking around wildly for a better hiding place, I headed between two enormous old metal saws, into a junkyard of abandoned trucks and other construction equipment. Crowe stayed behind me, maybe recognizing that I would have some warning if magic was coming our way.

And I did, but a moment too late. The bitter bite of ash and cinder hit me and brought me wheeling around. Darek stood with a gun to Killian's head, crimson *animus* magic coiled around both of them. Darek's other hand was wrapped around Killian's neck, and streaks of ebony marred the red ribbons of Killian's power. He was siphoning it and using it against his uncle yet again. "Thanks for bringing him back to me," Darek said to me and Crowe.

"Go ahead and shoot him," Crowe said.

Darek pulled the gun away from his uncle's temple and pointed it at Crowe and me. "Nah. I've got a better use for him."

Killian stared at him miserably while his own magic wrapped around his legs and his arms like the strings of a marionette. "You said you had someone else."

"You're the best, Killian. You've always been too weak to use your power, though. That's why I need it. I'll actually be able to put it to good use. Now, give me your knife."

Stiffly, Killian reached beneath his shirt and pulled out a sturdy knife from a hidden holster. The blade glinted in the moonlight as he handed it over.

"Head inside with the others," Darek ordered. "Use your power to make sure they stay put. I'll be there in a few minutes, and we'll get started."

Without another word, Killian staggered up to the logging mill, disappearing inside, leaving us well and truly alone.

Knife in one hand, gun in the other, Darek circled us. "You never really cared about me, did you, Jemmie?" His gaze sought mine. "I just want to hear the truth of it."

"Leave her out of this," Crowe said. "You and I have plenty of other reasons to kill each other."

"Quit trying to protect her," Darek snarled. "It only proves my point."

Slowly, I stepped in front of Crowe to face Darek, and Crowe let me. "I did care about you. I still do."

Darek's eyes flashed. "Once I do the cruori, I'll be the most powerful kindled who's ever lived. And you could have been by my side." His lip curled into a sneer. "Except for the fact that you're in love with *him*."

He shifted the gun to aim directly at Crowe's chest, and I instinctively stepped in front of it. "Don't!"

Darek grimaced. "It's true, then." He nodded, as if to himself. "You chose this." He tossed the knife to me. "Catch."

My hand snatched the blade from the air, compelled by ribbons of black-striped crimson wrapped tight around my wrists.

Darek held the gun up and shook it. "This one is for you, Crowe." Using Killian's magic, Darek forced Crowe to hold out his hand. Crowe's entire arm shook as he tried to resist the silent command. Darek set the weapon on his palm. "It's better if you don't fight it."

"Darek, you don't have to do this," I said. "You can stop all of this, and we'll forget it ever happened."

Darek scowled. "Forget? I can't forget. You used me, Jem."

"*I* used *you*?"

He didn't even have the good grace to acknowledge the irony, considering he was *wearing* my stolen magic. "You strung me along until Crowe Medici crooked his finger, and then you didn't want anything to do with me." Darek's eyes were full of rage now. Here he was, facing off against one person with a gun and one with a knife, but he was controlling both of us. "I wanted to do everything for you, Jemmie.

I would have, if you'd let me. But now I see that you never would have chosen me. It was always going to be him."

I glanced at Crowe. He was glaring at Darek with unrestrained rage. His amber magic was lashing at the shield around Darek, trying to find a way in, but for now, the stolen *locant* barrier held and Crowe couldn't touch him. Not with magic, at least.

Darek stepped between us. "Despite the heartless way you led me on, I'm going to respect your choice, Jemmie. It's my final gift to you."

"Please, don't do this."

"Sit," he said.

Crowe and I each dropped onto a stack of tires, facing each other, close enough that our knees were touching.

"Please." Tears welled in my eyes.

Darek sucked in a breath, and for a second I saw him, the old him, the one I thought was my friend. For a second, I believed that he'd end this entire thing and give me my parents back.

But that naïveté was what got me into this mess in the first place.

"I'm going to murder you," Crowe said.

Darek snorted. "Crowe Medici, so fucking powerful. We're gonna find out."

"Darek! Please!" Fat tears streamed down my face. I couldn't believe that I used to think he was a good person.

He turned to me and whispered something, and the black-and-crimson ribbons of stolen magic around him struck like snakes, burying themselves in my mind. Even through the chaos of magic around me, I could see that the same thing was happening to Crowe.

"Jemmie, if Crowe so much as moves, you slit his throat. Crowe, if Jemmie moves, you shoot her in the head." Darek's eyes met mine. "I really did love you." He sighed and walked toward the mill.

"Darek!" I moved to stand and Crowe cocked the gun and put the barrel against my forehead.

"Don't. Move," he said.

I froze in place.

"We have to stop him. He's about to do the spell."

"I know." Crowe's voice shook. Sweat shone on his forehead. "Please don't move. I'm really close to pulling the trigger, Jemmie."

"I'm not moving."

For a moment, we just stared at each other. Then Crowe spoke, as if every word was a struggle. "You have to undo this spell. You can see it. You can see how to break it down."

"I don't know if it works that way. I've only undone my own kind of magic. This is a whole other ball game."

"Just try."

I concentrated on the threads that bound us to Darek's orders. I could see the magic when I squinted: thick red ribbons of it zigzagging between Crowe and me. But when I tried to pull on one thread, the knots only seemed to tighten.

"I don't think I can undo this."

"Yes, you can."

"I can't, Crowe. We are going to sit here forever until one of us moves."

"Then I'm going to move," he said. "And you do what you have to—and then you find a way to stop Darek."

"What? Are you kidding me?"

"Listen to me. Jane said one of us would die tomorrow, but it's just past midnight. It *is* tomorrow. And I think she meant me, Jemmie. So it's okay." He gave me a brave smile. "No guilt, all right?"

"It's not you," I whispered. I gave him an apologetic look as his smile faded. "I grabbed Jane's hand as Hardy was dragging her away. She said it was going to be me."

Even in the darkness, I could see the blood drain from Crowe's face. "Tell me you're lying," he demanded, his voice breaking.

"If this is how I die, here with you, then I'm okay with that."

"Goddamn it, Jemmie. I will not be the one to kill you." His hand shook.

I closed my eyes, breathing deeply even as I felt the barrel of his weapon against my skin. "If that's what it takes for you to get out of this and go save all those people, then you have to do it. Your sister. My parents. Our friends. They're depending on you."

"What about you?" he whispered.

I opened my eyes. "I guess my story might end right here. But it'll be quick, right?" I sounded a lot braver than I felt. Hopelessness was tearing at my heart.

Crowe started to shake his head, then hissed as I brought the knife to his throat. He froze. "I can't be the one," he said in a low voice. "It would kill me anyway. I only ever wanted to keep you safe."

I offered him a tremulous smile. "Is that why you told me to leave Hawthorne?"

"You really want to talk about this right now?"

"What better time? This is probably the last conversation we'll ever have."

"Yes," he said quickly. "I thought you'd be better off far away from this place."

"You mean far away from you? From what you might have to do, now that you're president of the club? Is that why you got with Katrina, too?"

His eyes slid away from me and he swallowed, his Adam's apple sinking. "Yes."

"I think that's horseshit."

He smiled. "Did you just say 'horseshit'?"

"I'm serious."

"I can tell."

We fell into silence again. Crowe shifted his weight an inch on the woodpile, and without thinking, I pressed the blade to his skin. He pushed the gun harder into my forehead.

"Sorry," he muttered.

The harder I fought Darek's order, the less control I seemed to have over my body, the more compelled I felt to listen to my hand instead of my head. It was only a matter of time until one of us wouldn't be able to hold back the urge to kill.

I didn't want to die not knowing the truth.

"Did you ever love me?" I whispered. "Was I ever more than just a distraction?"

Crowe blinked. "Jemmie."

"If I'm going to die, I want the truth."

"Yes. I loved you. I *love* you. I've never stopped."

My shoulders fell, and Crowe seemed able to ignore the

shift in my posture, though his eyes squeezed shut and his gritted teeth were telling me it wasn't easy. I'd been waiting over a year to hear him say those words. Now he had, and it was bittersweet. Because I was going to die today, one way or the other. I could feel the finality of it settling in. I didn't need to have *omnias* blood in my veins to feel fate crushing down on me.

"Thank you," I whispered.

"I wanted to protect you," he said. "From me, from what I might become, and from everything that came along with that."

"And now?"

His gaze fell to my lips. "Now I just want you."

A smile. A sigh. I had a gun to my head, but I was ridiculously happy in that instant. "I'm yours."

His hand came up, like he meant to touch me. I dug the blade harder against his throat, leaving a small gash. Blood welled in the wound and spilled from it like melted wax over the edge of a candle.

The blood ran toward my hand, the one still clutching the knife. "I have an idea," I said, inching my palm up the hilt, toward the blade. I forced myself not to move any other part of my body except my fingers and prayed I wouldn't accidentally drop the weapon before I'd gotten what I needed.

When I felt the bite of the knife's edge, I smiled. Crowe's blood was streaming down the side of his neck, and mine was dripping from the pads of my fingers. I tried angling my hand a fraction of an inch to bring our essences together. Crowe's finger slid back to the trigger.

"What are you doing?" he said.

"Saving us."

"I can feel you moving. So you should either hurry up or stop it."

I counted down in my head. Trying to propel myself into action, coiling the necessary energy I'd need to move fast enough to dodge a bullet.

One.

Two.

"Jemmie," Crowe warned.

Three.

I pressed my right hand to the wound on Crowe's neck where *locant* blood met *venemon* blood for the second time. As the power surged inside me, I threw my left hand up, grabbed Crowe's arm and pushed it away. The gun went off inches from my face.

My ears ringing from the blast, I reached for the magic we'd just created together. It exploded out around us, gold and sapphire and the indefinable shimmer that was both of them together.

After this morning, I'd thought I knew what it felt like to work blood magic. But I didn't. Crowe had been in control this morning, casting the spell he'd needed to survive— I'd mostly been an observer.

Casting the magic in a blood-powered spell was ten times more potent.

Time stood still as warmth ran through me. This tingly-all-over feeling. Like velvet. Like rose petals. Like smooth chocolate melting in your mouth. Breathing felt like freedom. The beating of my heart was the thundering of a storm electrifying the air. The ground vibrated beneath me. Colors became more vibrant. Sounds more refined. My magic surged inside me, with his wrapping around it, breathing life into it.

It was like I was seeing and hearing and feeling the world for the very first time. With a grin, I reached up and drew my finger through the crimson ribbons of *animus* magic imprisoning us. Blue and gold twined together and cut through the crimson power. The mind-control power Darek had stolen from Killian shattered all around us, crumbling like an afterthought.

I slid off the woodpile, my body melting with the magic, and collapsed to my knees. Crowe caught me, hugged me close.

"Jemmie. Talk to me."

I looked up at him. Stupid, handsome Crowe. More handsome than ever before.

His eyes were black again, but so were mine. I couldn't see it, but I could feel it, the blackness of the magic bleeding into my eyes. It stung just as much as it thrilled. But I didn't care. The good far outweighed the bad.

"Get up. We have to go," Crowe said, letting me go quickly. "Darek is going to be doing the spell any minute now."

The euphoria of our blood magic faded quickly, just like it had before, and I climbed to my feet, Crowe's arm laced around my waist. I was here but not here, delighted and floating on the revelation of his love yet strangled by the certainty of my own impending death. But I was ready even though it was way too soon. I was part of this, and it was time.

Somewhere far away, I heard the whisper of the Undercurrent, where the blackness lived. And it was calling my name.

EIGHTEEN

"HARDY AND I USED TO PLAY HERE ALL THE TIME WHEN we were kids," Crowe said as he led me around the junk-yard, headed for the riverbank. "There are a few ways to get to that second floor."

We reached the bottom of a conveyor-belt ramp along the side of the building that must have been used to move logs up from the river to the processing facility inside. The ramp connected to a section of the second floor that jutted out over the Sable and was held up by a few rickety-looking wooden posts. Even from here, I could see that part of that floor had rotted away, revealing the lighted space inside the building. "This is my entrance," said Crowe, leaning close, his voice just a whisper. "He probably won't expect anyone to go in this way."

"Probably because it's crazy—be careful you don't end up in the river."

He grinned, hard and dangerous. "You can go in through the building and get up the stairs. How's your magic?"

I looked down at my hands, at the wisps of *locant* trailing from my fingertips. The blood spell had amplified my magic temporarily, but it was already wearing off, as was the feeling of euphoria, leaving me with only dread—even if we saved everybody, I wasn't going to make it out. "Not a hundred percent yet, but better."

If I told him it wasn't, he would feel the need to protect me, and I needed him to protect Alex and my parents and everyone else.

"That barrier around him is going to be wearing off really soon," I said. "Unless he uses my dad to recharge, that is."

"We'll have to take our chances. I'm going to get Darek as soon as I find a way in. At the very least, I can keep him busy. You focus on getting people out and protecting them from Killian's magic, since he's under Darek's control. Start with your dad, because he'll be able to help you shield the others from any *animus* magic. Then free Alex and Hardy. Can you unbind magic yet?"

I offered him a brave smile. "I'll give it everything I have." All I really had to do was get to my dad—if I failed or went down, he could do the rest.

"There are two staircases inside," Crowe continued, his lips brushing against my hair. "He's probably been using the one nearest the front entrance, but there's a narrow set of steps through there." He pointed to an old door, just crooked planks barely holding together, that was situated beneath a sagging overhang. "If he's got a barrier up to wall that entrance off, you'll be able to take it down."

"Be careful," I whispered as he tested his weight on the ramp. "Remember how many people need you. My mom—" My throat constricted over my last request. *Take care of her after I'm gone.*

He raised his head as if he'd heard it anyway. "This isn't the end, Jemmie. I won't let it be."

We stared at each other, and I drank in the sight of his moonlit face. "Okay. Go," I whispered, knowing that if I lingered a moment longer, I might lose my courage altogether. Now I fully understood what Crowe had meant when he said he didn't want to know when he would die for fear it would make him hesitate.

Crowe's long fingers tightened on either side of the conveyor belt, and he began to climb, ascending like a big jungle cat, silent and dangerous. I tore my gaze from his body and crept over to the rotting wooden door. It hung open slightly, leaving just enough space for me to slide through without having to pull it wide.

Guided only by the dim silver glow of the moon through filthy panes of glass, I began to make my way to a set of stairs that led up to the second floor. My parents and Alex and the others were directly above me—I could smell the faint waft of their magic now, all mixed together. I flexed my fingers and smelled the stinging mint of my own power, and I couldn't help but think that Alex would be so proud of me; I'd dug my power out from under all those layers of denial, as she had said I could, and now I was going to use it.

The darkness at the bottom of the staircase was nearly complete, but I could see where the steps ended near the ceiling in a trapdoor. There was no *locant* barrier there. Maybe Darek had been arrogant enough to leave it unprotected.

"Sorry, Jemmie," came Killian's voice from behind me—a moment before his arms slid around me—and his fearsome *animus* magic did the same, winding around my head and body like ropes before I could conjure any type of shield. A sense of numbness came over me, and I sighed. If Killian was here, it meant Crowe might have a chance. There was no point in fighting.

"Come on," Killian said as he tugged me up the sagging

stairs. His muscles were trembling. I swear he didn't want to be doing this. But I understood his magic well enough to know that talking wasn't going to change things.

We reached the trapdoor, and Killian swung it up and helped me through into a cavernous space. The ceiling had rotted away in some places, revealing the starry sky above as well as the huge missing section of the floor that we'd seen from outside—from here, it was just a black pit. Even though we were a few dozen yards away, on the other side of the space, I could hear the rush of the river below. Next to the giant hole in the floor was a stack of massive logs, which probably concealed the ramp Crowe was using. The floorboards creaked beneath my feet as Killian guided me out of the shadows with his mind, his hand resting lightly on the back of my neck.

Darek had lit lanterns he'd clearly stolen from the festival. They were placed against the walls. A big wooden trough sat in the center of the floor, maybe eight feet long and a few feet wide. Around it stood all the people we were missing. My parents, Alex, Flynn, Hardy, Boone, and Gunnar. Katrina and Jane were there as well. They stood on either side of the trough, their bare arms stretched out over it, palms down. Their eyes were unfocused.

"Mom!" I yelled. "Dad!" I wanted to run to them but couldn't get my feet to move.

"They can't hear you," said Darek. He was standing on the far side of the trough, looking triumphant. "I've put my uncle's magic to good use. They're deaf and blind. So are the others."

There were nine total. Alex and Gunnar stood across from each other, both of their faces stained with dirt, their hair a tangled mess. They'd fought, and they'd lost.

"Let them go," I said. Where was Crowe? I couldn't look for him. I couldn't do anything but stand like a zombie at the opposite end of the trough, completely lost in Killian's influence.

Darek was watching me intently. "I heard the gunshot and thought he'd killed you," he said.

"I ducked." My arms were slack at my sides as Killian's magic stroked at me, filling my nose with the smell of copper and salt and ash and sweat. Mine and Killian's.

Darek arched an eyebrow. "Is Crowe dead, then?" Around him, the *locant* shield glowed weakly, revealing a few spots that had worn away. It was still there, but fading fast. "He'd better be dead."

"Not as dead as you're about to be," came a voice from the darkness behind him.

Darek whirled around as thick whips of *venemon* magic flew outward from the shadows and slammed into his body, making the *locant* shield flicker and fade. With a desperate

302

sound, Darek dove for Flynn, who was standing nearest the end of the trough, right next to Old Lady Jane. Darek squatted low as he wrapped his fingers around Flynn's unyielding forearm while the older man merely stood placidly, as if lost in a dream.

Crowe moved into the lantern light, his power perfectly controlled and absolutely terrifying, like an army of vipers just looking for a place to strike. Each loop of it spiraled in the air, the ends narrowed to sharp, stabbing points. His lip curled when he saw Darek hunkered down behind the trough. "How's that stolen shield holding up, asshole?"

Darek let out a nervous laugh, still holding tightly to Flynn's arm. Something about it felt wrong, but I couldn't quite break through the numbing peace of Killian's magic to figure out why. "I guess you're as strong as everyone says, Crowe," Darek replied. "But you're not about to stop me."

"Wanna bet?" Crowe spread his fingers, and one of the golden vipers lashed out, slamming into Darek's shoulder. He fell backward with a scream, blood welling from what looked like a stab wound. He rolled over quickly, though, green *inlusio* magic slithering from his fingertips.

He'd just siphoned a hefty amount of Flynn's magic, and Crowe couldn't see it. He had no idea. The sight of Crowe stalking toward Darek, the urgency and need I felt to save him, tore at the bonds of Killian's magic inside my mind. But it wasn't enough. As Crowe raised his arms and his magic reached for Darek one last time, Darek flung his arm out.

The *inlusio* magic arced through the air and engulfed Crowe. Threads of it slid into his ears and over his eyes. He gasped and froze. "What happened?" he whispered, his voice cracking as he stared blindly at all of us. "Did I just do this?"

With a stifled curse, Darek pressed his hand to his bleeding shoulder and got to his feet. "How's the view from there, Crowe?" he asked with a pained chuckle. "Did your mighty powers have a few unintended consequences?"

My heart twisted as I witnessed something I never thought I'd see. Tears, streaking down Crowe's handsome face. "Alex?" he asked in a broken voice. "Flynn!" His arm rose from his side, reaching for them. "This can't be real," he screamed. "Jemmie? Answer me! I know this isn't real!"

But his expression said it all. It felt real. Way, way too real. Real enough to paralyze.

Darek looked over at me. "I'm showing him his worst nightmare," he said quietly.

Tears stung my eyes as I watched Crowe fall to his knees, just a few feet from the place where the floor gave way to nothingness. He clutched at his head, tearing at his hair. "I didn't mean to," he howled. "I would never hurt them!"

"You hurt everybody," Darek shouted. "Just like your father did."

It killed me, watching Crowe break like this. And that pain, that love, it was enough to penetrate the fog of *animus* in my head. As Crowe stared in horror at a scene I was sure involved the sight of everyone he loved dead in front of him, my fingers began to twitch, aching to reach for the crimson threads of Killian's magic. He stood impassively at my side, sweating and breathing hard, as if he was fighting as well.

"Crowe, I'm a compassionate guy," said Darek. He walked over to Crowe, who was now on his hands and knees, his head hanging, and grabbed Crowe's hair, pulling his chin up. As he did, I could see the golden skeins of Crowe's magic sliding up Darek's arms, being absorbed by his dark power. "I really want to help you get through this."

"It's not real, Crowe," I whispered, then huffed with frustration. I'd meant to scream it, but Killian still had a hold on me.

"Make it stop," Crowe sobbed, not resisting as his enemy siphoned away his magic, too caught in the illusion of his own personal hell. "I would never hurt them. I didn't mean to do it!"

"Make it stop?" Darek asked, turning to me. He pressed his hand to his bleeding shoulder and whispered an incantation, and the wound glowed golden as it healed. "Should I make it stop, Jemmie?"

"Crowe, it's not real," I said, louder this time.

Darek's smile fell away. "Try harder, Killian. Don't disappoint me."

Instantly, the ribbons of crimson *animus* tightened around me, stabbing into my ears, stealing my voice once more.

Darek's grin returned as he watched my mouth snap shut. "Much better. Now," he said, turning back to Crowe, "you wanted me to put an end to all your suffering."

"Please," Crowe whispered, his eyes locked on the imaginary horror. "I never meant to do this. I don't ever want to lose control again."

Darek approached Hardy. Ash and cinders hit my senses as he touched the side of Hardy's face and siphoned his magic. "Oh, wow." Darek stumbled back, his aura tinted orange with *invictus*. "It's awesome to be you."

He ambled back over to Crowe as I waged a battle in my own mind. I could see Darek's strength growing with every step, along with his intent to kill. Crowe knelt, helpless and in the grip of overwhelming grief. How Darek had known to hit him with this—not just the deaths of the people he loved, but by his own hand—I didn't know. It reeked of an evil and cruelty I hadn't known existed before that moment.

"I'm going to make this stop for you just like you asked," Darek said, leaning over Crowe. "You ready to join your old man in hell, big guy?" His fist shot forward and slammed into the side of Crowe's face. Crowe's head snapped to the side and he fell hard, blood pouring from his mouth, his body landing right on the edge of the hole in the floor.

Love and determination surged inside me. It was as if I could feel Crowe's newly shed blood calling out for me. I didn't know if it was how I felt about him or the blood magic we'd created together, but it was as if his heart beat in my chest. I was not about to watch him die. My hand rose from my side, and my fingers, sparking blue with *locant*, encircled one of the undulating ribbons of Killian's magic. It felt silky and loose as I yanked it away from my body.

As Darek stood over Crowe, preparing to kick him into the pit, I whispered protective incantations as I whirled around and let my *locant* tear Killian's crimson magic to shreds, ripping it away from Killian himself, who shuddered and staggered.

"Help me," I said. "Don't let this happen." I'd freed the two of us, but it was clear that all of Darek's intended victims were still held in helpless oblivion.

"Dammit, Jemmie," yelled Darek. As I spun around to face him, I saw that he'd left Crowe lying right at the edge of the hole and was running back to the trough. He bent over and pulled something from inside the basin—a hunting knife. With a cold glint in his eye, he quickly moved to my mom's side, and with sharp, brutal slashes, slit her outstretched arms from the crook of her elbow to her wrist. Her blood flowed into the bowl, streaking it red.

"No!" I screamed. Killian and I both ran forward as Darek deftly cut Alex's wrists, too, and then pivoted around and cut my dad's.

"I should never have protected you," Killian roared as he slammed into Darek, his *animus* magic winding around his nephew. They hit the floor between Dad and Katrina, who stood by, calm as sleepwalkers.

As Darek and Killian wrestled for control of the knife, I sprinted for the only person I knew could save my family— Crowe. I grabbed his shoulders and dragged him away from the edge of the pit, just far enough so he couldn't accidentally roll in. With clawed fingers and all the love that was in me, I muttered another protective incantation and ripped away the sickly green curse, leaving him groaning and blinking up at the fractured roof. "It wasn't real," I said, bending over him as Killian and Darek struggled by the trough.

Crowe's eyes met mine. "Jemmie?" he asked weakly.

"Yeah. I need your help."

"I killed you."

"Nope. Get up. How much magic do you have?" I yanked on his arm, trying to get him on his feet.

Blood dripped from his mouth as he swayed, trying to keep his balance and get his bearings. "I don't know," he muttered. "He took a lot." From the tortured tone of his voice, I knew he wasn't just talking about his magic.

As we started for the trough where my parents and Alex stood, their blood spilling into the basin below, Darek let out a laugh, and Killian screamed. Before we had a chance to intervene, Darek rose from the floor, the dripping knife in one hand and Killian in the other, bleeding from a terrible wound to his gut. Orange strands of *invictus* magic wound around Darek's arm, and he hefted his uncle upward before dropping his entire body, limp and bleeding, into the trough.

"You aren't worthy to call yourself a Delacroix," Darek said, then spit on Killian, who shuddered and went quiet, the blood from the others Darek had cut flowing over him.

Darek raised his head and saw me and Crowe standing between the pit and the trough, and then his blue eyes skimmed the people around the bloody basin, as if calculating. A tiny smirk pulled at his lips, and he lunged for Katrina.

He was going to try to complete the curse, and if he did, there would be no stopping him.

Crowe began to move forward, but I grabbed his arm and turned to him. "No," I said quietly, taking his face in my hands. "You heal anyone who's been cut, and hurry. You aren't the monster today."

Tonight, I was the monster. It had to be me.

Crowe looked down at me, and I watched the same love and determination I had felt spark in his eyes. I wondered if he sensed my heart inside him, too. He crushed his lips against mine, quickly, hungrily. Did he know this was the last time? Did he feel it, too?

"Go," I said quietly. "Save them."

Magic surged inside me. It coiled in my bones and in my veins. I charged Darek, calling forth a vault hex. Too late did I sense the glittering blue shield around him, stolen from my father as he bled. My hex bounced off him. Before I could stop my momentum, Darek lunged for me and jammed the blade of his knife into my stomach. Blood poured down the front of me, soaking my shirt and my jeans, squishing in my boots. My insides burned. It wasn't just a physical pain, but a mental and metaphysical pain, felt to the root of my soul.

"This is what you get for hurting me," Darek said with a low sob. He grabbed my shoulder, and with his other hand, drove the blade up, hitting bone when he reached my rib cage. A reedy, wet gasp escaped me.

Crowe roared my name from the other side of the trough,

but Darek threw up a barrier around him, imprisoning him inside.

I dropped where I stood, my entire body on fire, a strange whispering in my ear, calling to me. Mom had collapsed to her knees, her lips blue and her skin pale, but her arms were still held out. My dad bled out into the trough, too, though he was starting to sink to the floor. With Crowe trapped, beating his fists against Darek's barrier, Darek quickly sliced the wrists of Boone, Gunnar, and Hardy before going to the other side of the trough to cut Flynn and Jane. They stood helplessly, growing paler by the second, as their blood—and their magic—drained from them.

I closed my eyes. I was so tired, and so cold. "Don't do this," I whispered. "Please."

"I have to," Darek said, even though he had tears in his eyes. "This is my destiny, Jemmie. I'm going to be a god among men."

It hit my consciousness hard, awakening a memory from its slumber. Slowly, I raised my head. "No," I said. "You're the devil." I rolled onto my side and glanced at the gaping hole in the floor that stretched all the way down to the river below. It was only feet away.

Up onto all fours, I grabbed the hilt of the knife and pulled it out with one swift motion. Blood hit the floorboards, and my teeth began to chatter. I clutched an arm to my stomach, pressing hard as I leaned against the end of the trough. Avoiding looking at the carnage within, I raised my head.

Darek's spell had already begun. He threw his left hand over the trough of blood, and with one quick slash opened a gash across his own palm. When the first drops of his blood hit the rest, the crimson liquid vibrated and rippled outward, like a stone had been dropped in the center. Wind kicked up outside and ripped through the cracks of the mill, drowning out the sound of Darek's voice as he shouted an incantation. He plunged his hand into the trough. The magic immediately took hold and a mushroom cloud of smoke and light burst upward.

Darek rocked on his feet. There was no *locant* barrier surrounding him now, but his black *tollat* magic was coiling around him in ribbons, mixing with the other magic to create something new.

Something terrible.

Though I could barely feel my legs, I sensed that they were moving, propelling me to my own end.

Magic glittered like a rainbow of serpents above us, soaring up from the casting trough and arching back down when it hit the ceiling. Darek repeated the incantation over and over again. Bright red lines appeared on his arms, and spread up to his neck, and then up the side of his face.

He looked right at me with black eyes. The blackness seeped out, over the bridge of his nose and back toward his ears. He grinned at me. A devil's grin.

I took two giant steps and rammed the knife up and beneath his rib cage, straight into his heart.

Darek leaned into me with a groan. I staggered back, caught beneath his weight.

"You really think this will kill me?" he said. "A knife?" He laughed. "It's too late, Jemmie. I'm already immortal."

"Not if I take your power from you."

I gave the knife another shove and he gasped again, then I pressed myself against him, wound to wound, a grisly embrace. I felt the connection between us, our blood mixing, all the different kinds of magic running through our veins. That warm, fuzzy feeling washed over me again, strengthened my own magic in a way I couldn't describe with words. With my arms around him, I twisted in the ribbons of loosed magic, winding them around us as I staggered toward the open pit. Faintly, I could hear Crowe shouting, but it didn't stop me.

I was going to throw myself into the sea, and take the devil with me.

The skeins of magic began to weave themselves together around us, closing in. Using my *locant* power and the connection of our blood, I seized Darek's siphoning power as my own and bound it, gilding my own bones with it even as I wrenched it from his. Ashy fog billowed around me as I sucked him dry.

"No," he breathed as the magic abandoned him.

The blackness pulled away from his eyes, just in time for me to see them gloss over. I lost my balance as his body went limp in my arms and his face smoothed. For a brief moment he was just a boy who had once offered me a piggyback ride out of the swamp, a boy with a sweet smile and warm hands.

It was too late, though. For him and for me. My faltering steps had carried us backward, and we were already plunging through that hole in the floor. "Now the sea has us," I whispered as we fell toward the rushing river below and let the Undercurrent welcome us both.

NINETEEN

I COULD HEAR THE ROARING OF A RIVER.

Not the Sable River. This was different.

This was everywhere. This was bigger.

The Undercurrent whispered to me, called my name.

The rushing of water through my fingertips, the cold seeping into my skin, the blackness running through my veins. As I let the current carry me, I reached out my hand and brushed something vital, something huge and inhuman and very much alive, even in this place of death. It whispered to me in the voice of a monster, singing me a song of blood and power, caressing my soul with its long, spindly fingers, wrapping them around the very essence of me.

Distantly, I was aware of a pull, of something trying to yank me away from this perfection, and I fought it. But the creature that lived in the Undercurrent laughed while it dragged its fingertips along the seams of my soul, knitting me back together in its own image. *Go,* it said, urging me home, returning me to the living with its fingerprints all over my heart.

TWENTY

"You fix her, goddamn it, or I swear to God—"

"Try harder."

"She has no pulse."

"She's not dead, Jane. I can still feel her—"

"Crowe, I'm sorry. I'm not strong enough."

"Take my blood. Just bring her back!"

"Come back to me, Jemmie."

Light flashed behind my eyes. I could feel the distant pull of the ground beneath my legs and the grip of strong arms wrapped around me, the press of his face against mine. He was shaking. Shaking. And the earth trembled.

The roar of the nearby river was in my ears, and still he held me.

"Crowe," I whispered.

He pulled back. "Jemmie?"

"Am I alive?"

A beautiful honeyed glow broke over the treetops on the other side of the river, casting a halo of light behind his head. The sunlight. I could taste it on the tip of my tongue.

I could hear the birds in the trees and the worms in the earth and the fast beating of Crowe's heart.

I could sense every breath pulled in and pushed out. I could sense the world sighing.

A single tear streamed down Crowe's face. It glittered in the light.

And then he kissed me and the earth stopped trembling, and held its breath.

I was alive.

TWENTY-ONE

CROWE TIGHTENED HIS ARM AROUND MY WAIST, HOLDING me upright. My entire body had broken in the fall, and water had filled my lungs, but he'd healed me. I didn't have the heart to tell him I hadn't needed it. That my body knew how to put itself back together. I could still feel the aftereffects of Crowe's *venemon* magic and mine knitting my bones.

He led me to his car, where my mom and dad waited, looking pale from blood loss but otherwise alive. By some miracle and Crowe's powerful healing magic, the only people we lost were Darek and Killian.

I fell into my parents' arms and Mom sobbed against my neck, her tears soaking my hair.

"I'm so sorry," I said, though I wasn't sure what I was apologizing for.

When they pulled away, they both looked at me with those concerned Mom and Dad faces, the kind that said they were still worried that something might be broken, something they didn't know how to mend.

Something *was* different.

I was different.

I was better.

No one had to say it for me to feel it. The blood magic.

"Me next," Alex said, and pulled me to her. Her slender arms wove around me and squeezed me tight. Her heart thudded hard in her chest. "I heard you were a badass, just like I always thought you were."

I smiled. "I suppose I was. And I suppose you were right."

She let me go but held on to my shoulders. "I was so scared, Jemmie," she said in a choked voice. "And I was afraid he was going to hurt you, too."

"He did," I told her. "But I was stronger than he was."

She blinked and looked away. "Here," she said, taking a deep breath and turning back to me. She slid on a large pair of aviator sunglasses over my eyes. "Just for right now," she said. "Until it wears off."

I nodded and thanked her and kissed her cheek.

It wasn't going to wear off.

I'd caught sight of my reflection in the window of Crowe's car. The blackness I'd seen in Darek's eyes that had bled across half his face now had a home in mine.

It wasn't going to fade away. It was a part of me.

Whatever I'd taken from Darek and bound to me, it lived inside me now, rooted at the heart of my soul.

Crowe fed a puffed-up story to the media, blaming Killian's and Darek's deaths on the collapse of the mill—which had no doubt actually been brought about by Lori and Boone and their *terra* magic. There'd been a party, he claimed. A bit too much revelry. No one questioned it. The building was now just a pile of rubble.

I still wondered what Crowe would have done if I hadn't woken when I did. He was somehow more distant than before, but closer, too. He didn't say much to me, but he wouldn't leave my side, either, and his hands were constantly on me.

In the quiet moments, I could almost hear his thoughts.

Something is wrong with her.

She's different.

I couldn't keep her safe.

I'd died and I'd come back to life thanks to the blood magic brought about by him. He'd mixed his own blood with Old Lady Jane's, and together they'd created the kind of magic that could bring a dead person back to life, the kind that could tear me out of the hypnotic pull of the Undercurrent, the kind that could make whatever had embraced me in that river...let me go. But some part of the old Jemmie had stayed dead, and something new was birthed in the aftermath.

"How are you feeling today?" Crowe asked.

We lay in the bed in the big, bright room in the back of a Devil's safe house. I'd asked Crowe if I could stay there just until I felt better, and he had quickly said yes. Of course I'd meant I'd stay there alone, but he'd moved in with me.

"I'm okay."

He stared at my eyes, unsure if I was staring back.

I was.

"It'll go away," he said.

"I know."

It wouldn't, though.

"Your mom and dad want to stop by this afternoon. See how you are. Your dad texted me early this morning. He's worried about you."

Everyone was. I could see it written on their faces. It was why I wanted to be alone.

"Old Lady Jane wants to stop by, too. I think you should see her."

I nodded and rolled into him, my finger tracing along his arm. He was shirtless, in nothing but black pajama pants.

He shivered beneath my touch.

"Jem," he said, his voice reedy.

"Yeah?"

"You'd tell me if something was wrong, wouldn't you?"

"Of course."

"I feel like you're lying."

I was. But he wanted to fix me, and I didn't want to be fixed.

My body was still buzzing with magic. Even though the spell hadn't really been completed, even though all the kindled who Darek had kidnapped were still alive and slowly regaining their strength, something of their blood and power had stayed with me and embedded itself in my marrow.

The kindled world didn't deal in money; it dealt in power. And I now had power in spades.

I could sense that Crowe felt the shifting sands beneath us, the hierarchy reshuffling, with me at the top.

"Could you make me some breakfast?" I asked, and looked up at him. I needed him to leave.

He shivered again, but this time it wasn't from my touch, it was from the blackness in my eyes. I'd told him I was his, but I think we both knew that wasn't completely true, not anymore. I had left a part of myself in the Undercurrent, and it'd been replaced with something else, something bigger. Something *more*. Something that was not his, and never would be.

I was still trying to figure out what it all meant, who I had left behind and who I had become. Just a few days ago, I'd felt like I didn't belong, not good enough for someone as powerful as Crowe. Now everything was different. Crowe Medici bowed to no one, but he was no longer the most powerful person in the room, and he never would be when standing next to me.

"Sure. What do you want?"

"Cheese omelet."

He climbed out of bed. I watched him as he walked toward the door, muscles and bones dimpling in his back beneath the skull tattoo nestled between his shoulder blades. I was ravenous for him. I wanted his hands on me and his lips on mine. I wanted his body wrapped around me. But I couldn't tell him that. I was afraid I'd devour him whole. Distance was what we needed. I needed to put distance between us again, for his own protection.

Just because I didn't belong to him didn't mean I had stopped loving him.

When he was gone, I slipped from the bed, set my feet to the hardwood floor. Scorch marks appeared beneath me as I crossed to the small bathroom. Electricity ran up and down my arms, bolts of it webbing between my fingers. Wild magic permeated the air, smelling of ash and dirt and charred wood and the musk of a wolf's pelt. The hair on my arms rose on end.

I flicked on the light and looked at the girl in the mirror.

She grinned a devilish grin, black eyes glinting in the fluorescent light.

But I wasn't smiling.

Whoever that was in the mirror, she wasn't me.

I flicked the light off, letting the darkness bleed back in.

ACKNOWLEDGMENTS

THIS WAS A HARD BOOK TO WRITE. AN EVEN HARDER ONE to edit. It had nothing to do with the book and everything to do with me. I would have lost myself and this book if it hadn't been for the incredibly patient and incredibly wonderful people in my life.

I have to thank Sarah Fine for being all-around awesome, for being patient and kind and extremely generous with her time. This book would not have made it to book form without her!

As always (and forever and ever until the end of time), I have to thank Joanna Volpe for being a miracle worker, for being incredibly understanding and supportive, and most importantly, for being such a badass. I constantly ask myself how I got so lucky as to call her my agent.

Huge thanks and much gratitude to my editor, Pam Gruber, for her unwavering belief in me and this book when I had lost faith in both. This industry is made better with an editor like Pam, who not only uses her intelligence and intuition to make our books better, but who also has the kindness and patience required to deal with the craziness of a writer (or at least this writer)!

Thank you also to the teams at New Leaf Literary and Little, Brown, who work tirelessly behind the scenes. You guys need superhero capes!

Thank you to my friends and family who continued to support me, even through the rough patches.

Thank you to Lisa Cooper for letting me take long lunches to write and edit! But thank you also for lending an ear and a shoulder when I really needed it.

Lastly, and most importantly, thank you to the readers. Thank you for picking up this book, for giving it and me a chance. Thank you for all the love and support you've given the Altered Saga over the years! Those boys (and this writer) love you for it!

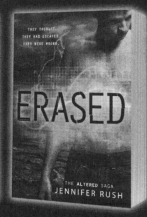
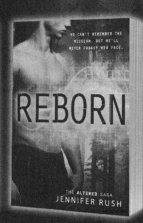